The harmony between humans and fianna, a species of shapeshifting deer, begins to wither as racial tensions and deeply rooted resentment turns violent.

Ruthless hunter Finn Hail and prophesied liberator Adelaide may be heroes to their own species, but they are enemies to each other. With war on the horizon, the reluctant pair must team up to find the most elusive of prey: the god of the Forest.

As enemies press in from all sides, true intentions begin to show. For Finn to save the boy he cares for most, he might need to aim his gun at the very god he seeks. And Adelaide, with her festering hatred for mankind, will have to determine if peace holds true salvation for her people.

FOREIGN TO YOU

Jeremy Martin

A NineStar Press Publication

Published by NineStar Press
P.O. Box 91792,
Albuquerque, New Mexico, 87199 USA.
www.ninestarpress.com

Foreign to You

Copyright © 2018 by Jeremy Martin
Cover Art by Rozenn Grosjean Copyright © 2018

Printed in the USA
First Edition
February, 2019

Print ISBN: 978-1-949909-80-7

Also available in eBook, ISBN: 978-1-949909-79-1

Warning: This novel contains scenes of bloody violence and the death of a secondary character.

Finn

IT IS STRANGE to sit in the Forest with a rifle, bullets, and the intention to kill. The Forest is meant to be a place of harmony, where the order of things is meticulous, spontaneous, and beautiful.

I am a blemish in an otherwise blissful system.

My only justification for upsetting said balance is that I am here, with a gun, to silence another disturbance.

"To the right," Jay whispers, his words turning into clouds similar to a furnace expelling smoke. His voice is so soft the branches seem to lean downward greedily, as if the leaves could catch each of his words like raindrops. With the meek backdrop of the Forest, Jay's features are highlighted and prominent. His sturdy jaw, light stubble, and bright eyes were all a combination of classic handsome.

I, on the other hand, am classically average. Brown hair, dull eyes, and a nose that's a little too big.

After waiting in the same spot an unholy amount of time, my body had sunk deeper in Pa's musky leather jacket while my muscles and thoughts had stiffened from neglect. The slightest stirring from Jay startles me out of my daydreaming and from my cocoon of warmth. Unlike me in the present moment, Jay's attention and energy are crisp and alert while his entire body leans forward in anticipation.

"Do you see him?" Jay murmurs with thinly veiled anxiety. He scrambles for his rifle with shaky fingers, brings the scope up to gaze through. I blame the cold, or my own fleeting concentration, but I cannot see what he does. The only abnormalities I see in the surrounding Forest are the slabs of meat Jay strung up on the branches like decorations to attract the ferals.

With a huff of frustration, he angles my line of sight with his rough fingers, squishing my cheeks, and gripping my head. Within an instant of the contact of his skin on mine, my mind sharpens.

Allowing my gaze to soften so I can absorb more of my surroundings, I finally see the tiniest of movements. A flash of white that doesn't belong to the never-ending bark. A drifting smudge in the sea of stillness. Yet, the Forest is so dense the leaves tend to bunch together like armor, protecting its inhabitants from invaders. Between one blink and the next, the Forest returns to its previous state. Not a twig out of place. Nothing exposed.

"Found ya," Jay says, his voice trembling. I study his nervous movements. Gloved fingers twitching individually. Teeth tugging at his bottom lip. Chest barely rising and falling as he forgets to breathe. For he has the skills of a great hunter, but not the heart for it. Jay was the boy who once found a rabbit with a broken leg and attempted to nurse it back to health. He was the same boy that cried for four days after his father snapped the creature's neck to put it out of its misery.

I'm not good at vocalizing emotions, making them into pretty little words, which is a genetic trait from Pa. All I can tell Jay is, "Stay calm," and that doesn't sound like near enough. I wish I could tell him that we should head back to town, that he deserved much more than loud rifles and dirt.

But I don't say those things.

I move past him, my boots squishing in the mixture of mud and snow. Each step is heavier than it needs to be, and my impatience starts to hum within my ears with each *squish, squish*. As I stalk, I strain to find the distortion of the brown that slipped away.

"It was probably a raccoon," I tell Jay, despite knowing we are meant to be silent. Loud hunters gain no prizes. "I bet you got caught—"

A snort comes from my right, and as I turn, I find a beast stationed between two oak trees.

Its massive frame looms before me with red-rimmed eyes, thick and building black veins, patchy fur, and teeth bared. My eyes soak up every inch of the deer, my heart hammering in time with his exhales. From this distance, the beast is nearly magnificent, practically the size of a horse. His nostrils flare as he paws at the ground, catching all wayward smells while each muscle twitches and throbs. Unlike his cousins, this stag does not flee at the sight of a human. Instead, he lowers his brow defiantly, his antlers posed daggers.

It is an unholy combination of god and devil.

A loud crack fires off behind me, and before I can even blink, the bark of the nearest oak shatters into a thousand shards.

With fear leading it, the stag rears back onto his hind legs and lashes out with hooves strong enough to break bones. I attempt to leap backward, but my boots do not leave the mud willingly. As I fall onto the ground, my rifle skids across the Forest floor. I scramble for the dagger stored at my hip, but my gloves make the hilt as slick as a trout. As the stag brings down the weight of its body with an aggravated snort, I roll to my side so that the hooves bury themselves into muck, not flesh. I manage to free my knife and drag it across the beast's torso before I make a dash for safety.

The buck, alarmed by the sudden pain, moves his eyes frantically, rolling them around his skull and exposing the whites. Its scream, a noise rivaling that of a horn being blown, attacks me even from a distance.

Another gunshot fires off too close, missing once more. As mud rains down from the misfire, the stag flees, taking blood and the stench of rot with it deep into the lush green.

Crawling out from the bush I dove into, I can hear Jay abandoning his usual stealth to reach me. His right boot slips in the slush as he nears me, causing him to crash down beside me. "Shit, Finn. Are you okay?" His hand creeps near my knee before stopping inches from it. "I thought—"

"What even was that?" I snap, pointing at the crude hole in the ground. Instantly, Jay's cheeks flare red, his face hardening defensively. "You were aiming for it, right?" Jay is deadly silent. I work my jaw, hoping to alleviate the ringing still echoing in my eardrums.

Jay curls his fingers into fists. "Next time would you rather I let you go? You seemed to be handling it well," he bites back with sarcasm.

At the lodge, Jay will find any reason not to pick up a gun. Instead, he studies the plants, tinkers with complex traps, and vanishes like a frightened barn cat at the sound of a rifle exploding. I shouldn't be surprised he's an awful shot, considering his lack of practice.

"Well, I'm alive," I tell him, wanting more than anything to be on the move again, and to distance myself from the anger that quickly rose to the top. "But maybe leave the guns to me?"

After a quick smile, Jay squares his shoulders and flexes his hands as the facade of a hunter starts to settle back over him. As the best parts of him get stuffed away. "I'll find him again," he promises, and I have no doubt that he will. It's often teased that Jay has a nose more acute than a hound. He carries a rifle for formalities, but his talents lie within his knowledge of the land. Animal droppings, tracks, and broken twigs are all parts of Jay's trade. It's what makes him valuable to a band of killers. "We are losing daylight," he points out. "And we're approaching Falling Rock."

Are we that far out? I think, dazed. With Jay, time isn't something I usually keep up on. When we were young, I would battle fatigue for one more hour with him.

I scratch at my neckline where sweat starts to bead. "Well, I left you a blood trail, so my portion of help is exhausted." I let the edges of my lips rise, and Jay accepts it with a nod. This is how comrades treat one another.

Right?

Jay rises, body hunched close to the ground as he follows the red through the bushes.

Once upon a time, back when it became evident a gun only felt natural in one of our grips, Jay tried teaching me the art of tracking, taking great pride in his skill. But at that age, when I was young and full of pride, I pretended it didn't interest me. Eventually, after I'd declined his guiding hand enough many times, Jay stopped trying to explain his methods to me.

Today, Jay is further removed, his words shorter than usual. The same tension sparking between us with the simplest of blunders, or the slightest of nods, because this is the first time Jay is tracking a feral.

The first time I have been tasked with killing a feral.

This feral is a rarity. The majority of the ferals stay in the Forest, killing what crosses their paths. Yet, this particular beast had entered human territory, killing a farmer and his wife before peeling back into the trees. It makes our mission important. It is more than just killing.

It is justice.

After a rough mile of trekking over minor cliffs and rocky outposts, Jay brings me to a halt with a snap of his wrist. As he shrinks down, I mimic him. Pointing at the snow, he shows me a large divot in the otherwise perfect layer of white. I don't need to be a tracker to know the buck must have slipped on ice, crashing into the remaining snow and splashing against the fluff like a sponge full of red paint.

I pop two bullets into my rifle, check the safety, and snap the chambers shut. Slinging the gun onto my back, I notice that Jay's eyes barely leave the blood, lost in the color. Doubt is starting to build upon his shoulders, gnawing at his edges.

"Are you ready?" I ask. He doesn't know it, but the same uneasiness lines my stomach.

"We've come this far," he tells me. He takes a bold step forward, and I can do nothing but follow. Despite the ground dropping away into a steep slope, it is clear the feral struggled up the side of the mountain.

Jay begins climbing first, taking fistfuls of roots and rocks, to propel himself along. As we move, the blood remains consistent on our right. Before long, Jay crawls over the top of the outpost, disappearing for a moment before reappearing to hoist me up. Once we are on even ground, I want to thank him, crack a joke, or anything, but my words are swallowed up as I look over Jay's shoulder and across the plateau.

I follow red snow until I find the once four-legged stag wobbling on two legs, erect for a breath before plummeting onto his knees. There is blood all over his body, tainting his skin like a rampant infection. Even from here, I can see his muscles quivering and shaking, his body burning off the gentle flakes that land on his shoulders.

His frail human shoulders.

Every part of him seems at war as he spasms and writhes. Despite the fur drifting off his body in decaying clumps, his antlers still hang from his brow, holding steady in the air with crimson stains along the tines.

I snap my rifle in front of me.

When the stag turns to me, he tries to raise his hands. Hands that should be human but are jagged and blackened. A droplet of blood creeps from his eye and down his cheek and drips onto his bare leg.

It is clear he is suffering, caught between two bodies.

I hear him mumbling, but I can't make out the individual words. Despite my head screaming, *don't get any closer, you idiot*, I find my boots propelling me forward. As I near the fiend, his voice breaks like a young boy in puberty. "Begin again," he raves. "Begin again, begin again—" he lets out a tangle of screams, his claws tearing into his cheeks. "Pain, pain, rebirth."

"Finn," Jay says, grabbing my shoulder with his giant hands, startling me from my daze. "It might not be too late. We might be able to help him."

"He is sick," I say. I stare at a point behind the beast, letting my words flood me with false confidence. "He is just an animal." It is Pa logic. Town logic.

"Wait, Finn," Jay pleads. None of the other hunters would hesitate to kill the feral, I want to tell him. Not after the feral's hands were stained with blood. Blood from Norsewood.

"He's changing—"

"It's too late for that," I tell him sternly. "He has already done enough damage."

Jay looks away, squinting into the distance. "Something doesn't feel right."

Killing never feels right, I want to tell him. But in the seconds I take my eyes off him, the feral lunges at me, fangs angled at my throat.

Adelaide

ONE BLINK.

Blue sky.

Another blink.

Lungs filling with air.

I squirm, my body cumbersome and clumsy and different. I stare up into the clouds as blood creeps into new pieces of me.

Two hands. Ten fingers.

Stretching my arms, I realize I never had fingers before...but when I move to inspect them, I find that I can't raise my hands. They are stiff and unresponsive beyond a squirm of activity.

Two legs. Two feet.

I struggle to move once again, wondering why two legs don't seem enough.

I raise my head, finding a pink, strange body that I know is not mine. I see thick corded vines holding my body down while dirt is packed tightly within any exposed crevice. As I stir in my confinement, several birds become frightened by my movement and take flight into the blue overhead.

"This..." I hear myself say. Never have I heard my own voice. "This is not my body."

You...are...human, my mind murmurers, gently, reassuringly. As if the force of these newfound thoughts could shatter me if they aren't soft enough.

You are human, they restate boldly.

I attempt to sit up, but the roots and vines are reluctant to let me leave. Panic, traveling through my veins faster than blood, adds extra power to my limbs as I grit my teeth and attempt to free myself. My arms break loose first. With my hands free, nothing prevents me from excavating the rest of my body.

"Where am I?" I ask out loud, looking for someone, something, anything to ease this acute sensation of being alone.

Propping myself up, I turn to see trees, trees, and more trees, surrounding me like sentinels. A tug blossoms in my chest, the rocks and bushes beckoning at me. A pull that reassures me, *you will be safe. Safe within the trees.* The thick aroma of nature clots my nostrils, luring me, yet a stench overpowers it all. A scent that is encoded into my being.

Blood.

Having mistaken it for dirt, I now see a thin coat of red along my skin, bright as berries. But it cannot be my own. I find, after a studious glance, that I have no wounds. Nowhere for the blood to have come from.

Holding my palms against my head, I attempt to calm my frantic...mind. This new, evolving consciousness that informs me blood is bad, blood means danger. It is not accidental. It is the result of fangs around throats, of legs caught in traps, of bullets—

I am torn from my concentration by a nearby rustling. I turn, but there is too much around me to pinpoint the origin of the noise. The wind, further numbing and clouding my senses, whistles through the treetops savagely. I attempt to stand, but I am not accustomed to balancing the entirety of myself on two legs. Finally, with both feet spread apart, I remain upright.

Then, from the underbrush, a figure creeps forth. A man. Initially, I am startled by the creature's appearance. By its two legs, upright posture, and its humanness. Yet, how can I now fear a being that remarkably resembles myself?

Yet...something is not right.

Two antlers tower above his brow, glistening sinisterly. His mouth is angled into a snout, his dark nose dripping blood while one pointed ear swivels around frantically. With my limited knowledge, I can't understand why the man's body is mostly human...but partly animal.

"Are you...fine?" I ask. A single, painful moan comes from the man. His fingers sway, snapping back and forth, while the bones figure out where they belong. "Let me..." What can I do? My fear grounds me, stealing away my voice. I find that I cannot push myself forward, only further away. "I'm sorry. I don't know how to help you."

Throwing back his head, the man unleashes a guttural roar before he charges at me.

My reaction is not quick enough to prevent his hand from connecting with my stomach and lifting me off the ground. I fly through the air with the grace of robin until my back collides into the base of a tree. Pain, immensely bright and hot, latches onto my bones as I roll to my side. As the man nears me, I raise my hands out to him, words with no meaning rushing from my lips. I hear, with each step, the man crying and moaning in agony.

No amount of pleading will slow him down. He is hunting.

And I am the prey.

Looming before me, the man swings his antlers downward, ready to deliver his final blow. Having misjudged the distance, his tines dig into the bark of the tree above me. As the man snaps his teeth at me viciously, he only sinks his horns deeper. Saliva and blood splash onto me as his mouth gets closer and closer.

The man gropes for my limbs, trying to pin me down and make his kill easier. I pull my arm free and reach for a rock pressing into my hip. Grasping it in the palm of my hand, I swing with all my might and slam the rock into the cheek of the beast. It roars as teeth fall out of its mouth.

My attack pries the antlers loose from the wood, allowing the beast to dive for me one more time. I react instinctively by shielding myself with my forearm. I scream as the man's fangs separate my flesh, and bone hits bone in a dizzying moment.

Desperate, I grip his throat, prying my fingers into the tender skin. I hope to dislodge the teeth, but the fiend is too strong. With all his weight bearing down on me, I have no chance of warding him off.

My body, turning against me, sends a blinding pain streaking through my arm, landing in the hand that grips the fiend's throat. Reacting to the heat beneath my skin, the creature shrieks in horror and recoils from me in disgust. He fills the air with howls as he rolls along the dirt, claws tearing into skin to ease himself of the torment.

With a snap, five white flowers explode from the beast's flesh.

For a painstakingly long time, the beast rolls and screams while white lilies repeatedly burst from his skin. Eventually, he stills, resting on his knees, looking like a bush of wildflowers. While there is beauty to it, unease overpowers me.

When he arches his head back, I brace myself for another scream, but the fiend's jaw is frozen, nothing but gurgles coming forth. With a full body shudder, a final white lily erupts from its open mouth, blood splattering into the air like pollen.

Then everything is tranquil.

First, the fur on the male's body starts to fall to the ground in fistfuls. Gently at first, then rapidly until only pink skin is showing. Then, with a gentle quiver, the antlers topple from his forehead.

A breeze ripples through the air, snatching the lilies from the fiend's body until only one flower remains, the one with petals resting upon his lips.

Hugging my bloodied arm to my chest, I approach the human. Close, I see that all the blackened veins and animal qualities have disappeared from him. I place my hand against his chest and notice, with a start, that he is no longer breathing, his features locked in place.

I tangle my fingers around the base of the lily and wrench the flower free from his jaw with a snap.

As soon as the bloodied roots slither from the man, he is brought to life with a gasp.

Tears roll down his cheeks, red until clear water can push all the color away. The wounds on his body shine as bright as fireflies as they crawl shut ever so slowly.

Those eyes, golden like sunflower petals, find my own and refuse to let go. A jolt nips at my heart as I take in the male's features. Those eyes.

I know you, I realize as purely as I know to breathe or to flee.

With the might of a sudden rainstorm, an endless array of images crashes upon me. Memories. He is there, in most of them, traveling beside me on four legs and with a body that spooked predators.

I reach my finger out and trace the edge of his nose. The...smile that decorates his skin warms me in ways I thought only the sun could. He does not pull away as I smear blood on his face.

"Caleb," I say, putting my arms, blood and all, around him. I hold him tightly, and the ache within me starts to dull.

"Maiden," he says, barely audible between his rugged inhales.

Finn

BULLETS HAVE A certain magic to them. They are so loud, so abrupt, that they consume all other noise around them.

There is no sound as the skull of the feral shatters like dandelion seeds blown by the wind. Only blood spouting in intricate patterns. It is a sight that disables me, scatters my thoughts around, but eventually, I can numbly tangle a rope around the mutilated human form of the feral. I make a tight knot at the beast's ankles, flinching each time my fingers brush its flaky, loose skin.

"No, no, no—" Jay chants like a prayer. He dropped his rifle on the ground and part of me wants to focus on that one taboo and chastise him. Cling to something childish so I can't study what's before me, the body, the blood, or the bone. "Did you see him?"

I use the complex form of the knot as my cornerstone, how it coils and twines, to keep me moving. I force my eyes away from the face with the jawline of a man and the eyes that are already milky white. I don't want to recognize how very human he is.

"Help," I request of Jay as I pull the rope taut. My bare fingers ache from the cold, and my teeth chatter together from snappy wind. "Help," I repeat to him in minor contempt.

I don't understand why he's upset, my thoughts growl. *He didn't even pull the trigger.*

Jay, doing the opposite of what I ask, collapses in a bundle of leather, his legs giving out. His cheeks glisten, his attention worlds away as he stares at the ground. "Did you see that?" He rubs his palms into his eyes with enough pressure that I'm worried he'll burst them. "He was human."

After a few fruitless tugs on the rope, it snaps, and the released tension throws me onto my back. For a moment, I do not move, but continue looking at the setting sun while the chill of the night locks me up like a statue. "He wasn't human," I recite. It has been taught to us over and over. By parents, elders, and the hunters' guild. The words have been beaten into us until they ring alongside our blood.

The ferals and fianna can look human, don the same smile and laugh and words, but that does not make them such. Humanity goes deeper than skin.

"Be a man," I fire at Jay. They are words that belong to Pa, to his crude lips and rough beard. They do not taste right on my tongue.

Jay flinches.

I stand back up and grab hold of the feral's antlers. As the weight settles onto the focal point, one of the horns gives way from the rotted flesh and fragile bone. Gore, pus, and blood spew from the gaping hole.

I vomit until the only thing I can offer up to the earth is rank exhales.

I rub the edges of Pa's coat along my mouth. "We need to get moving. We can't be out here after—"

"Finn!" Jay shouts, and the volume of his voice is as loud as any bullet, demanding my attention. "I saw his skull explode. Shards of bone—" Flustered, Jay can't even allow himself to finish the sentence. He shakes his head as vigorously as a wet dog. "That was like shooting a person."

"He wasn't human." I reinforce the point because I am over this conversation, done thinking.

"But—"

Shut up, shut up, shut up.

"Jay, I need you to shut it!" I scream, my control a fickle being at the moment.

Because we did nothing wrong.

A noose secured around the neck of the feral, I start to drag the body with all my ebbing strength. I ignore Jay as he sits immobile, mumbling over and over again with his nose and eyes running.

I take several breaks dragging the body through the Forest, and each time I find Jay following like a wounded animal begging to be put down. When we break from the trees, I stay close to the border between land and Forest, seeing the distant glow of Norsewood on the horizon.

Stumbling from the ferns like a newborn calf, Jay pops from the brush, arms wrapped over his gut, trying to hold back all his discomfort with the pressure. "I can help," he says, rather bashfully.

"You can help?" My voice starts to shake, because I am trying my hardest to keep my cool, and after hours of neglect, my jaw is a block of ice. "You could have helped hours ago."

Defiance sparks in him. "Stop being a dick."

I long to snap, to tear into him with my exasperation and frustration, but I catch a singular glance at Jay's eyes, and my rage ebbs away. Pity steals anything else I feel when I see his chapped cheeks. Jay's not very good at hiding his inner emotions, which is yet another quality most of the hunters possess that he lacks.

"Grab some of the line, then." Stretching out the rope further, I make it possible for both Jay and me to pull. With the combined muscle, the body scoots along the ground easily.

It is there, with Jay's body close to mine, that the cold isn't as insufferable.

The lodge looms in the distance like a castle, all sharp angles and devoid of any eye-catching features. The building is the size of at least three commoner's homes, and much too colossal for a handful of rowdy men. Rumored to be strategically placed, the lodge rests dangerously close to the edge of the ocean's cliffs, endlessly teetering.

This is a home to killers of ferals.

Outside the lodge, there's a fire vigorously burning. Several of the hunters are situated around the ring with mugs of beer, clumsy limbs, and crude jokes. There's a roar louder than the sea as the men try to talk over one another, rivaling to be the voice that dominates all others. Each hunter is decorated with matching scars, broken facial features, and beards of various girths. From afar, they all became a blob of man.

It is a stark reminder of everything I am not. The lodge, and those who inhabit the moldy walls, are Pa's definition of masculinity. Yet, no matter my rank with the hunters, no matter the few hairs that sprout on my chin, I was *other*.

Making our way into the light of the fires, I find Garth centered amongst them all, like the king of a usurped kingdom. He is by far one of the ugliest men I've ever encountered. His forehead is too large, his teeth are either missing or crooked like a child's, and his beard is patchy and scraggly. Yet, all of that is overlooked, due to him being the leader of the guild and cunningly ruthless.

Standing, the man causes the rest of the hunters to look out into the darkness.

Indistinguishable faces turn to the two of us, not initially impressed with the novices who stand before them, but after a collective study of the feral's body behind us, they explode into cheers and celebration. Rough hands rip me free of the roped carcass I feared I may never release and into furious embraces and painful back slaps. Like the lull of the sea, I am torn from Jay and cast into the body of hunters. Voices upon voices stack as they ask details of the expedition and the death of the feral. Questions that I'm sure were asked a thousand times before, but never had they been so loud and so personal.

I once felt jealousy at the attention the hunters gave each other so easily, at the comradery I felt displaced from. It was something I thought I craved. Validation I was confident would bring pieces of me together in a neat little harmony.

"Was it a clean shot? My first kill was a gut shot—"

"You didn't even skin him? Make a blanket outta that son of a—"

"Last one I got, I blasted off its hind leg. A bloody clean shot—"

Two hunters who smell dangerously flammable stretch out the embers of the fire, until its perimeter has tripled in size. They stack logs in crisscross formation, as if building up a cabin for children to play in. Without a single reaction to touching cold, dead skin, a hunter by the name of Gerald hoists the feral's body up by its lifeless arm. The limb starts to rip apart, but with a huff and a grunt, the body is flung, without much care, onto the top of the fire's structure.

The corpse lands with a sickening thud, the sound similar to that of blood-slick meat smacking the countertop.

The hunters roar as the body cracks and pops in the flames.

With calculated precision, Garth plucks me from the cramped space of hunters and places me in front of the gathering. Rowan, a handsome and quiet hunter, has acquired Jay and sets him on the opposite side of Garth as one would do when returning a wandering child to its parent.

Garth raises a slender pistol into the air, fires once, and brings the clamor of the hunters to a halt.

"Brothers," he starts, his voice thunderous like a deity. Yet, there are still lingering conversations. Garth, not a man of hesitation, aims and fires his pistol. The bullet causes a hunter's mug to explode, shards lodging themselves into his hand. As all the other voices and conversations die, only his whimpering remains.

Garth rolls his shoulders, pleased with the result of his shot. "Before you stand two fledgling hunters. Jay Alder and Finn Hail." My cheeks flush as the collective cheers and chants our names gallantly. Garth allows them a moment of praise.

"Today, they were sent into the Forest as boys. They were but children, killing wildlife and pigeons from the rooftops." The men snicker and elbow one another. "They were boys sent to track a killer. A subhuman that claimed the lives of two citizens of Norsewood."

I look to Jay, with his face tilted at the flames, wanting to say, "*See*? We did something good."

Because, from a young age, we are taught the difference between ferals and fianna. Both races exist within the Forest, and both can be deceivingly human. The fianna shift in the spring and walk into Norsewood with two legs instead of four, but the ferals are fiends who are beasts stuck between animal and human nature.

We are taught to tolerate one and kill the other.

"Boys do not kill demons," Garth explains, making eye contact with me as my pulse responds. "They cry and suck from their mother's breast. Boys do not belong in the lodge. But these two..." he tells the bundled crowd who waits on his every word. "These two are men now."

A sliver of me, a brave and foolish part, wants to tell Garth that demons shouldn't be able to cry. That the being I killed in those woods was as far from a demon as he was from a saint.

"I am proud to declare these two defenders of Norsewood. Two shining knights who shall lead with valor and grace," Garth ends with the constant joke. Because the guild is no better than a prison for Norsewood. And one that doesn't work. The guild is a collective of murderers, thieves, rapists, and so on. Anyone charged with a crime by the town council is sent to the guild leader for evaluation and if they don't pass, they are sent back to Norsewood with a death penalty stamped to them.

"Welcome to the guild of hunters, you shits," Garth announces with a smirk.

The clamor from the hunters is deafening.

As Garth sneers at me, I can remember, to this day, the first time I met him. He had wandered into Pa's house like it was his own. It was then he demanded that Niall Hail's only son be recruited into the hunting guild. Garth had told my father this was the condition for his silence. For Pa had a dangerous secret only Garth and I knew. One that would bring a swift execution if it was revealed.

Pa didn't seem bothered, only said, "You might be able to toughen him up. Right now, he keeps his hair too damn long."

The flames start to curl possessively around the feral, finding kindling in the rotten fur. When Garth gives us a shove, I worry that Jay might go charging into the fire, believing he could rescue the feral now.

Ironically, as they pull Jay into their celebration, they save him from himself.

The gathering trickles back into the lodge. After the threshold is passed, the building expands into unknown dimensions with insides as bland and featureless as stone caves. Hunters don't need cabinets to store goods, grand kitchens, or much else. Just a place to drink beer, a surface to sleep on, and food to eat. Weapons, placed wherever their owner feels inclined to leave them, carelessly litter the lodge. The corners, where the shadows are deepest, have become home to delicate spiderwebs.

The rest of the ample space was filled with *noise*.

The initial beer is thrust at me. Knowing my thoughts will blur at the bottom, I chug the contents of the mug until I can slam its empty shell onto the table. Before I can blink, another is magically placed before me.

And thus, the night continues.

Since the rest of the guild started indulging themselves into a coma long before Jay and I arrived, the evening dies off quickly. Bodies land on the wooden floor, others are draped across furniture like blankets, but all of them snore in sync with each other. Jay disappeared within the madness at some point, no doubt escaping back to his family's home.

"Bastards, hm?"

Rowan is perched across the table from me, and I would be lying if I said I detected him before he spoke. "What?" I ask, my lips sluggish and my actions delayed.

"They'll find any excuse to get drunker than a skunk," he comments. Rowan himself is teetering on the edge of oblivion, but he keeps his stature. His fingers occasionally toy with his chin-length hair, which is usually pulled back to highlight his slick features. "But I suppose congratulations are in order? Kind of ironic, due to how much Jay loathes holding a gun."

I try to shrug, brushing off his attempt to pry into my psyche. "Did you notice when he left? Jay?"

Rowan spins his empty mug.

Back in the day, he was the best tracker in the guild. He had become an official hunter right when I was recruited, and lost his ruling position of lead tracker when Jay volunteered himself into the lodge soon after. I can never tell if Rowan is bothered by Jay trampling on his turf, but Rowan usually doesn't have a reaction beyond a sigh and a leisurely eye-roll.

"He left not too long ago." Burping, he continues, "He was not enjoying himself, as per usual." Jay is known to drink like a fish until he becomes a calamity on two feet. He is the kind of drinker who will boast that he "didn't feel a thing" and then suddenly, wham, he's beyond saving. "Something troubles the tracker." With a not-so-sly look, Rowan asks me, "Do you know anything on the subject?"

"I don't." I might.

My eyes, sloppy and tipsy, trace the lines of Rowan's lips once he's smiled. "You don't think Jay should be a hunter."

"No, I don't," I say without much thought. As soon as the words leave my mouth, I regret them. I glance all around me, but no other hunter besides Rowan and me are conscious at this point. It could be due to the alcohol, but my tongue becomes especially clumsy. "Nothing chains him here. He could go anywhere else."

"You'll have to remind me because I forget, but what keeps you around?" Rowan asks. By now, he has leaned close enough that I can smell the musk hovering against his skin.

I have always been interested in Rowan's backstory. What did he do that would classify him as a criminal in Norsewood? He's too pretty to do evil. He's much more suited to the role of a knight than a rogue.

"I am a Hail." There isn't much else to say. We are pariahs labeled by a name and a repeated madness.

"You say that like it makes a difference?" Rowan pushes at my forehead with his finger.

I attempt to swat his hand away, but I completely miss.

"Have you ever trapped a wild animal, Finn?" Rowan asks. Yet, before I can answer, he has already continued his tale. "Once, I caught this coyote, but by the time I got to my trap it, was gone. How did I know he was even there, you might ask? The bastard had chewed off his own foot, leaving it behind, all because he was caught. His life and his freedom were much more powerful than anything I had. Don't do the same to that boy, Finn. Or you'll lose another part of him."

Rowan passes me a mug full of beer. I look into his eyes for a moment, and I know this conversation will reach no other ears. Rowan, unlike the others, could be a man of worth.

"Don't make Jay chew his own foot off."

Adelaide

IT BECOMES EVIDENT early on that traversing the Forest on two legs is a chore. While I know I am far less nimble without hooves, it still feels as if the vegetation maliciously reaches for me with each step. The temperatures, once dulled by thick fur, are felt much more potently on my human skin. Yet, the songs of the birds are much lovelier to these new ears.

"That healed up nicely. Unnaturally quick, if I may be honest," Caleb comments as he runs a hand down my once wounded arm. The only proof that remains of his bite are tiny sections of healed, shiny skin. Caleb is silent as he stares at the marks, his voice hollow when it finds me. "Again...I am sorry."

I gently pull away, tucking my arms behind my back. "Tell me everything."

We have been walking for at least a day, and my fatigue only grows. "You are a human now," he starts off. The word comes to life within my mind like a bird flashing between the leaves.

Human, human, human.

"Before...I was an animal, right?" Four legs, black snout, more fur.

"Yes. That space in your mind, where it gets hard to see, like morning mist? That's your memories as a beast. Proof of your before and after," he tells me. "If that makes sense?"

Caleb has a head of curly brown human hair and the start of a human beard. He is sturdy like a bear, built with muscle upon muscle. He leads me through the Forest, forging a path for me. "I do understand," I tell him, because there is a clear separation between before and after. My conscious mind is aware that I am a new creation. "But why did I become human now? This isn't your first time as a human, right?" Caleb shakes his head in response.

"You will find no simple answer for that," Caleb tells me as he holds back a branch. When I pass, he reaches into a nearby bush and plucks a handful of blue spheres. He encourages me to eat them as he plops them into his own mouth. "Like the leaves, the fianna change with the seasons. When the air grows cold, we adapt and shift back into furs. When the days are long and hot, we shed. Some fianna will become human, others will not. It is all...random. Wild and without order. Similar in ways to nature itself."

"For only a season?" My mind whirls and strives to make sense of each word laid out by Caleb. I nibble on the berries before deciding to devour the rest.

He nods. "The Stag blesses us with the chance to walk between two bodies. A good portion of us use this time to learn as much as we can about the humans, to show them proof of the Stag's miracles and to build a relationship with them, but others simply enjoy all that comes with being human."

"Is the Stag not the god of man as well?" I question.

Caleb hesitates in the middle of a smile. His mouth hangs sideways. "The humans are interesting. It was said they once believed in the god as deeply as us, but after time, they decided to believe in only what they could see. And create."

My ears fill with the song of the Forest, and my eyes absorb the hues of the earth. "What more evidence do they need?" I ask as I inspect the Forest, for I see signs of majesty everywhere I glance.

Caleb scratches at his chin, turning to face me as he spoke. "As you remain human, you will find complexities that go beyond anything you've experienced. You will begin to understand pain, happiness, and possibly love," he tells me with a soft grin, one that shimmers like the sun. "Yet you will also begin to understand doubt. I've met plenty of humans who want to believe, but..." Caleb's mouth hangs open, the flow of words coming to an end. Quickly recovering, he waves his hand before me, dismissing himself. "There will be plenty of time for debates and theology. For now, enjoy the walk."

I do not point out that we have been walking all day, and I am finding it not so enjoyable. "This is not the first time we've met," I confirm.

Caleb stops before a trickle of a creek. Bending down, he takes deep swallows of the water, then he rinses the blood and gore from his skin. I join him, running my fingers through the icy stream. "You are special, Maiden. Maybe in ways I can't describe, but thankfully others will be able to help you with that." He aids me in washing my skin until not a trace of red can be found. "It doesn't matter what body I inhabit, it doesn't matter how my mind twists, I will always know you are family."

"What is a family?" I ask. I know Caleb is a vital piece of me, wedged stubbornly into this human heart, but I'm not sure how.

Caleb stands back up and flashes his teeth at me.

He smiles, my mind clarifies.

"A family is like a herd. A collective of beings that honor and protect one another." Caleb wipes the final trace of blood from my arm with the remaining moisture on his palm. "Sometimes, family is more of a feeling. It is a bond that connects you to others."

"You are really bad at making this less confusing," I confess. While the words are truthful, I find that I can grin around them.

Caleb reflects the action. "I did tell you I may not be the most qualified to help you. If you wait, we shall shortly be amongst brighter minds."

There is something enticing about learning more about this new existence. To prove Caleb's point, I know that I could follow him anywhere, that he would protect me with his own life. I don't know how, but I feel it. I feel his care for me in the core of me.

He continues to explain the lay of the land as we travel, but I find none of it interests me near as much as this human body does, for everything that surrounds me can easily be explained, it is either that or this, but my heart is as complicated as three Forests stacked on top of one another.

I flex my fingers, shrug my shoulders, and tug at my hair. All these things make up me. I study Caleb, but he does not move with a single doubt. He is completely at ease in this body. Not many creatures in the Forest could move with such grace.

Caleb pivots so swiftly that I nearly collide with him. "We have a few more hours of traveling. Are you okay?"

I slump over in exhaustion. I don't need to know how long an hour lasts to be certain that I won't make it. My feet are aching like a wound. "I'm sorry, Caleb. I don't know if I can go much further."

Caleb closes one eye while keeping the other open.

He winks at me. "I'm only joking. There," he tells me, pointing in the distance. "The village."

Shapes huddle against one another in the dying mist. Lopsided and covered with a thick layer of moss and vegetation, the...buildings could have been another plant the Forest gave sanctuary to, not something man birthed. The fianna village is squat and crowded together like the jagged fangs of a wolf. Gaps run along the walls for...windows, but those have long been shattered and left open for inhabitants of the Forest to build homes within.

"It is...ugly," I decide. Caleb shepherds me to the beginning of the village where a path is laid out before me. Even from where I stand, I see both the start and the end of the village. "Why is it empty?"

"It is rumored that the humans once made this village for themselves. But eventually, the Forest kept growing, forcing them to move further inland. Away from..." Caleb does not explain who the humans ran from. "It is empty because when we are animals, no one cares for this land. But the Forest watches over the settlement."

"Do the humans not come here?"

Caleb does not answer right away, and I wonder if he has even heard the question I posed. He treads into the village before circling around to me and saying, "It was decided long ago that it was best for our two peoples to have separate regions to live in. The fianna belong to the Forest, and it is where we are most comfortable. Only the children of man come here. They dare one another to enter the home of the fiends." He pulls back his lips in a fake snarl.

As Caleb walks through the...streets of the village, I am very uncomfortable. We pass few others, most of the empty spaces filled with monsters from my imagination. The birds and insects, no matter how close they may feel, can't sing loud enough to cover the sound of my bare feet slapping the stoned streets.

My eyes travel to the side of one of the homes. Noticing...carvings on the side. Of flowers. Flowers that bloomed from Caleb's skin.

Once we are at the center of the village, a place where a single bucket hangs above a hole in the ground, I notice another human. This one, a female.

She is as slender as a crane. Her long legs give way to a tiny waist, and her brown hair rests along her...collarbone. As she turns to me, her eyes lock with mine, and I find they match Caleb's.

Eyes like a mountain cougar.

Eyes unlike humans, I realize with a start, the fact rippling through me.

Joy expands along the features of the female. She lets out a yell before she latches onto Caleb with enough force that one could, from a distance, mistake it as an act of aggression. She is speaking with a speed that crams all her words into each other. Before I can decipher any of them, her arms are around my shoulders, squeezing my throat. I struggle frantically against her hold, but Caleb is there with laughter and smiles.

"Anna, Anna." He bats at the female like a pesky bird. "Her mind is still expanding. You must explain your actions beforehand."

Releasing me, the female bounces backward, tucking her hands behind her and grinning...sheepishly. "I'm sorry, I'm..." She bites her lip and jumps one more time. "It's really you! I can't believe it!"

With a slight pinch of pain, my mind flashes several images before me. They are of a doe, always close, always patient. She teaches me in the Forest, she guides me. She is a constant in the winter...a ghost in the spring.

I peer into her eyes and I say, "Anna," because that is who she is. As the declaration leaves my lips, emotion invades me with such force, water bubbles into my vision.

Tears, my mind reaffirms.

"Anna," I say once more as I reach for her. Anna pulls Caleb into us, and for a moment, we are three bodies so tightly pressed together that we resemble a sturdy oak.

This is what Caleb meant when he described a family. This much I am sure of.

Once she pulls away from me, Anna wipes the tears from my cheeks. She revolves, facing Caleb. "And you!" she exclaims. "Are you a ghost?" She grins as her hand touches his very solid skin. "I must be losing my mind."

Caleb places his palm against Anna's skin, and I watch as she leans into the touch. I see such...care in the embrace.

That is because they're mates, I realize.

Caleb clears his throat, and he looks to me. His eyes are filled with...gratitude. "A few seasons past, I didn't turn human. I got stuck in the transformation. It is an ailment that occasionally cripples our kind. Changing shapes is hard. It is messy. There are times when we don't make it completely to one side."

"It happened to Caleb." I can see the fear that remains in Anna's eyes, how she is still unsure how much of Caleb she has regained. "We don't recover from losing our minds. It doesn't happen naturally." Then, she turns all her joy towards me. "You saved him."

"A maiden of the white lily will awaken to harvest the lost," Caleb recites plainly. "The doe with fur as white as snow who would save us all. The Maiden."

"Enough of this." Pushing playfully at her mate, Anna comes up against my side, her arms encasing me. "You must be cold."

I notice that Anna is not...naked, but tangled in strips of fur. I only take into consideration now that Caleb and I are both bare. Nothing hides us from the world. Yet, I feel no shame.

"Go with Anna. She will prepare you to meet Willow. She is a human woman, who is much wiser than I," Caleb tells me as Anna pulls me by my hand. "She will have the answer to everything you wish to know."

Anna stops before a looming house. Shooing off Caleb, she tells him, "Search for the other fianna. You were not the first two lost in the shrubs, I am sure. I will make sure the Maiden is safe while you are gone."

"Adelaide," I say to them both. The word is small at first, as insignificant as a pebble on a stream bank. But then it builds up in my chest until I am able to say, "Adelaide," because it is the only thing that mattered. "Please, call me Adelaide."

Anna beams, planting her lips to my cheek. "I've missed you, Adelaide."

Finn

THE NEXT MORNING, I groggily make my way home after peeling myself off a sticky tabletop. The lodge and the Hail household are on complete opposite ends of the human territory, and the sun casts down its merry light to personally torture me as I waddled along. My head pounds with each step as though aiding the elements in trying to quell me.

I count my blessings as I finally make it to the dirt path that leads to our secluded home. With a backdrop of the Forest, our stark white house was so ugly it could be found by even a blind man. Paint peels from the siding and half the shutters are missing. When I was young, Pa and I had lived in town, nestled in with all the other citizens of Norsewood. I remember the tiny little home with warm colors and the distinct scent of spices. The home Pa bought years later was too large in comparison. Shadows and ghosts lived in the vacant rooms, or so nine-year-old Finn had believed. Noises would travel through the empty spaces at night, and sometimes I imagined ghouls of Pa's past dancing in the hallways and all the way down into the sealed basement.

As soon as I enter the house, I can tell that Pa is not in a pleasant mood. In the living room, his favorite chair is overturned and one of the vilest lamps ever created is lying broken on the floor. I right the furniture and sweep up the glass shards, then continue following the mess, as talented as Jay when it comes to tracking Pa.

It isn't long before I find Pa huddled in the corner of the kitchen, clutching a knife to his chest like a woman would her babe. His salt-and-pepper hair hangs messily down past his ears, his gray eyes are fixated on the cracked tiles beneath him, and I wonder, not for the first time, if this was the man Garth wanted my father to become.

Norsewood is laced with myth and lore. Tales of a hunter and a fianna who created the world, of how Norsewood was founded, or why the sun rises and sets. All of them in a collection of endless stories.

And my father, Niall Hail, is another one of those legends.

At a young age, Pa had shown promise in Norsewood. His parents had been renowned bakers with a son who rose in popularity like bread full of yeast. Pa was promised a future and a place in Norsewood, with the possibility of owning his own shop and meeting a pretty lady to settle down with. But one day, the family bakery erupted in fire. When the citizens finally put out the flames, it was only Pa left sitting in the ashes, the bodies of his parents inches away from the boy. There were rumors that the troubled Hail boy's demons coaxed him into lighting the fire himself. Pa was taken in by another family, but it soon became evident that he was of the troubled variety.

Pa was sent to the hunting guild without much of an argument.

Rising through the ranks, Pa killed feral after feral with unmatched skill. Eventually, Pa sat upon the throne of the guild, becoming its infamous leader. A few years later, he met Elinica, daughter to Lon and Messena. Pa, with what little sanity he still possessed, wooed the daughter of the farmer. After Elinica had given birth to their only son, Pa bought her a home in Norsewood and snuck into town under the moonlight whenever he could.

Then, Elinica vanished. She was declared missing, and Norsewood looked to Pa for answers, but he slowly descended into madness. Garth, sensing weakness, tore the leadership of the guild from Pa and pushed him further into darkness.

Crouching before Pa, I ignore the ramblings that escape his lips and start to remove the knife from his hands. After I secure the blade, it takes Pa numerous minutes to register that I am before him.

"I thought he was coming," Pa tells me, standing up and snatching the kitchen knife back from me with a confidence missing seconds ago. He turns his back to me, using his curt anger to cover up his embarrassment. "Let me finish dinner, boy. Leave me be."

Pa never clarifies who "he" is, but I always assume he is haunted by the man who stole everything from him.

As he chops up vegetables from the garden, I start to stitch up the tears in my tunic, studying Pa's movements as I work. Part of me wants to tell Pa about the feral, about the hunt, but I don't have the energy to endure the conversation. Instead, I prick myself with the needle as I try to sew.

"You finish this up," he tells me abruptly, throwing the knife aside. I watch the metal bounce across the counter. "I think it's too cold in the basement. Do we have any extra blankets?"

What the public didn't know was that Garth was able to dethrone my father because he had found out Pa's darkest secret. And he kept it like one of those pinned-up butterflies, using blackmail to rule the guild and demand Pa's son join the hunters as soon as he could pull back the string of a bow. I had thought Garth recruited me to torture Pa further, but as I grew, I could see that Pa barely paid any attention to me.

"Should I tell her you said hello?" Pa asks me, unlocking the basement with the key only he possesses.

I suppress a shiver and focus on the task of making dinner. "Please."

For Niall Hail did not kill his love. I remember the night Pa staggered into the townhouse, a bloody Elinica rolling across the carpet as his strength failed to hold her in his arms. The way he cried, so broken and raw, was proof enough to me that my father didn't kill her. And I guess that was all that mattered to me; it wasn't Pa who'd done it. After that, I accepted her death. She was gone. Other than hazy memories, her existence had no impact on my life.

Pa, in a moment of weakness, invited his apprentice, Garth, into his home. He begged the young man for help, but Garth was not a kind person. He looked at the man sobbing before him and began crafting the plan to topple Pa.

So, Niall Hail escaped out of Norsewood, taking a boy and a secret.

My mother's corpse lay stagnant in what had been her resting place for so many years...

Niall Hail's basement.

Adelaide

"YOU LOOK PRETTY," Anna tells me. She has draped furs along the frame of my body and smeared bright berries along my lips. When she shows me my reflection, "pretty" is not the first word that comes to mind. My hair, which used to cover every inch of me, hangs only from my scalp. It is pale and curly. My eyes, golden like Anna's, show no emotion.

Taking me by my hand, Anna ushers me back through the streets. The Forest constantly tempts me to return to the shade and the lullaby of the rustling leaves, but Anna's grip is stronger. She only lets go once she brings us before a giant of a building. With a high roof and a spire that stabs into the sky like a needle, it gives off an unsettling vibe. The entrance is a detailed arch wide enough to fit several bodies through. As we enter, I can see there are rows of benches lining the expansive room. At the end of the structure is a statue carved from wood. A man stands beside a stag, his hand resting on the neck of the animal as they both stare out into the dust-filled room, patiently waiting on worshipers.

"Marvelous, isn't he?"

The voice echoes throughout the room. A woman, human by her telltale blue eyes, appears from behind the statue. Her hair reminds me of a heavy rain cloud, gray and voluminous. When she smiles, I do not see much happiness in it. Just the baring of teeth.

"Adelaide, this is Willow." Anna makes the introduction. "She has been offering up information on human culture and tendencies while we are visiting for several years now. She is a kind—"

"Child, you do not need to butter me up. And you," Willow says as she moves to me, her shoes clicking as she marches, "no introduction is needed." She stands before me, collecting my features with the sharp eye of an observer. She bows her head ever so slightly. "It is an honor, Maiden."

My mind pulls forth various replies I can give this woman, and the first that comes forward is "the pleasure is mine," but I do not say anything, for my stomach churns with unease. I decide to nod and give her a partial smile.

"We have much to discuss before the Festival, no?" Willow asks. Gliding back to the front of the room, she runs her fingers over the figure of man and stag, her nails long enough to carve extra details into the icon. "Where do you wish me to begin?"

"Anywhere," I say when I really want to say everything. Tell me it all. "I will take anything you offer. First—" I collect all the empty space "—tell me what this place is."

"This is what the humans dub a church. A place to go to worship gods and goddesses alike." Willow, as though she were addressing more than two bodies, centers herself on the stage. "Centuries ago, the fianna were believed to be figments of the Stag's very soul. Creatures that became human to teach us, govern us, guide us. Yet, it has been a long time since this building has spoken such sermons."

I push past the current subject, finding it heavy. "What is the Maiden?"

Willow seems to hold plenty of information she is giddy to part with. "Again, there are no definite answers. The Maiden is said to be a doe of snow-white fur. She is born into a human form and tasked with leading the sick and wounded deep into the Forest. There, she will 'heal them amongst a field of white lilies.'"

"You assume I am something special because of the color of my fur?" I face Anna and notice, for the first time, that much of her features are vastly different from mine. While my hair is as light as the stars, hers is the color of fresh mud. Do such minor details in our design cast us into completely separate roles?

A soft cough echoes from behind us as Willow builds up her response. Anna and I turn to see Caleb, his body and parts of him deemed "inappropriate" for public sight covered with colorful clothes. The material does not take away from the might that Caleb carries with each step.

"The pigment of your fur is but a sign of your greatness, but the proof is with that man," Willow tells me, pointing at Caleb as he struts down the aisle. "There is no known cure or practice to eradicate ferals—the fiends who go mad during transformation. The fianna have been going feral for ages, Maiden. They go mad, they kill without hunger, and they roam the Forest endlessly. The humans of Norsewood hunt and kill them to protect their own people, but it is not enough. I am under the assumption that you found him in the Forest?"

I nod. I do not indulge her with the details of said meeting.

"I was worried I would fall to ash before I saw a Maiden, yet, here you are," Willow exclaims, a deep pleasure stretched across her lips.

"Why does the Maiden only appear at certain times? And if the other Maidens have found the Stag...have 'saved' the ferals...then why hasn't it stopped?" What was broken, I want to ask.

Willow spins a single finger through the air in a tantalizing circle. Around and around. "It is a cycle. The ferals rise, the Maiden arrives, then silence for a few generations. Humans do not know what the Maiden does to ward off the fiends, for the fianna consider the journey a very sacred matter. Thus, only you can answer that." Taking note of the frustration I am inept at hiding, she adds, "In short, a permanent solution does not seem to exist."

I fight a sensation that tries to crawl its way up my body. I don't know what to name the pressure in me, but it is crippling. "Is it possible you are mistaken? I don't think I'm any different from Anna or Caleb."

Willow nods apologetically. "Being a human isn't all that grand. Prone to emotions and sin, we are a cluster of a mess. But I assure you, Maiden, you are every bit as special as the ones who came before you."

I open my lips, but no words crawl up my dried throat.

"It's a lot to take in, I'm sure." Willow coils strands of her hair around her fingers as she speaks. "But don't worry yourself on such things till after the Festival. Drink, be merry, meet new faces."

Caleb further explains by saying, "The Festival is an event the humans host at their city, Norsewood. It is how I, and most of the fianna, have met the humans. It is a night of celebration and communion."

"They'll be expecting you, Maiden. A grand number of eyes will be watching you." Willow starts to walk to the exit of the church, her hair trailing behind like a fog. She stops, once she stands by my side, and touches my shoulder as light as a butterfly. "I'm sure you'll enjoy the humans of Norsewood very much."

Finn

NORSEWOOD SITS SQUISHED between rolling fields and blue skies. Each brightly colored house and shop is scrunched up beside its neighbor, their roofs peeking against each other, their chimneys releasing smoke at seemingly rehearsed intervals. Every other home has planted the same rose on their windowsill, and the same orange tomcat is seen in at least ten windows. The stone cobbled roads cut through the masses like overlapping snakes. During the day, people spill from the shops and houses like bees leaving to collect honey for the hive. The space expands and courses like rivers. Shops vary from weapons, to cooking, to dresses, and back to livestock. All of it presses into me, molding me.

Norsewood, despite the size, is a place of many faces. It is the hills that stretch toward the sea, the bonfires that reach skyward, and the salty-sweet candies at each shop. It is everything the Forest does not take from us.

Walking through the streets is the easiest way to see the activity taking place. Typically, Norsewood is full of everyday chatter and stained stands bursting with merchandise. The bustle can be too much to handle at times, and the people underwhelming, but not today. Doors are thrown wide open, floral decorations are fashioned and hung, lanterns are strung up high, bakeries are popping out snacks, streets are being swept to no avail, greetings are being passed, and most importantly, there are smiles spread openly.

Because, in a few short days, it will be the Festival.

Beer is drunk, regardless of the hour, children run around playing tag while their parents prepare, and women gather while sewing new dresses for their daughters. Dogs bellow, horses snort and stomp their feet, and cats run along the joined rooftops, escaping the noise and commotion like bands of thieves. A few people have brought their instruments into the alleys to tune and prepare their notes for their grand performances.

It is moments like these that I see as much beauty in Norsewood as I do in the Forest.

A group of children spin in a circle, gleefully chanting the old nursery rhythm, "Lily, lily. Lovely lilies. Bloom, wither, begin again. Lovely lilies."

Norsewood yawns and starts to wake up from its sluggish routine. The blood is rushing, sweeping us along.

I take a lungful, inhaling the scent of cinnamon and hoppy beer.

"Personally, I think kids singing is kind of creepy."

I had forgotten that Jay was following me until now. He trails behind me several steps, distracted by all the commotion. "I don't think you should have any children. Ever."

"You think?" he baits.

Without answering, I find my eyes clinging to the chiseled remains of a statue set square in the center of the town. It has been like that, jagged and dangerous, since I was a child. The elders claimed that a man and deer once stood there together, carved from the mightiest of stones. A tribute to the legend of the First Hunter and the Maiden, a farfetched fable of creationism. The statue had, possibly after ill construction, met its demise. There have never been any attempts to repair the damage.

Like the statue, Jay has changed.

He isn't a completely new species, just a slight variation from the boy with a crooked smile. I grew up beside Jay Alder, practically his shadow, so there was not much about him that I couldn't figure out. Back then, I thought the only thing that divided the two of us were our family names. The Alders are a notable house who live a luxurious life. His family trade is fishing, something only Alders and a few select houses tampered with. It's strenuous work, going into the sea's clutches and stealing its inhabitants. When spring finally breaks through winter, the Alders are gone, lost at sea and to the lull of the waves. Every year, Alders went to the water, and every year a few didn't return. They controlled the docks like monarchs, and Jay was handed a crown fit for a prince.

But Jay hates fishing. He hates the scales, he hates the slime that coats their skin, he hates the smell of the ocean, and he hates the motion sickness that accompanies it all. Jay often teased me about entering the hunters' guild, but I always thought it all jokes. It wasn't until he was seated awkwardly on the lodge steps that it all cemented.

As the years stretched, I began to see that more than our families divided us. Jay was growing up into a man who I didn't know well. He was someone I thought I had completely mapped out, and there was comfort in the certainty of that Jay.

"Is Garth too lazy to walk into town on his own?" Jay asks me, cutting my thoughts apart.

Garth had requested—nay, demanded—that Jay and I pick up the coins due to the guild. Because most of the hunters barely stepped inside Norsewood, minor errands became the responsibility of those still in good standing with the town.

"All I have to do is stop by the Hall and pick up the completed bounties and then return to the lodge. I can handle it myself," I tell him. I want Jay to be able to enjoy the Festival's preparations. Despite him being an official member of the hunters' guild, he still has the grace of his family name to protect him in Norsewood. He can linger in the streets without even a side-eye glance. It is an immunity I envy.

Jay pinches my arm. "You think those puny arms are gonna carry all that coin? Pfft. You need me." Folding his hands behind his head, he finishes with, "You should be begging me for my assistance."

I rub at the tender skin. "Is that how it is?"

Inside the Hall, Urkan, a stout man with a horrid temperament, scowls fiercely at the two of us. He mumbles and groans as he checks the files for the money due to the guild. Each bounty and each death compiled is an ugly price for the town. They tried to bring down the cost of each hunt years ago, but Garth merely laughed and passed it off as a joke. In reality, we could charge double and still be in service with the town. The guild is indispensable. While the town might cast us aside, they know not a single citizen would be safe without our protection. No one enters the Forest but the hunters.

Once we have two burlap sacks full of coin, we make to leave from the Hall. Before we can pass the door, Urkan shouts for my attention. Handing me a sealed envelope, he tells me it is an urgent message for Garth.

"The lead hunter has submitted several reports for the council's review." The council is a group of old conservative farmers who hold sway over the direction of Norsewood, usually creating rules and regulations that are no longer relevant. It is a wonder Garth even plays with them. I do not interrupt Urkan though. "Here is their response. Please see to it that he is given this letter."

As we depart, I tuck the envelope into my jacket and promise the councilman it will have a safe trip.

When our feet slap the cobbled streets, Jay swings his bag purposely, the coins glancing off my shoulder. "Damn, I can't tell you the last time I've seen this much coin."

"Too bad Norsewood banned brothels long before your time," I kid. "You could have rented the entire building out."

"Yeah, a pity, indeed," he says with a casual eye roll. "But really, I've been thinking lately."

"Someone notify the authorities; Jay Alder is thinking."

Jay's face scrunches up as he tries to hide his grin. "Screw you. I'm being serious. I know living in the Forest is 'forbidden'—" he creates two pairs of crude air quotes. "But what if just a few people left? No one would notice."

"You wanna live in a cave? Take a bath in the stream?" I roll my eyes. "You wouldn't last a day. You're so pampered you'd come back crying."

Jay continues despite my interruption. "I could build my own house out there. Further from the fianna village. And I'm sure that if I took my time...no one would notice."

"You're telling me that you know how to build a house?"

Jay shrugs. "I could do it. I would just have to teach myself."

"You'd get mighty lonely out there, all by yourself." In this fantasy, Jay would be removed from Norsewood, as if he never existed. He would be a ghost, some name children whispered around fires. "Not to mention, you'd still have to dodge the ferals and some pesky fianna."

"I wouldn't have to be out there all alone," is all Jay says.

"Yeah?" I weave through two men shouting over a heated purchase. "Planning on running away with some farmer's wife?"

"I don't think I could handle that," Jay admits softly. "All the girls in this town want...stability, a family, that perfect image. I can't give them that."

I want to tell him he is wrong. That the Alder family has the strappings to lead that picturesque fantasy. Wealth, status, influence, you name it. Just having the surname of Alder ensures said life. "So, what other options do you have, then?"

Jay looks to me, his hair tickling his brow, while sunlight exposes only half of his face. "I guess I always imagined that you'd be there."

My throat constricts, accepting only the tiniest amounts of air.

"You know," he continues, "so you can be my gardener."

We both laugh as I cuss him up and down. And just like that, we are thrust right back into Norsewood, and further from the exposure of Jay.

AS WE LEAVE the town and enter the waist-high grass fields, Jay continues to plot his hideaway home in the Forest. I humor him with playful questions as we pass by grazing cows and horses, and each answer seems thought out and precise. He has plenty to share as we make our way to the hunters' lodge.

As we near the building, I deduce that it isn't vacant. With even a single hunter in the building, music, vulgarity, and laughter seep from any seam available. Silence does not follow the guild members around.

Once we are within the belly of the lodge, several of the hunters flock to us. It is Garth who dashes through the masses, shoving men left and right until he can herd us past all the chaos and into the cramped room at the rear of the lodge, into his personal space. After the door is shut tightly behind us, Garth starts to divvy up the coins into mini towers designed for various hunters.

Handing him the letter from the Hall, I tell him Urkan's message and prepare myself to leave, ready to pull Jay behind me. Garth stops us with just a raise of his hand. We wait in silence as he tears open the envelope and starts to skim the words before him. After he is done, he crumples up the paper and throws it into the fireplace.

"I have an assignment for you boys," Garth tells us, leaning back in his chair and holding his fingers together into a steeple. If it weren't for Garth's ruthlessness, I wonder if men would follow him naturally. I have seen him break a hunter's nose out of simple annoyance. Garth often leads through examples of violence while I'd believe the hunters would follow anyone who made sure they had enough coin and booze.

"What would that be?" Jay politely asks. Garth has never intimidated Jay. He's used to ruthless men. Growing up with a father who's known for cruel words and loose fists prepared him.

"Several of the hunters have reported that more and more subhumans are pooling into their village. 'Tis the season and all. Willow has already deployed herself, but as I'm sure you are both aware, the witch can't be trusted." Garth rolls his eyes to the common knowledge, dismissing the woman.

Willow is a citizen of Norsewood, but just as much of an outcast as the hunters. She is known for her lionization of the fianna and their ways. Once the previous ambassador of the humans died, Willow was all too eager to take the infamous position. In reality, Willow does nothing of actual value. Aiding the fianna in finding Norsewood in the peak season is the majority of her "help." Yet, she deems her station worthy of a crown.

"There have been sightings of a white-haired doe within the Forest," Garth tells us, and my interest is piqued immediately.

Jay's spine snaps into place, expanding his stature by several inches. "Are you referring to the Maiden of lore?"

"The exact."

Jay tugs at his earlobe. "They see a deer with white fur and suddenly assume it's her? When was the last time one was even sighted? A Maiden, I mean. They only show up every..." He looks to me for confirmation, but I can only shake my head. "Every hundred years or so."

Garth throws his hand in the air, waving off the superstitions. "I'm sure there is record of it somewhere, but I don't give a damn about your wives' tales. All I know is that apparently the subhuman princess appears once the ferals rise in numbers. And as you can see," he finishes with a thumb jabbed at the board behind him, "we have plenty to see." Sheets of paper hang loosely, all of them sightings and completed hunts on ferals. Within the last few weeks, the board has been filling in like a bird's plume feathers.

No one understands the conditions of the ferals' birth. It was a study abandoned long ago. They, unlike other animals of the Forest, do not follow the laws of Nature. They kill for the pleasure of it, not for subsistence. Many hunters of the guild simply follow a trail of corpses to find their marks. The feral Jay and I took down recently was the killer of Ragnar and Ruth, two middle-aged farmers near the edge of Norsewood. Steadily, the ferals are leaving their domain and trekking into human territory.

It is a swell obvious to all.

"Our ancestors were content to follow along with the fianna mythology and lore. 'A Maiden of the white lily comes forth and is the savior of its people,' they'd holler." Garth snorts fiercely before spitting a wad of phlegm into the fire pit. "At the expense of human lives, we've allowed such tales to prevent the safety of our kind. The council wants to seek a more permanent solution to the ferals." Garth stands up and throws several logs into the flames. "I have gotten the approval of the council to have two hunters travel to the subhuman village and confirm the arrival of the Maiden. We are requesting that she accompany her people to the Festival and meet with the human council. And with me," Garth adds, a sneer plastered to his lips. He winks, implying his words have a double meaning.

"With the arrival of the fianna, is it not normal to have hunters stationed at the village anyway? It seems odd the town wants further protection for the fianna," Jay comments.

Garth sighs and glares at him. "The closer you watch those beasts, the easier they are to kill. All of them are storms waiting to erupt. If a single fianna shows signs of turning feral, we have every right to send a bullet through their skull. Yet this girl. She may have secrets useful to humanity. Sniff them out."

"Humans have tried that before," I state rather boldly. There was once an entire cult that worshipped the Stag as wholly as the fianna. They tried to glean the details of the pilgrimage from the Maiden of that time, but they were massacred by ferals after they followed the Maiden through the Forest. Garth turns to me with a fire in his eyes. Despite my courage, I swallow hard. "The fianna keep their beliefs and secrets close. The Maiden will not enlighten us on her pilgrimage to her god."

"She will have no other option," Garth's voice cracks. "Both of you are to report to the fianna village tomorrow morning. Find the location of the Maiden, take notes, and then report back to me. Hazel and Noah Golding are already at the village. Make sure you switch off with them when you arrive. Is that clear?"

Jay and I shoot each other a swift glance. For neither of us consider Hazel being at the fianna village a wise move. Many a man has questioned Hazel Golding's position in the guild due to her being the only female hunter in the history of the lodge. Yet, all those men have ended up with gouged-out eyes, bruised genitals, and broken pride. She is as dangerous as a fox caught in a trap. Her twin brother, Noah, is the only one who can escape Hazel's wrath.

"Before you go," Garth adds as he leans across his desk. He angles his words in the direction of Jay, but they collide with me all the same. "You may need to toughen up, boy."

Jay tries to remain unresponsive, but the muscles along his jaw tighten in an effort to restrain himself. "The weak have no place here. I know you are only succeeding by being close to that one," he says, pointing at me. "And you should know that devils don't make good allies."

Silence hangs in the air so thick that I think it is strangling us. I want to be angered by Garth's statement, but my mind is clogged, unable to move past the fact Jay's act is no longer working. Until now, I've assumed I could pick up the slack, that I could cover up the parts of him that are different.

You were wrong.

"You must not be watching close enough," Jay comments. "Because it was me who shot that feral first. If he hadn't been moving, I would have been the one to kill him."

Garth returns to his seat, fingers coming together in a steeple. He studies Jay as if he can still see the bloodshot eyes and the tears running down his cheeks. "I see. I look forward to you continuing to correct me. You two have your orders. Now, get lost."

When we stand outside the lodge, Jay turns to me but doesn't say a word. There is no accusation on his lips, no judgment in his eyes, but he waits for me to say something, all the same. I'm not sure what he wants. The things inside me, the thoughts currently raging through my mind, aren't the things he wants to hear. I'm too caught up in the notion that I am not a devil. That Jay can and should always consider me an ally.

When frustration takes over and Jay leaves me, I know I am a coward.

If I was brave, or had a fraction of courage, I would stop him. Tell him to come back. Tell him everything I keep bottled up.

But I don't. And this is how I know I am a coward.

Adelaide

JUST AS BEARS know when to hibernate, the fianna instinctively migrate towards the abandoned village that was more Forest then manmade now. They are pulled into the confinement of mossy planks of wood and concaved roofs like it was written in their blood.

"Do you think it's true?" I ask when Anna finds me in the village streets. Despite the new faces, all of them seem to know who I am. It is the kind of intimacy that startles me.

Anna runs her fingers through my hair, combing it while she hums, "Hmm?"

"That I'm the Maiden?" I finish.

Anna pauses for a moment. "The Maiden is white as snow, as delicate as a lily. You are all of those things, and more."

"Those things don't seem very...important." How do things I can't control change how this world perceives me? "I also do not feel as delicate as a flower. I feel as mighty as a bear."

"You can be both fragile and mighty," Anna tells me as she pulls my hair upward and places pins within the folds. "But remember, badgers can't be foxes, and the birds can't help but fly. You were born special and you can't change *that*."

Before I can further express my angst, Anna stands up, holding her hand down for me to grab. "You should come and greet them. You give them courage."

I stare at her hand before allowing her to pull me up beside her. Just because I am not confident in my role doesn't mean I can't support my species.

The first fianna to approach me is a female. She is heavyset, and her smile is kind. Without hesitation, she wraps her arms around me and squeezes. She greets me as the Maiden and continues her way into the village with such ease that one would think she had only been gone for a day, not half a year.

"Most of the fianna rejoice in their time as a human," Willow informs me. She was at the entrance to the village when we arrived, cheerfully helping the fianna trickle through it. Just as effortlessly as the fianna can name me, they seem to identify Willow. "It is when they can truly be themselves. All parts of them."

"They are their selves before they become human," I state, trying to ignore the heat itching my skin.

Anna pretends to swat me away like a fly. "Let her be. She has pretty words." While she speaks, Caleb stalks up behind her, laughing once he causes her to scream. Caleb attempts to bring her into a hug while Anna bats at him in mock anger.

Appearing from the tree line, a buck staggers forward as his front legs crumple beneath him. I watch, terrified and captivated. His head collides against the grass, and no matter how the soil has thawed, I know there is pain in the contact. His body spasms, legs thrashing in the air like a fish out of water. The deer continues to roll on the ground, multiple cuts starting to form on his brown hide like crudely drawn lines. With a mighty effort, the buck lifts his head once more and brings it back down onto the soil with an audible crack.

Still as death, the buck seems to have left this world entirely. Then, only the muscles start to shift. Something underneath the skin wiggles and pokes through the furs. The front legs crack, the meat on the marrow twisting and growing until the fur can no longer contain the pressure and bulges and tears. A hand extends from the black hooves, the digits dark and stiff, but soon works out into five fine pieces. The other arm follows, and the knees buckle forward until a human male peels away from his old skin. The antlers, still attached, splinter away like dead wood, dissolving elegantly. The tumble of blond hair that cascades down his brow pushes the bones onto the dirt.

The fianna stays kneeling in the remains of his old body, now merely furs and blood, his new form only moving to take in breaths, hands curling around the gore.

Then he screams a harrowing sound.

Caleb lets out a mighty breath, one I felt everyone was holding. "Our transformations are becoming more difficult. It is not a good sign," he admits. "It is then, between those shapes, that the fianna can get stuck." Pushing past us, Caleb moves until he crouches by the male's side. His lips move as he speaks gently and slowly to the fianna, striving to calm him down. Caleb helps the male rise to his feet and continues to hold onto him until his first few steps transform into a confident gait.

"This must be his first time as a human," Anna concludes. "Shifting is painful...but it shouldn't be that difficult."

"Do you remember yours, Maiden?" Willow asks, not affected by the scene before her. Her curiosity does not seem gentle, but suspiciously dangerous. Like a predator. "What it felt like to become human?"

Anna scoffs.

"I do not," I say, still captivated by the male Caleb brings closer and closer. "I awoke...in dirt," I say. "In a hole covered in petals." With the words—

begin again, begin again

Anna looks at me with worry.

"Well, you certainly are special, hmm?" Willow teases, patting my arm lightly. "Sprouting from the ground doesn't happen to everyone."

As the Forest begins to still, I notice from the corner of my eye that two figures rest amongst the trees, unmoving. One male, one female. The girl holds a rope that is attached to a...

"Why does that troubled girl have a goat in the Forest?" Willow questions.

The girl in the distance pats the animal's fuzzy head as it cries repeatedly, a look of playfulness tugging at her lips.

"Who are they?" I ask.

"Hunters," Anna informs me.

"What are they doing?"

"The Forest hasn't been a safe place for some years now. It was decided that only hunters should be able to enter the domain of the fianna." Willow waves at the hunters as they slither through the tree line. "That girl, by far, is the most dangerous creature in the Forest right now. Stay clear of her," she tells me, tapping a nail to my shoulder.

"Do not let her scare you, Adelaide," Anna tells me. "You will love the human town. Endless things to do, so much to see." She squeezes my arm, her joy contagious. "Soon, you will see that there is nothing to fear."

"Being human seems very...complex," I admit to both Anna and Willow. Fianna and human.

By now, Caleb has passed the male fianna off to Willow who wraps him in clothing and showers him with kind words. As he passes, I see his fingers are still twitching. "It is important that we deal with these issues ourselves," Caleb tells me. "The humans, with good reason, are afraid of even the slightest proof of ferals."

I yelp as a loud pop rings through the treetops, disrupting roosting birds. "What was that?" I ask, pressing a hand to my chest to find where my heart rages about.

Caleb goes very still. "The hunters."

"They caused that loud noise?"

"That is the sound of the hunt," Caleb tells me as he ushers us back into the village. "The sound of a gunshot. And the sound that accompanies death."

Finn

I'M AWOKEN EARLY in the morning to Pa stomping through the house frantically. As I roll around my mattress, the wind outside beats against the house mercilessly, adding to the general ruckus. Blurry-eyed and groggy, I descend the steps and find Pa rummaging through the cabinets.

"I need my pistol," he proclaims. "Dammit, have you hidden my pistol?"

"No," I tell him. "Where do you plan on going?" I ask after I inspect his boots and the pack slung across his back.

"The fianna. They arrived," he tells me as he spills the contents of a cabinet onto the floor. He does not flinch as fragile items shatter. "I must go into the Forest."

It is a legend on resurrection that has kept my father going. Mystery and myth hung around the fianna, but only a few adopted such beliefs. Pa had lost his last remnant of sanity along with his wife, and his devotion shifted until he clung to the lore of the Stag and his powers.

For it is said that the blood of the Stag is life itself.

Generations ago, Norsewood was home to a band of fanatics who believed in the Stag god just as devotedly as the fianna did, but for other purposes. They believed, amongst many things, that the blood of the Stag was mystical. That if it was captured and drained, the substance would give humans otherworldly powers. Entwined with the belief was the theory that the blood would prevent death itself. Immortality could be achieved.

Pa was a practical man, but the theory snagged his soul and claimed him.

"All I need is a little more blood," he informs me. "If I can just do a few more tests, I will have everything I need."

I rub my knuckles against my eyes. "You can't do that, Pa. Hazel and Noah are patrolling around the village." I don't need to remind him that Hazel is comparable to a mother bear in ferocity and ruthlessness. She would enjoy beating back my father. "Don't give the town any more reason to hunt you down."

"Don't tell me what I can and can't do!" he screams. His shout is horrendous, a sound that cracks as it leaves his throat. It is a complete jump from his previously hushed tone. "I have to—I can't stop—" Pa rambles, his sentences clashing together.

I imagine what it would be like to tell Pa that the Maiden was sighted. What would he do, to what lengths would he go, to find a creature said to be directly connected to the Forest deity?

I massage my temples, knowing Jay will be here soon, and I don't need him seeing Pa like this. Years of growing up side by side with me has given Jay a hint of the storm that brews inside Pa, but I was quick enough, smart enough, to make sure Jay was always distant when Pa could no longer hold himself back.

"You wouldn't be able to get close," I tell him as I realign the sofa. "It has been a long time since you were in the Forest. It isn't as safe as it used to be."

"Plenty of them get lost in the woods. I'll just—"

A knock sounds off at the door.

"Please, promise me that you won't go into the Forest," I beg.

Pa looks out of the nearest window, temperament rivaling that of a toddler. I know I can't hold him to his word, so I'll have to trust that I hid the weapons well.

Another knock at the door.

"Hold on!" I shout as I tear the pack from Pa. I find a stray shirt on the floor and throw it over my head while disgusted by the amount of filth that can collect in this house. "Stay here. You understand?" Pa does not respond. I kick some of the mess under the sofa before I head for the door.

When I open it for Jay, he immediately glances down with raised brows. "I'm no expert, but don't you need pants for this?"

"I'm working on that," I say as I slam the door in his face.

I KNOW HAZEL intended to be spotted as soon as I see her golden braid falling down her shoulders. Hazel is lethal in the Forest, able to shift through the layers of the trees like a mountain lion in her element. To be so noticeable is no accident.

"Well, well, well," Hazel sings, her voice high pitched and sweet. Her ugly bangs, indubitably cut with rusty shears, sway in the breeze. She slings her bow across her back with practiced ease and skips up to Jay and me. She gets close enough that her nose brushes my lips. "Come to keep us company?"

I peek over her shoulder and wave at Noah. "Hey there, bud."

Noah, who silently stands beside his sister, does not grin, does not move. More of a boulder than man.

"We don't need backup," Hazel informs us. "We are more than suited for the task, aren't we, Noah?" To emphasize her point, she shows off her blood-stained hands.

For the years I have known Noah, I have never heard him utter a single word. Some say that after he watched Hazel butcher their mother, he lost his ability to speak. It was hearsay, but not impossible.

I doubt he even has a tongue.

"We are here to relieve you of your..." I scan Hazel's bloody tunic. "What are you doing?"

"Don't worry about it." Hazel, deliriously herself, licks her lips in an attempt to be seductive, yet my stomach churns instead.

"Welp, how about you go back to town? Or! Go stab some squirrels. Murder a family of porcupines," I recommend. "I personally think you would love some poisonous reptiles."

"Your low opinion of me is truly alarming," Hazel tells me. "I would never hurt a squirrel. Besides, I'm busy taking some billy goats for a walk."

I look to her brother. "I bet your happy chattiness doesn't run in your family, huh?"

He only blinks.

"Makes sense that Garth would throw you into the center of this mess," Hazel teases. "It'll be fun to watch you scramble."

I grab Jay's arm and pull him behind me. "Ignore her. She's insane."

Hazel's laugh bounces through the Forest long after she is gone.

TWO BULKY MALES stand in surveillance at the entrance to the fianna village, their golden eyes taking us in. The gun on my back suddenly feels hot. Jay states we are here with the guild to offer the fianna protection and the two don't protest. They offer us grins and greetings as they move to the side, allowing us entry.

We circle the perimeter of the village twice before moving inward, sliding past buildings hung with ivy and moss that look more like graves instead of living quarters. The entire settlement is suited more for ghosts, not anything living.

"How do they even survive?" Jay mutters while simultaneously smiling and greeting a couple of fianna.

"They have a farm," I say, pointing into a patch of the Forest that has been stripped away. On the night of the Festival, Norsewood gifts the seasonal fianna with produce and crops to help sustain them until their own food flourishes, but with such a small time frame to grow anything, the fianna usually resort to foraging in the Forest. Technically, they're scavengers," I say. "They're used to eating grass."

The center of the village is nothing spectacular, simply a location where all the paths and "streets" meet up. I avert my eyes from numerous fianna walking around nude, trying to minimize the rosy tint of my cheeks.

"They look so similar...yet they are clearly different," Jay comments, not nearly as displaced by exposed genitals.

We have been taught from a young age that the fianna look human but are not such. Old Norsewood doctrines has told us each human possesses a soul that will travel to the afterlife. Fianna, like foliage, belong to nature and the "cycle." It is a novel concept, being compared to plants and life, but in the end, the fianna are still being called soulless. Less than.

When I was a child, the concept that I could be so easily deceived frightened me. Yet, as I grew, I found that even men can bear no soul.

"We should start by looking for Willow. I wouldn't be surprised if she's crawling around on all fours by now," I say. Even when the fianna are animals in the woods, Willow can still be found wandering the empty village like a mourning ghost. A phantom who clearly doesn't clean or tend to anything.

"Wonder why more people from Norsewood don't come visit," Jay comments, almost to himself. He seems to be fixated on a fianna male dusting out a shadowy home.

I think of what people like Pa would do in a place filled with so many fianna. "It isn't exactly the safest travel destination. With all the death and stuff."

"So, we force the fianna to stay in this dump?" Jay sighs. "We could do more to protect the village. Actually try. Set up a system. Try and give a shit."

"You speak so highly of them," I say. "The hunters."

Jay shrugs. "You know they aren't the best of the best."

"And that's why I'll never understand why you joined," I say. Jay looks to me, confused. "The guild," I clarify. "You know how screwed up they all are, and yet you stay? You could do anything else in the world, and you chose this?"

"Where is this coming from?" Jay asks. By now, he has thrown himself on the ledge of the well, taken off his boots, and is massaging his feet.

"All I'm saying is that if you weren't in the guild, you could be...a baker. You could build homes. Farm. Settle down. Raise a family." As I outline each of Jay's possibilities a sharp pain increases in my chest. All these chances he has at normality and he just spits on them.

"'Cause I don't want to be a fucking baker," Jay snaps, the familiar tension between us flexing its massive muscles. "I don't need any of that to be happy."

"You don't get it," I insist. "Ennon, Rowan, all of them. They could be tried and executed. Maybe Garth was right." I hate how the words sound, how I don't struggle at all to speak them. "You can't trust hunters."

"Then why are you in the guild, Finn?" He turns the decision around to me with dizzying quickness. Jay has never intruded on why I am in the guild myself. It is a conversation neither of us wanted to have. Yet, here we were. "I know that you have no dark sin. There has to be a reason, even if it isn't one you can admit, that you are a hunter. Why don't you start, Finn? You first, and I'll follow suit."

A chill clasps my heart. I wonder what Jay would say about Pa. If he knew it all. Because while I'm not the one with the "sins," not the sinner, I'm protecting him. That makes me pretty much an accomplice, right?

"This isn't about me," I growl. I tell my thoughts to jump off a cliff and I focus on Jay.

"It's never about you," he snaps back. "Never. It's always me who should leave the guild. It's me who isn't strong enough to hunt."

Jay's eyes glisten, but I can't look straight at him. Because I just can't.

"So, what about you, Finn? Why are you in the guild?" He drops down to the ground, barefoot, and stops when he is inches from me. "'Cause, I'd follow you anywhere, Finn."

"My, my."

I virtually leap out of my skin as Willow, with her hair pulled back, exits one of the abandoned buildings. She squints with the intensity of someone inspecting bugs that have invaded her kitchen. "Here to replace those menacing twins?"

I can only blink at her.

"I mean no disrespect, but two fledgling hunters doesn't seem like adequate protection."

Jay moves past Willow's sarcasm faster than I can, forever being a better person than I. Despite being raised by Ben Alder and his raging emotions, Jay is careful with words. "Plenty of hunters are patrolling the Forest. We were sent to guard the inner parts of the village."

"And here I thought you were just visiting me," Willow sneers, acting like the fianna village is her home. "You can tell Garth that everything is swell. The fianna will be at the Festival. As they have years before. They will drink, they will mingle, and the children will point and stare. All will be the same. Also—" She crosses her arms with annoyance. "Let Garth know we don't have enough supplies this year. We've almost run out already."

"Garth does not control the guild," I say, but I can see in her eyes that we both know it isn't the truth. "Orders come from the council."

"You know just as well as I that Garth has his claws in too much." I have never tackled the concept of bad blood pooling up between Willow and Garth, but, at surface level, it looks deep. "Please pass that along to your master."

Jay looks to me, silently asking for advice. "We were informed of a fianna with white fur," I tell Willow, ignoring the warnings that Garth's interest in the Maiden may be confidential. I straighten my back unnoticeably. "Know anything about that?"

"An albino," Jay interjects.

"Who wishes to know?" Willow asks. "Garth or the council?"

"None of your business," I tell her. "You can—"

"Does she plan on attending the Festival?" Jay asks Willow. While he may have cut the flow of my words, the war between Willow and I is being fought now with body language. "You know the myths. A Maiden being born would explain the rise of ferals."

"Odd," Willow says while she places a finger between her teeth. "I didn't know you cared much for maidens."

Before I can snap back, Jay has his hand on my shoulder. Turning to look at him, I see he is pointing further into the village.

Straight at a girl. With hair so light that the sunlight turns it nearly invisible, she is a clear variation amongst the other fianna. Her eyes are the lightest tint of honey, and her face is perfectly symmetrical, which isn't something I think I'd normally take into account. Her lips are thin and brightly colored. Her sturdy body is hidden beneath an elegant dress fashioned from the fur of animals. A set of intertwined antlers rests on her brow like a crown.

For the first time in my life, I'm looking at something new.

Trailing behind her is a petite female with chin-length hair the color of a raven's feathers and a male who could easily rival a bear with huskiness. When they stand before us, they are the image of fairy tale royalty.

Willow, taking on her role, introduces the three fianna. "Maiden, Caleb, Anna, this is Finn Hail and Jay Alder. They are residents of Norsewood. They come with blessings and goodwill."

"We are just here to make sure that you are well and safe for the Festival tomorrow. The humans of Norsewood are very excited," Jay tells the three fianna, an uneasy smile on his lips. On one hand, he isn't lying. The humans are excited for the Festival, with the snacks and the start of a new year. They are not always excited for the visitors. "I trust you will inform us if anything is amiss?"

The Maiden glances to me, and for some reason, an unknown heat prickles at me. It is not the Maiden who speaks, but the female at her side. "Thank you for your kindness. We are fine."

"That's good to hear," I tell her. I do not like the way the Maiden's eyes latch onto me. She seems to study every piece of me. "If you need us, we shouldn't be too far away."

"What do we need...protecting from?" the Maiden asks, speaking for the first time.

I know that I have a chance to build a bridge between us. To say the right words. But Pa never taught me how to speak kindly.

"Have you not seen them?" I say. "The creatures that roam the Forest killing?"

The brute beside the Maiden stiffens. "Thank you for your protection. Will you be needing anything else?"

Willow laughs at the escalating tension. "They have direct orders from the town to keep the Maiden safe. The more eyes on her, the better, no?" She aims to reassure us all.

Anna, the other female fianna, skips forward. "I think that is lovely. Thank you," she says to Jay and me. "We are grateful. Right, Adelaide?"

That's a pretty name, I think before I can silence the thought.

Adelaide does not answer right away. "All I ask is that you don't hurt them," she says, aiming her voice to me. To the one with the gun. "I don't know how, but I will save them."

"That is the role of the Maiden," Jay interjects. "Until then, we will protect you. No matter what the cost is."

Adelaide looks to the mass beside her, at the grim male. "Caleb was feral. But I found him. I saved him. What if you would have killed him?"

"What if he tried to kill someone?" I fire back.

"He didn't." Anna places a hand on Adelaide.

"He could've," I say as Jay jabs at my back with his knuckles.

Willow claps her hands together, but that Maiden and I still glare at one another. "Well, we all have places to be, no? I think you and Jay have plenty to think on."

Despite it all, the impracticality of saving each and every single feral, I can't stop myself from imagining who that beast may have become if I hadn't killed him in the woods.

Adelaide

I START TO develop a fear of darkness when the sun flees from the sky and the shadows of the Forest grow large enough to devour me. No matter how close Anna sleeps next to me, it isn't close enough. The furs beneath me and on top of me aren't enough protection from what I fear.

And each morning I am exhausted.

"I think this looks stunning on you," Anna tells me as she pulls and teases at my hair until it is piled behind me like a beehive. Those words are hauntingly familiar at this point with Anna having said them over and over. Having placed me before a mirror, she fusses over every angle of me for the entire day. I decide, rather quickly, that I do not think I can ever be as pretty as Anna. When I look at her, with her human smile, I doubt I could ever exude her confidence in new skin.

"It should be you who wears this crown," I tell her, my fingers moving to remove the half circle of flowers and horns resting on my brow. It is Anna who possesses grace and beauty unlike any other. No matter how much time passes, I do not feel like a Maiden.

Could it be transferred just as easily as I can hand Anna the makeshift crown? If I could, would I allow her this legend? To go and be something special to our people?

My fingers hesitate.

"You are meant to wear that," Anna tells me. Her smile is warm, genuine. "I'm much too simple for such a task."

"What happened to Caleb?" I ask her as she peels me from my reflection. Despite her continual attempt to tame my mane, I see her frown. "Did you think he was dead?"

Anna makes herself busy, beginning to clean up the mess she caused to make me pretty. "Our memories from before are confusing. Yet, somehow, I remember the last time I saw him. He had been chasing me through the Forest. Prancing and throwing his body around youthfully..." Anna's fingers brush the smile resting on her face while she reminisces on a time other than now. "Then...I was human. Between one step and the next. Caleb was there, his body trying to follow me. But he didn't. He..."

I place my hand on her arm, and it seems to pull her back here, into this room with me.

"You brought him back." Anna's face seems... complicated. I expect to see her eyes filled with longing or joy, but her gaze is far away, lost almost.

A knock on the door signals Caleb's arrival. He, like us, is decorated for the Festival. Placed upon his head is half the skull of a buck, antlers and all. Black mud is smeared along his facial features, exaggerating each angle fiercely. Most of his body is exposed, as if giving the humans proof that he is one of them.

"Both of you look beautiful." When he says the words, I have no doubt he means them. I see pride all over him. He pulls Anna to his chest, and while she playfully squeals, he plants his lips to her forehead. It is so human...and adorable.

Anna swats at Caleb, dancing out of his hold. "Are you ready?" she asks us both grandly. "To meet the humans?"

I look at the room and the low light that trickles through the openings, a panic clenching me. "Is this supposed to be home?" For the next few months, will these walls be all I see? Will it matter, though, if Anna and Caleb filled up the empty spaces?

"It's nothing spectacular, I know, but it's...cute." I scrunch my nose at the word and Anna giggles. "Tomorrow, we can go pick some flowers for the den. You'll learn to love it."

"But right now, you have a Festival to attend, Maiden." Caleb places his hand on my back and confidence bubbles in me. Anna and Willow have been teaching me the procedures and rituals of the humans of Norsewood, but touch is still startling. "Are you ready?"

I nod. "Of course."

The other fianna are much more prepared than I am. They huddle together in excitement, preparing fledgling fianna and sharing stories of past Festivals. Several fianna stop me and bless me, but I am too awkward to do anything except thank them and move on. Instead, with each conversation, I take just a pinch of their excitement and it begins to build within me.

Graciously, after the swarm of bodies became too strong, Caleb captures my attention and he declares to the herd that we will begin our descent into Norsewood. As physical as a warm summer breeze, the varied emotions of the fianna cascade my body. Their nervousness, their fear, their excitement.

I take a deep breath, consuming it all with an intoxicating potency.

It is the first time I will see the human village. The first time I will be submerged in their world.

While I prance behind Caleb, finding it so easy to laugh and smile, a scream splits the air.

At first, I mistake the noise as a part of the anticipation. Like how a wolf howls before the hunt. Yet, the scream is accompanied by another, and another.

Then it's *bam bam bam.*

The herd shifts uneasily, trying to identify the source of the yells. As I search, I see a figure coming down the path, approaching us leisurely. It is hunched, walking on all fours, black veins visible, and its crooked antlers drip with blood like melting icicles.

Feral.

I spin my head and see another one. Moving as quickly as a fox, the feral cuts into the herd and sinks its fangs into the exposed neck of a female. The brightest red I have ever seen flows from the feral's jaws as the dying fianna gurgles a warning.

Then, chaos.

Caleb pushes bodies away as he reaches for Anna and me. Once he has ahold of my hand, he leaps from the village square and into an alleyway. He does not stop running, pulling with a force that threatens to tear my arm free.

Crashing through glass, a feral tumbles into the path before us. When it collides with the adjacent building, the feral's neck crunches at a horrid angle. As the fiend rises, it hisses guttural words at us like a snake. Swiftly, Caleb removes the skull off his head, breaks the antlers apart and poses them before him. The feral lurches forward, and Caleb is prepared. With a sucking sound, Caleb sinks the antler into the throat of the beast. The feral claws at Caleb with its remaining life, but when Caleb retracts the horn, the fiend collapses in a heap.

"This is wrong...this is wrong, wrong, wrong." Anna has her hands tangled in her hair, blood from the feral speckled along her face. "Caleb, we need to get Adelaide out of here."

"You didn't let me save him," I state, but it seems I am the only person who hears my words.

"Caleb!" Anna screams, taking hold of his face in her two hands. "Listen to me!"

Caleb places his bloody palms on top of hers. "Take Adelaide and run for the town. I'll hold them off."

Tears spring from Anna's eyes. "No! I'm not leaving you. You need to come with us—"

"Take her and run!"

"Caleb," I say, my voice shaky. "Please. Come with us."

Flicking his wrist, Caleb swings some of the blood off the horns. "Adelaide, I need you to protect Anna. Please. Take her and get out of here. Run straight out of the village. You'll find the town once the trees vanish." I do not move at first, stunned by all I hear and see, by the burden cast on me. "Now!"

I reach for Anna and pull her behind me, running despite the terror that locks onto me.

Finn

JAY AND I are climbing the stairs to an abandoned building in the fianna village, the boards of moldy lumber creaking beneath us while we discuss the inevitability of twin babies being mismatched at birth.

"Where the hell is this even coming from?" I ask Jay, unable to hold back my chuckle.

"All I'm saying is that when Gregor and Brent were born, Gregor was Brent and Brent was Gregor, but since they looked so similar as babies, they will forever suffer from an identity crisis," Jay replies once we reach one of the few bedrooms. He pulls out a notepad and jots down a few details on yellow pages about the Maiden, her features, the fianna that surround her, and so on. "All because of lazy parenting, we now have two unstable men in Norsewood."

"I honestly can say I have no idea what you are talking about." And that's the truth. Jay is a fan of outlandish conversations, ones that might confuse and frighten eavesdroppers due to how strange they truly are. "So, what solution would you offer to the parents of newborn twins?"

Jay presses his pointer finger to his chin in mock concentration. "To be fair, I didn't have to worry about this with my twin brother."

"Mhm?" I say, knowing fully well that Jay is an only child.

"Because I ate my brother in the womb!"

Jay and I laugh as I launch several punches at him.

It is only the second day Jay and I have been in the fianna village, but I am already dreading when it will end. Outside Norsewood, in the space between the trees, Jay's layers unravel until only the fun-loving boy who tells corny jokes and sometimes snorts when laughing too hard remains. It is the Jay from years ago.

The Jay who wasn't a hunter in the guild.

"What now?" Jay asks once his breathing levels out.

"The Festival is tonight," I tell him. As I peer out the glassless window, I see the fianna gathering, their anticipation reaching even me. "Are you going to want a rematch at the ax toss this year?"

Jay rolls his eyes dramatically. "I think I'll pass. It's unfair that someone as puny as you can whip an ax like that. Frankly, I think it's cheating."

It is my turn to roll my eyes, but Jay can't see it.

In the thick of the fianna, I see the Maiden. The others step out of her way, giving her a path through the streets. They reach out to her, dance around her, and laugh like birds singing in the evening. "Do you think she's pretty?" I ask Jay absentmindedly. "The Maiden, I mean."

"She's gorgeous. Shy. Sweet. You could learn something from her."

"Sorry I can't be as pretty as her."

Jay smirks as he stands, the setting sun lighting up his face lazily. "You are such—"

Boom.

The first shot stuns both Jay and me. It isn't unusual to hear a few shots this far out in the Forest—

Then, shots fire off consecutively. *Bam, bam, bam.*

When we hear the screams, Jay and I hang out of the window, scanning the streets down below. I see the first feral bursting through the trees with the second close behind, running into the village on all fours, arms and legs animalistic.

"No," Jay stammers. "This isn't possible." A few more shots sound off in the Forest. "Do you think Hazel and Noah have been overrun? Aren't there more hunters out there?"

"Not important," I tell him, grabbing my pack and heading for the exit. "If we leave from the east gate, we can hit the creek and—"

Jay does not move from the windowsill. "We have to help them."

I blink at him, baffled. "Are you kidding me? We don't have to do anything! We can't possibly take all of them out."

Standing, Jay swings his rifle in front of him. "I'm not leaving."

A loud crash sounds from beneath us, a gurgled scream accompanying the noise.

"Hells," I sigh as I throw my pack against the wall in frustration. I know, with the way Jay sets his shoulders, he won't budge. "You stay right here; do you hear me? If you even leave this spot, I will personally skin you alive."

"Where are you going?" Jay asks.

"Guns are loud. You'll be painting a target on yourself." I stand in the doorway, wanting to say something inspirational or motivating, but instead I tell Jay, "How about you aim this time?"

I take the steps two at a time while Jay's shots ring out. Once I land at the bottom, I find a feral with his deer-like snout tearing through the thin flesh of a fianna beneath him. The sound of my heavy footsteps causes the beast to rear his head up, his eyes locking with mine.

As I reach for my rifle, the feral dashes off the wood with his hooved feet, faster than an ax dropping.

The feral is within my space before I can aim. Instead, I drop to the floor, and when the feral's momentum causes its body to loom above mine, I stand up, bringing my shoulder as hard as I can into the feral's sternum. Continuing the beast's trajectory, I toss the feral against the wall. Thankfully, its body careens through a window and out into the neighboring alleyway.

Running out of the house, I see blood and bodies littering the streets like dead leaves. I raise my rifle and snipe the closest beast. As it drops, I reload. I want to call out, ask for backup, but only madness exists here. I peek up to the second floor where Jay is stationed, watching as fire explodes from the tip of his gun.

I bring my focus back to my own shooting. After my second feral falls, I stop counting. My mind screams for rational thoughts. Never before have I seen so many ferals in one area. They never attack as one unit, like a swarm uncontainable.

Sharp teeth clamp onto my calf.

I unsheathe my knife and bring it down onto the back of a feral. Once the blade hits meat, its jaw separates in a moan of pain. I spin, cock my foot back, and slam the steel-toed boot into its nose. I don't need to aim as I fire into the feral's forehead. Wet splashes against my pants.

Panic laces through my veins. I continue through the fianna village, but my wounded leg handicaps me. The teeth sunk deeper than I realize, and each shuffle is a painful endeavor. In panicked flight, a fianna barrels into me, racing out of the village perimeter. He is only a few feet into the trees when a female feral pounces on him and tears his body apart.

A force presses into my side, and before I can struggle, Jay's voice is in my ear. "I'm here. I got you." He hoists me up, taking the pressure from my calf.

"I thought I told you—"

"Yeah, well, I didn't listen, did I? Let me save you this time."

I bite my lip as each step sends a new thump straight to my head. "We need to find cover," I say, my voice achingly weak. Matching gore covers Jay and I don't know how he got it, but I do know it looks so very wrong on him.

"We'll bunker down and wait until morning to go back to town," Jay informs me while turning a street. "By now, the ferals are mostly concerned with the fianna. If we stay in cover and bandage you up—"

A few steps ahead of us, a feral steps into view, blocking the road ahead. It is larger than the others, with black fur lining its legs and chest. A stern chiseled face gazes at us, while horns, unnaturally thick and coiled behind its head like the horns of a ram, continue to grow and become impossibly large.

Jay, with all his strength, shoves me off the street and through the opening of a dusty building. I land in a pile of leaves and items that belonged to past inhabitants. My leg bounces against the floor and I bite back a yelp.

As I struggle to right myself, the battle outside commences.

Jay, legs spread, rapidly fires at the charging demon. With shots too wide, the feral is able to dodge the bullets without much effort. Swiping, the feral is close enough that his hand knocks the rifle from Jay while leaving an intricate slash along his forearm. Jay jumps backward, giving him space to brandish his own knife. As the feral advances, Jay is too slow to dodge all the blows, unable to track the randomness with which the feral attacks.

A surprisingly intentional and solid kick connects to Jay's chest, sending him careening backward and onto the stones and dirt like a baby bird falling from the nest. The feral lunges through the air and lands on top of Jay, and as they twist and turn, I lose track of where Jay is and where the beast ends.

On the final roll, the feral comes out on top, clawed fingers tight around Jay's throat. My heart sinks when I see more blood on Jay than skin.

With a snarl, the feral brings his antlers down.

"Jay!" I scream as I hear the tines shred and crack against the street.

I can't see where the horns land, not with all the wayward points, but Jay continues to move relentlessly, whether he was hit or not. With the opening, he uses one hand to grip onto the feral's antlers while he brings his other arm up, dagger becoming a blur.

The feral freezes as the blade opens up his throat.

The world is silent as the body drops on top of a battered Jay. There are no more screams, no more gunshots. Just the remains of something evil. Jay crawls from beneath the corpse, nearly unrecognizable, and shakily makes his way to his feet.

For a moment, Jay is victorious. My entire body unravels with relief. Yet, when he presses a hand to his stomach, his face scrunches up in pain.

When he removes his palm, it is soaked in blood.

His eyes find mine, and his lips quiver. "Finn?"

And he drops.

The pain in my leg is absent as I rush to his side, turning him onto his back and into my arms. Jay's hands reach for me, grasping every part of me like he's drowning and I'm the only thing to prevent him from sinking. I take his knife and slice the rest of his tunic off, trying to be as careful as I can while my mind screams at me.

Along his stomach are several punctures. Deep, ugly wounds that endlessly pour out blood.

"I'm so sorry." Tears slither down Jay's grimy cheeks. His fingers stretch to find the gashes lining his chest, but instead, I grasp his hand in mine and squeeze as hard as possible. "I'm sorry–"

He is trying to talk, but it becomes gurgles. When he exhales, it is a cloud of blood splattering over his lips. I don't know what I am saying when I talk, mostly a tangle of words and confusion.

Jay keeps trying to talk, and I keep trying to put his stomach back together.

"Please no," I say. My voice is rough as I shake. My vision won't stay clear but damn it, I need to see. "No," I plead.

Jay is staring at me, no longer trying to speak, but just watching me. He offers me a bloody smile, one that tears through me ruthlessly, and a million versions of Jay flicker through my mind. The boy who was afraid to fire a gun, the one who swam in every creek possible, and the man who was brave enough to join a band of killers.

But I know the Jay I see now is the one I will never be able to forget. This version of him will haunt me for the rest of my life.

When Jay goes limp, I don't let go of his hand.

Adelaide

I RUN AS fast as my two human legs will allow. Anna and I leap over logs and stones, but our pursuers devour the little distance we create. To our right, the Forest spews out vicious-looking ferals. Bodies already coated with blood. Anna shouts for me to duck, and I drop underneath a low hung branch right as a feral collides into the wood.

Run.

Run.

I can't think of anything else. My thoughts start to jumble together, blurring into single actions.

Run.

Flee.

Hide.

Clenching my jaw, I command myself to continue through the pain. An ache throbs deep within my muscles, and my bones snap and slide against each other. With a start, I realize my body wants to change. To adapt to the situation.

A sound that rivals thunder cracking causes a feral to buckle mid-run. Blood and mush spray into the grass as he stills. Looking over my shoulder, I see two ferals pierced through the throat with sharp arrows. Anna slows down, her steps coming to a halt as she inspects the bodies behind us, chest heaving in exertion.

"You continue to the humans," she tells me. "I will go back and find Caleb."

"I don't think you should do that," I reply. I care for Caleb and pray to the Stag that he is safe...but I am terrified. I do not want to be abandoned. "Please, don't—"

The words are canceled as an arrow swipes past my shoulder.

The blond-haired human girl from before is pulling back another arrow, a smile across her face. "I see another beastie."

"Wait!" I scream, desperate for her to understand. "I am not—"

The second arrow slices my skin open, just shy of finding a place to sink into my body. I clasp a hand over the wound, but the blood refuses to cease. Tears blur my vision, but Anna becomes my eyes, pulling us between trees in zigzag directions. There is a boom, and bark rains down on Anna.

"We aren't feral!" I scream. To Anna, to anyone that will listen. "They don't understand!"

"Keep running!" Anna shouts. "Don't slow down."

It is so dark now that the world around me blurs and loses all definition, but Anna crosses the Forest floor naturally.

And in one blink of an eye, the trees vanish around me, and I fall into emptiness.

There are no trees here, just endless grass, and...sky. The stars spread so thick above us that it seems they shine to guide us to safety.

Too much open space, my heart tells me as it pounds with such force I am afraid it will break. It is not safe.

Anna keeps running, but I try to pull free.

"The town is this way, Adelaide!"

"Please," I tell her. "Please."

I am afraid.

"You can't stop!" Anna's voice breaks under the stress of her shout. "You are being hunted. You have to look over fear, and you have to run."

The adrenaline of being hunted, of being prey, runs through me no matter what form I may be in. It is so strong it follows me between two lives. I am able to grasp that fear, to allow it to consume me, for the benefit of my safety.

I take a deeply needed breath and allow instinct to latch onto my limbs. I ignore the voice in my head and I give myself over to the sensation of the tall grass tickling my calves.

We run across the endless plains, further away from where I felt safest.

WHEN NORSEWOOD COMES before me, it is unlike anything I've seen before. The humans' homes are pressed so tightly together that the light can only go upward, like a beacon. The structure of the entire town looks like a mound of rock, not something etched with time and patience.

Fires burn around the perimeter of the town, sinister and glossy and unwelcoming. The closer we get, the mass of humans waiting outside their town, faces and bodies rugged with anticipation, becomes more identifiable. Their offspring run and play, and...music hovers densely in the air.

I am so close when my legs snap beneath me.

Anna does not notice I have faltered until I cry out in agony. She attempts to pull me up, but her strength is also ebbing. She calls for help, but the humans have started to scatter and panic. I look over my shoulder and see countless ferals tumbling down the hills of Norsewood. Humans start to scream back and forth, and a select few men surge forth with bows drawn.

With a thud, the first feral falls to the grass with a screech. Anna has given up trying to move me and instead pulls her body over mine in protection.

"Please, go," I tell Anna as the sounds of chaos start to overpower my senses.

Anna does not respond but stays with me, eyes clenched tight as my body begins to alter itself.

Finn

A TOXIC CALM settles over the fianna village. It is just the bodies, blood, and Jay. I, even with my wound, attempt to drag Jay away from the graveyard that was once a village. My eyes can't clear themselves, my vision constantly blurry. My body shakes ferociously. My stomach no longer has anything to vomit.

I'd do anything for you, a ghost seductively laments.

I trip over a detached arm and fall onto my side, the wind whooshing from my lungs violently. I lie there for what seems like an eternity, hoping the carrion birds will mistake me as a corpse, or a feral will find me weakened. To come and end me. So that I can be with Jay in whatever afterlife will have me.

I'd do anything for you, I hear Jay tell me. His eyes on mine, alive, alive, alive.

Rage bubbles through me like the crack of a rifle. Rising to my knees, I pound my fists into the ground, hard, then harder. My knuckles become as red as a rose as they crash against the dirt, and the ringing in my ears won't stop. They are filled with the words of Jay.

Over and over, I see him.

When I look up, I see his body lying in the distance, propped against a building, but—

He is not dead. He is smiling at me.

I move to rise to my feet, but then I hear Jay call for me, and when I find him, he is lying outside the village, his arm draped over the fence carelessly. He calls for me with an unhinged jaw while his skeletal fingers stretch out for me.

Yet, when I get close, it is no longer Jay.

I cover my ears and close my eyes when everybody becomes Jay and all of them are screaming at me, begging for my attention, but I can't hear it, I can't—

I can't, I can't, I can't—

I'M ON THE path back to Norsewood.

Through the entire Forest, I do not see a single feral, animal, or bug. Everything keeps its distance as I make my way into the farms that dot Norsewood.

My feet drag on the dirt road, and the closer I get to Norsewood, the more corpses appear. They are sprawled along the fields like cattle. Fires grasping onto the bodies hungrily.

"Someone," I say, my voice hoarse. "I need help."

Jay needs help.

Norsewood peaks in the distance, and all I can see is chaos. It looks as if the sea has crashed into the town, waves swirling around the streets. It isn't until I focus that I realize the waves are bodies running to and fro.

The hunters stand at the town's entrance, firing and slashing into the approaching ferals. It looks like the stories Pa used to tell me about foreign worlds and wars waged over women and thrones.

I reach for my gun, only to remember it is back in the fianna village. Back with—

Jay.

Hands pull at me, and I try to fight off the restraints, but the hold is solid.

"Calm yourself, hunter," the large fianna tells me. He had been with the Maiden. The Maiden who came and brought destruction.

I notice Willow beside him, not a hair out of place. "You can help him," I say, reaching for her, but she recoils at the sight of my gore-encrusted hand. "You can save him."

"He is mad—"

"No!" I shout. I pound at Caleb's chest with my fists. "Go back." I almost drop from Caleb's arms as I squirm like a trout out of the stream.

"Do not struggle," Caleb roars. "I have you."

But he holds nothing. Just a shell of a boy.

Adelaide

"TWENTY-THREE CITIZENS of Norsewood and two hunters from the guild. That is the final count of the dead."

A man as ancient as an oak nods as he hears the information presented to him by another stout human male. Seated in a half circle are the four delegates of Norsewood, their skin drooping like rotten fruit and their eyes as lifeless as lizards. I am seated between them all, with Anna to my right and Caleb to my left. Behind us is an endless amount of humans.

After the massacre outside Norsewood, Anna and I were collected by nameless hunters. I was carried through the streets as humans stared in fright and disgust as my body continued to shift and revolt, white fur tearing through the seams of my human flesh. Both Anna and I were placed in a room with instructions to stay put. Eventually, Caleb was brought to our room, and Anna sobbed endlessly in his arms while trying to clean the blood from him.

I had gotten no sleep. I had lain awake as my legs slid back together and pieced themselves into whole structures.

"Last night, the demons known as ferals attacked Norsewood—"

"As well as the fianna village," Willow interjects. While I do not know where she spent her night, she looks as rough as we do. She stands with us, speaking for us when we don't know what words to say next. "Innocent lives were lost there as well due to the lack of protection provided to them. If I'm not mistaken—"

"You may speak when addressed, Willow," one of the old men decides. His lack of hair reminds me of a robin's egg. "You meddle in affairs that do not concern you. Remember that."

Ever since we've met, Willow has appeared to be an unshakable force. A human who looks upon the world with a grin.

Now, she is terribly silent, her eyes downcast.

"We have never seen an assault of this scale. According to our records," the youngest of the leaders informs the room. "The ferals, from the little we know, tend to stay in the Forest killing wildlife. The guild has noticed a steady increase in not only the number of ferals, but also in their ferocity and unpredictability of their movements. Would you say that is correct, Garth?" The man points to the corner of the room where a mound of a human stands with his arms crossed across his chest. His smile reveals missing teeth and a hideous gleam in his eyes.

"That is correct, your honors. My men are reporting more and more cases of ferals leaving the Forest. But thankfully, the hunters protect the town from most of these threats," he clarifies, seeking praise for his actions. "There was nothing we could do with an invasion this size. I lost good men."

Willow snorts beside me, shaking her head slightly. "Several witnesses confirmed that at least half the guild's hunters were missing from Norsewood at the time of the attack." Her eyes are red and the edges dark. "Where were the hunters, Garth?"

"First, we aren't providing the fianna with enough protection, but now we are being criticized for not having enough hunters to defend ourselves?" The center man shakes his head in pity. "Listen to yourself, woman. You are making arguments against yourself. If we didn't offer protection to the fianna, which we do from the graciousness of our hearts, those hunters would have been stationed around Norsewood. I'm sure I'm safe to assume you see the dilemma, Willow?"

She does not respond, but her emotions simmer.

"A change must be made," the leader insists, and the room agrees with him, several voices rising in a single sound. It becomes as loud as a roar. The leader lets it go on for just a few seconds before silencing them again. "This is a vicious cycle put on repeat for years on end, and I grow tired of burying our people." Next, the man turns to me. "I am to believe that you are the Maiden?"

The entire room shifts uneasily to me, waiting with bated breath, for this is a question that no other can answer for me.

"I am," I proclaim. My blood pumps as only my voice fills the room for a brief amount of time. I want to tell myself I have nothing to fear here, but I can't lie to myself.

You are being hunted.

"My son died because of you!" I hear a crash and turn to see a large man being held back by two men dressed in the colors of the hunting guild. Before, the hunters had been clothed in furs from the Forest, but now they wear thin tunics of brown and golds. The man keeps cursing until he is removed from the room, all the while screaming a word that I dare not repeat to myself.

Once he is gone, I breathe, "I am sorry."

"What is your role to your people?" the man asks. "I'm sure the citizens of Norsewood have heard the fairy tale of the Maiden and the First Hunter. Yet, fairy tales are for children, not men at war."

I swallow, because I have never faced a predator like this before. "I must apologize, but I don't have any—"

"If you are truly to be the ruler of your people, we demand a plan of action. What precautions are you going to take? How do you intend to aid Norsewood in the feral increase?"

My pulse continues to climb until I fear my veins will split. "As the Maiden, it is my duty to—"

Another man silences me. "Again, your legends and myths are...admirable, but the humans of Norsewood can't rely on such childish beliefs. Our protection can no longer be free if it means putting our own lives at risk. Now is the time when you must be more than a mythical entity. You must be a diplomat, my dear."

Anna places her hands on the stand before her, face a picture of fury. "She has just become human. She is not prepared for this."

"Then step aside," the middle councilmember offers up. "Find another member of your species who can properly lead your people."

I remember how I wanted to give over the crown of antlers to Anna, to pass off the responsibility of the Maiden mere days ago. Now, before these humans who believe me as less, I can't imagine ever allowing someone else to suffer like this.

"You must allow us time to come up with a...plan," I say. "But I can't ignore that I must search for the Stag." The humans begin to murmur once more, but I ignore their squabbling. "While the humans may have varied beliefs, I know that I was born to find the Stag. There, I shall save the ferals."

"How will you find this god?" the man named Garth asks me.

It goes against every instinct to stand up to a predator whose teeth seem far too sharp. But I find it within me to keep going. "I am not sure of that yet. I just know—" The humans roar in defiance, but I roar louder. "I know I can find him."

"You wish for us to sit around and wait for you to complete your pilgrimage? Must we continue to supply you with protection as you frolic through the trees?" the lead hunter asks.

Caleb, blessedly, steps forward next. Even as a human, he is menacing enough to confuse his foes into accepting that he outranks them on the food chain. "We know, as well as you all, that we can't return to the village right now. Walking back into the Forest at this point would be dangerous. We would ask for protection, as well as hospitality for this season."

"This is a tall request, you must understand. You aren't just asking for a few hunters, but residency as well?"

"Please," I beg. "If you give me a little bit of time, I will have a solution to the ferals. I will go into the Forest and find the Stag. And when I do, I will make sure the humans of Norsewood are repaid for all of their kindness."

The councilmembers huddle close together, their words muttered and soft. They continue to discuss privately without a care to the people waiting.

It is an achingly long time before the center man focuses his attention back on me. "It has been decided by the council that Norsewood will harbor the refugees of the Forest while the Maiden begins her pilgrimage. But she shall not be alone. There needs to be proof that she is being faithful to her word."

"Of course," Anna says. She waves her hand at Caleb. "We are the Maiden's retainers, we will make sure that she completes—"

"We are sending a hunter along with the girl. You two shall stay in Norsewood and tend to your people," the councilman snaps.

Anna shakes her head with a grin half formed on her lips, almost in disbelief. "Well, that would be impossible! A human cannot travel with the Maiden on her journey. That is why the two of us were born. We are meant to protect and guide her to our god."

The lead hunter, Garth, pushes off the wall. He walks until he is standing before the three foreigners. "I don't think you or your people are in any position to negotiate. We only wish to have someone we can trust guiding the Maiden. We have a very qualified hunter who has offered to assist you. His skills at killing are superb."

One of the elderly men finishes Garth's statement with, "If you refuse this offer, the fianna will be forced to leave Norsewood and fend for themselves within the Forest. Norsewood can no longer sacrifice resources that our own people need."

The crowd is silent. They do not protest.

They do not defend my people. They do not fight for me.

"I will comply," I tell the council as I stare at Garth. "I will allow a hunter to travel with me. I will offer up whatever proof is needed to keep my people safe."

The crowd starts to rattle like a nest of snakes.

"Excellent," the lead councilman tells me, yet it does not feel very *excellent.* "We thank you for your cooperation. You and your guardians can lodge at the inn several streets down. We will provide you with a room while you visit Norsewood."

"Thank you very much," I must force myself to say. Meanwhile, Anna takes a hold of my hand, and for some reason, I fear I've just agreed to my own execution.

Finn

I WAKE UP tied to a bed with coiled rope. The ceiling and walls are unidentifiable, but the figure waiting in the shadows is unmistakable. Arms tucked against his chest, Garth brings himself into the light as soon as he notices that I am awake.

"You should be thankful that subhuman knew where to drop you off." I remain quiet. "How is that leg, boy? Should be nice and patched up."

I do not answer. I tighten my calf, and while the pain has lessened, it is not gone. I'm sure someone with a needle and specific herbs tended to it while I was asleep, which is a nicety that numbs me.

"You sure missed one hell of a fight. Where were you? You were brought to us in the arms of a fianna, crying like a babe. Your father would be proud."

I do not snap at the bait that Garth swings before me.

"Untie me," I plead.

"Not before we have a talk."

"Now."

Garth pulls up a chair to the side of the bed and toys with the ropes but makes no move to free me. "Can you do me a kindness? I have but just one question." I presume Garth tries to hide his smile, but it bursts forth anyway, his enjoyment impossible to mask. "Where is Jay? I can't seem to find him."

I lurch at him, but the ropes are unyielding. No matter how much I thrash and spit, Garth is too far away. My hands reach for him, wanting to tear his throat out, to watch him bleed and bleed.

"Are you done crying?" Garth scrapes his knife fearlessly beneath his nails, dispelling blackened dirt. "With a father like Niall, I'm sure you know men do not act like this."

I try to control my breathing.

"So, here is what I think—"

"Fuck you."

Garth acts surprised, placing a hand to his chest and batting his eyelashes rapidly. "My! How my heart aches. I thought we were pals, Finn. Buds who look out for one another. You hunt for me, and I keep your father's head on his shoulders. Isn't that our deal?"

Each word produces a thick red to clot my vision. My skin blisters at the heat I conjure. I am but a coal in a hearth.

"I'm done," I snap before I can consider the words or what they truly mean. But even as I process them, I find I have no regrets. "Slit my throat, feed me to the ferals, hell, go after Pa—" My throat clogs up.

"You don't mean that." Garth takes a sip from a nearby mug and flinches as the contents burn down his gullet. He coughs before saying, "I know what you really want, Finn. I truly do."

"You know nothing."

"Will you let me take a guess?" Garth is almost polite. "If I'm right, maybe hear me out?" Garth must study my face, the hatred I let line every inch of me, before he tells me, "Look to your right."

For a moment, I defy Garth. I deny him the gift of obedience. Yet, eventually, my pride is not enough to conquer my curiosity.

When I turn, I see a single bed beside me, and lying across the top of the sheets is a body.

Jay's body.

I vomit, but it has nowhere to go. It soaks into my hair and down the side of my cheek. As I revolve to look away, Garth's meaty hand pushes me back into the mattress and into my bile, forcing my vision to stay zoned on Jay.

"Take a good long look, boy."

It hurts to keep my eyes closed.

Garth lets me go and waits for my breathing to even out, but I do not think I can be calm ever again.

"I need you to listen very close to this next part," Garth mumbles in my ear, his breath moist against my ear. I can't tell if it is his breath or my vomit that makes me retch. "Because I know you, boy, better than you would have yourself believe. You would never end your own life."

I hate myself, but a sob rips through my throat.

"Hazel retrieved his body. I wanted to make sure we kept him in a safe place while we work some things out." Garth continues to pace around the room, his voice encircling me, boxing in my senses. "I need your assistance in a little matter. The Maiden, after failing to keep the subhumans at bay, has been given a chance to fix her wrong. She will be allowed to—" Garth grips my jaw with enough force to bring more tears to my eyes. He angles my face close to his own. "Are you listening to me?" I try to nod, but Garth shakes my head. "I will not repeat myself, boy."

Please stop, please stop, please stop.

He lets go of me. "The Maiden will begin her pilgrimage to find her god. And if I'm not mistaken, the Hail family seems to be rather religious when it comes to that deity."

I think of Pa, of his feverish rantings. And of course, Garth would know of them.

"A drop of the Stag's blood and...Jay could come back. Is that a tale you believe, Finn?"

I do not answer.

"You have two options. You can either trust in the myth, or not. But if you think there is some merit to it, and you hunt down this god and gain his blood, you would have much to gain." He points to the body of—

I look away.

"And in the end, if it isn't true, you don't have anything else to lose." Garth leans into my vision with a smile that could scare bears from the woods. "Seems silly not to consider. But, if that isn't encouraging enough, let me tell you this."

Garth begins to cut the restraints holding me down. He cuts and talks. "The death of Jay Alder was seen by no one. It happened, supposedly, in the fianna village. Away from Norsewood." *Snap, snap* go the ropes. "The only one with Jay at the time of his death is another boy. Finn Hail." *Snap, snap*. "And he returned with a body and hardly any wounds himself."

When the final cord is torn, I sit up as quick as I can, aiming to punch Garth in the throat, but the man blocks it simply. He brings his hand around my throat and squeezes it until I barely have enough air to remain conscious.

"If you don't follow my orders, the death of Jay Alder will be placed on your head." Garth tightens his hold. "Not to mention the death of Niall Hail. Your father."

My nails dig into Garth's arm, but I know I can't win here. I know I can't beat him.

"Let your anger fuel you, boy. Let the desire to kill me fill you with vengeance," Garth offers, taunting me. He welcomes any who would challenge his throne, but not one person has yet been a match for the ruthlessness that Garth commands.

When he lets go, I remain seated, immobile.

"Perfect," he commands as he claps, the sound rivaling two slabs of meat colliding. "We have some work to get done."

Adelaide

BEFORE THE SUN can even gather itself to rise, Anna tears me from my cocoon of blankets. I've barely had any time to marvel in the wondrousness of a bed before being asked to leave it. Anna presents me with a new wardrobe and pulls back my hair into a tail. The room given to us by the town is cramped and has an odd smell to it, but Anna doesn't seem to notice any of that.

"Surely, you can let me rest a little bit longer," I plead. I know recent events tower over us, but the bed, the warmth, and those blankets are so tempting.

Yet, the threats and decisions that must be made do not hinder Anna when she offers me a pure smile. "I want to take you to a bakery in town. Their pastries are so delicious that you'll debate if you should ever eat anything else!"

I don't want to tell Anna that everything I've eaten since last night has made me cautious of past food choices. Caleb had tried to convince me that everything we were presented with at the inn was second best in human cuisine, but my stomach wasn't convinced.

"Do you think it's appropriate?" I ask, aware I may squash Anna's joyous mood.

"It is now, more than ever, that a morning pastry is important."

As Anna leads me from the room, I see Caleb bundled under layers of blankets and I laugh softly as Anna compares her mate to a hibernating raccoon. She taps his arm gently before exiting.

I'm grateful for the furs protecting me from the morning chill as we make our way through the human town. Unlike the previous day, the town is calm like a steady rain. As I pass bodies, I peer into their eyes, seeking other fianna in the human fold. By the time we stop before a brightly colored shop, I have seen but one fianna in the streets. Anna slips past the open doorway and returns with two brown masses. She passes one off to me, but I'm not entirely sure how to handle it.

"It's dripping!" I shout at Anna, panicking. The waxy paper wrapped around the pastry is not enough to hold back the moisture and goo that encroaches onto my skin.

Anna is already biting at hers, making quick work of the meal. She speaks around the treat. "You have to eat it fast. And messy." I snort out a laugh as she displays the disarray around her mouth. Despite the several humans gawking at her, Anna doesn't allow herself to be anything but herself.

Following her lead, I sink my teeth into the pastry. Instantly, the cream and spices coiled within the bread start to drown my senses. After that first taste, I can't help myself from devouring the rest. When we are both finished, Anna and I look at each other, stunned by our appearances. Swiftly, an uncontrollable sensation takes over me.

I laugh.

Anna and I are cleaning off our sticky faces when a hunter, dressed in his brown and green tunic, approaches us. His body, lean like a sapling, seems unburdened as he approaches us. It is the same ease deer have approaching another in the Forest.

"Maiden. I hope that I am not interrupting." He bows his head as he addresses me with my title. His black hair stays pulled back like mine. "My name is Rowan. I'm from the hunting guild. I'm sure you are well aware of who and what we are."

I do not respond for he already knows the answer.

"I felt it would be polite to let you know the council has decided that the hunters should tend to the dead today. I'm aware that our cultures are different, and I wanted to be sure you get your chance to honor the lost before they are buried."

Coupled with the reminder of the horror that arrived with me in Norsewood, I find this human's kindness jarring. Is it possible that this hunter considers the ferals to be more than beasts? "Thank you," I finally say.

"I would hurry. They don't mobilize for much, but when money is involved, they're faster than foxes." He shrugs without a care. The lust for wealth clearly does not sting him.

"That is kind of you," Anna tells the man.

Uncomfortable, he rubs at his neck. "I was just here for a snack." He points to the shop we had just left. "I wasn't going out of my way or anything," he concludes as he walks through the entrance.

When Anna sighs, it doesn't sound heavy or troubled, but lighthearted and playful. "Humans sure are strange."

WHEN MY FEET touch the grass of the fields surrounding Norsewood, it's as if the chill of death creeps up through the soil and into my legs. The rising light hits each of the bodies that lie outside of Norsewood, illuminating the horrors I had tried to suppress the day before.

I move to the closest corpse and bend over the feral. Her face, right hand, and right foot are still human, but the rest of her is tangled around her bestial form. I look into her eyes which are staring up at the clouds.

I wonder if she was someone else's Caleb. Was there someone waiting for her right now? For her love, her caring?

I notice a white glimmer near her shoulder.

When I flip the feral onto her side, I find a single white lily poking from an open wound. The petals are spread wide against her thin skin, soaking in all the morning warmth. With my fingers at the base, the flower comes away willingly.

Anna leans over my shoulder. "A human once told me that when something dies, its body returns to nature. They decay and return to the dirt that once created them." She straightens her back with a huff, stretching. "I can't understand how the humans wouldn't see the Stag in the cycle of life."

I take a slight sniff of the flower, and then I hold it to my chest, noticing the human corpses without lilies. "What are these?" I ask Anna, holding out the flower to her, but she is distracted by birds swinging through the clouds. "Do we have something to put these in?" I ask, louder this time.

When Anna returns with a burlap sack, I already have a handful of the flowers. Once countless lilies are safely stored away, I sit down in the grass far away from any of the blood and dismemberment. I lose myself over what the lilies could mean. I had taken one from Caleb, but it withered shortly after. These lilies, no matter how many times I peek in on them, remain luscious and whole. "I wonder if the flowers mean they were cured...even through death."

Anna pats my head with a sad smile. "What will you do next?" I do not know what she refers to, considering all that stands before me. What will I do about the ferals? About the ritual? About the humans?

"I don't know," I admit. "I think I'm lost. How do I begin to search for a god I can't even feel?" Because I am supposed to be the Maiden, I should be able to find the Stag by closing my eyes and pointing.

"It is more than just feeling." Anna picks at the blades of grass beneath her feet. "Believing in something takes faith."

I look at her skeptically. "What do you mean?"

"Well, what do you feel right now?"

I glance down at my palms. "Human."

"And that is all right." Her fingers brush my chin. "The Stag gave you a human body, graced you with a brain and a heart that is confusing and troubling, but you can trust those things. Have faith."

Several hunters have started to walk into the fields. They drag the bodies onto a wagon led by a monstrous black horse that paws at the ground with a colossal hoof. It is hard to watch the hunters cast the ferals aside like lumber.

One of the men in the fields does not linger around the carnage like vultures over fresh kill but instead makes his way for Anna and me with precision. I wonder if we are so still that he assumes us a part of the dead.

"Is it my fault or the Stag's that so many perished here?" I ask Anna, my darkest question flowing from me unpredictably. "Who is to blame?"

"That is not your—" Anna's answer is taken from its privacy when the hunter known as Finn stands before us. His eyes are angry and the muscles along his jaw twitch as he holds back something ugly. He looks worse than the dead.

"Is everything—?"

"Maiden," he says as introduction, cutting off my worry. He does not address Anna but continues facing only me. "I have been assigned the task of guarding you within the Forest as you begin your pilgrimage."

I dust off my legs as I stand, leveling myself so that I may better see his face, to stare into the eyes of the man meant to "protect" me. "At least we are not strangers, hmm?" Finn does not answer. "Let's try to understand—"

"We are strangers in all ways that matter, Maiden. The sooner we accomplish this ritual, the sooner we can focus on our own lives. Meet me here tomorrow, and we will begin our hunt." Without another word, the hunter walks past us and disappears into the edge of the Forest, where I wonder if he lets out whatever pain he held so closely.

"Be careful around him," Anna warns. "His bite might be nasty."

"He does not scare me. Like he said, we are but strangers."

Finn

PA COMES UP from the basement as I'm chopping up vegetables. His hair is slicked back from grease and hygienic negligence. With a disheveled exhale, Pa collapses like a crumpling building onto one of the dining room chairs. The wood scrapes against the tiles as he slumps into the seat without much care. He puts his head against the table, and I wonder if Pa has fallen asleep right there as his body sags lifelessly against the grain.

"Where is his body?" Pa asks me. "Did they bury him?"

My next breath is jagged and sharp. Pa can't see, but my hands shake so fiercely that it stops me from preparing my lunch. I close my eyes and let my fingers trace the outline of the knife in my hand. The sensation of the blade works my mind into a loop, canceling any other thoughts.

"The guild has it. Garth is holding it for reassurance," I say as clean as possible.

Part of me resents Pa. Garth knows my father raised me on the belief, or the hope, that death itself wasn't permanent. He knows that, despite all I do to prevent it, poisonous thoughts of hope taint me.

What if.

What if Jay can be brought back?

"That man is a fiend, I'm telling you. Holding you hostage. You can't allow him to manipulate you," Pa tells me, and it faintly sounds like parental advice. "What does he want you to do?"

"A special fianna arrived after the feral attack," is all I say.

Pa snaps his head up. "The Maiden?" His hands grip the table edge. "She's in Norsewood?"

"Under watch and protection of the hunters. If she suddenly vanishes, that's your head on a plate. So, don't be stupid."

"She is meant to find her god," he tells me, gaze distant. Not a question, but a statement. He rises and places a hand on my shoulder and I wince out of habit. Usually, Pa does not touch me unless to strike or correct. "What will you be doing? Will you search for the god? Could you—?"

"I'm to record her ritual. So that the town can have it for themselves. That's it. Once I'm done with her, I'll work on getting Garth off my back." Pa takes in the information, stroking his beard as he paces the kitchen. Even in the dark, I can see the mud he smears on the tiles. "What did you ever do to him?" I ask rather boldly. "What made Garth ever decide to come after you?"

After me.

"Boy, evil does not need reason. That man saw power and imagined what it would be like to have a throne." Pa produces a piece of paper already crowded with his notes. "I have so many things for you to gather. You will need—"

"I'm not helping you." I declare. "Let the dead lay."

"How dare you say that about the woman who gave birth to you?" Pa snarls. "Did Jay mean so little to you that you'd spit in the face of such an opportunity?"

"Jay doesn't need—"

"That isn't for you to decide!" Pa slams his fist onto the countertop, shaking plates and glasses. His rage is the only noise in the entire house. "Don't be so damn selfish. If you aren't helping Garth for the blood, then why are you aiding him?"

I bite back my reply, but it sings through my blood, causes my heart to race.

It is all I can think of.

I do it for revenge, I want to tell him.

BEFORE I GO to Adelaide, I slink into the streets of Norsewood. Since the massacre outside the gates, the citizens are as skittish as stray cats. Their eyes flicker from alley to shadowy corners, looking for demons and monsters. When they take me in, gun on my back, boots still crusted in blood, it's easy for them to ignore me. I'm simply a demon they are accustomed to.

I say not a single word as I make my way to the butcher.

The shack perched oddly between a tailor shop and a bakery has a constant rhythm of knife meeting flesh in a sickening *shump*. A gray-haired bear of a man flings another pig's carcass onto his countertop as I round the corner. Two little boys stand on the street, huddled close to each other as they watch the severing of flesh and bone.

The butcher flicks a chunk of fat at the boys who in turn run away screaming. "Ya little shits!" he shouts at their retreating shadows. Catching sight of me, he narrows his eyes, expecting a challenge. "You."

"Me," I say as I drop a pouch of coins. "Should I ask how you are, Leo, or is it pointless?"

Leo scoops up the money and points his knife at me, unthreateningly. "My day will not be of importance as long as men like you continue to be my top buying customers."

Leo slaps three pieces of rose-red meat onto the counter and doesn't even bother to wrap it up for me. When he turns, I snake my hand behind the counter and steal enough paper to bundle up the flesh. "As always, a pleasure, Leo."

When I find the Maiden, she is by herself, standing dangerously close to the Forest, an apple in her hand. With caution, a thick doe creeps from the bushes and onto the open field. Her head whips back and forth, looking for any sort of danger. The Maiden is there, coaxing her and saying gentle words and—

When she tilts her head, I see the purest smile ever created.

The doe is inches from the Maiden's raised hand, the shoulder of the animal level with her forehead. With a final push, the doe has her head in the Maiden's palm, snatching at the apple, eyes fluttering shut in peace. The Maiden brushes the coarse fur of the doe, scratching her like a hound. My fingers twitch for my rifle out of instinct.

I see the Maiden's lips moving, her smile never wavering.

A crow screams in the distance, and the doe looks at me with solid black eyes, confirming she is just a beast. The wind shifts so that the breeze pushes against my back, and within two sniffs, the doe catches my scent. Both girl and deer turn and face me like two angels of death. The Maiden leaps aside in fright as the doe darts back into the Forest at the sight of man.

I walk up to the Maiden's side. She takes deep breaths, her chest heaving.

"That seems careless," I say, finding it ingrained in me not to trust anything that comes from the Forest. "Are you harmed, Maiden?"

"You can call me Adelaide, please." Standing, she moves the hair from her face. "I know your name already. Seems fair it goes both ways."

"Adelaide it is," I say. I rub the back of my neck, battling with myself for what I know comes next. "I apologize for my rudeness yesterday."

Adelaide looks sheepishly at the leaves and bark. It is clear to see how tense she is with her clenched fists, frown, and crinkled brow. When she looks at me, for a mere second, her fear is heightened. I am not soft and good with words.

You are not Jay.

"I know it is not easy for you right now. I'm sure you are not happy to be here with me." She pauses, and I wonder if I should reassure her that being with her was bearable. "What is the plan?" Adelaide asks.

"The council is going to want proof of your miracles," I tell her, and she flinches back. "I'm thinking if we can solidify that you are the Maiden, it'll ease their minds and give us more time to...search. I know you saved the fianna that guards you."

She just nods.

"Think you could do that again?"

"How?" she asks me.

With one step, I enter the Forest and leave Norsewood behind. Instantly, my ears and senses are bombarded with everything that encompasses the Forest. Green and *life* fills me up while flushing out all remains of Norsewood and humanity. "Ferals are attracted to blood and meat. Like wolves. It has also been said, in old tomes, that the Maiden may exude a smell that attracts the ferals."

Adelaide scrunches up her nose, raising her arm to give it a gentle sniff. "You think I smell?"

I allow myself a grin as I wait for Adelaide to catch up. "I'm sure you smell lovely. I'm sure it is a scent that can only be detected by bestial noses."

Adelaide blinks twice, lips pressing tightly together until they are but one pink line. "That would explain why the ferals followed me to Norsewood."

My heart sways frantically, painfully. I don't respond but keep moving through the layers of the Forest.

Eventually, I come to a halt when we reach the bank of a pond. I throw my pack off my shoulder and turn to find Adelaide staring at me intently. "I'm going to begin setting up. I was thinking we could try and lure a feral."

"That seems dangerous."

I nod. "It is, but we are close to the edge of the Forest. Ferals are not known to be pack animals. Instances like…" I collect myself, unable to finish the earlier sentence. "Ferals are lone hunters, typically."

"Why here?" she asks, indicating the pool of water.

I point to the cliff that rises steadily behind it. "With our backs to the rocks, we have fewer angles to worry about. We are close enough to the edge of the Forest, but if we need to, we can retreat into the water. The ferals are afraid of water, after all."

Adelaide cocks her head to the side. "Really?"

"No," I tell her. "I made it up. Did it make you feel any better?"

"Until you just now told me it was a lie. Now, I don't feel very comfortable at all."

I remove the meat from my pack and notice the rank stains it leaves behind on the fabric. I unwrap the first piece and chuck it into the foliage. It tumbles like a stone, collecting dead leaves to it as it rolls. The second piece I bind with a rope and hang from a branch.

"I'll be in a nearby tree, gun out. You'll be perfectly safe. But if anything were to go wrong, I need you to get to the middle of the pond."

Adelaide looks puzzled. "What if I don't know how to swim?"

"I'm pretty sure deer are good swimmers." I hold out my last piece of meat. "Hold this."

Adelaide eyes the soaking paper. "Can you set it down? I don't…"

Heat of embarrassment licks at my cheeks. I aim to apologize for my thoughtlessness, but instead I let the meat fall from my hand. Lastly, I pull out a canister of blood. I open it up carefully and pour a thin stream onto the bases of nearby trees. "I'll whistle once I'm positioned. That way, you know where I am at all times." Adelaide stares at the blood, the meat, and lastly, at me.

"What if I can't do it again?" she asks me softly. "Turn a feral. What if it wasn't even me who saved Caleb?"

I don't know how to answer her because of how much depends on this. The burden of it all, of Garth's manipulations, anchors me. If Adelaide can't prove her worth now, at the very start of this all, then I should start running. Initially, a stout rage blisters in my gut, but when I look at Adelaide, I only see a girl.

Not a leader, just a pair of fright-filled golden eyes.

"You have to have faith in yourself," I start with, because it sounds like something Jay would say. It sounds brave and right. "And if that doesn't work out, we'll just fake it."

She doesn't move at first, but the words seem to freeze her. Then she nods.

"You don't have to worry," I tell her. "I'm here to protect you." The words sounded different in my mind, but once they are out in the open, they sound too familiar. They are too painful.

"I trust you," Adelaide confesses. I don't know if she means it or if she is trying to instill a false sense of hope. It doesn't work either way.

"Then let's get started." I turn, never letting the Maiden out of sight for more than a few seconds, and walk several yards before finding a tree with sturdy branches that support my weight. Once I'm halfway up, I straddle a limb, pull my rifle onto my lap, and find Adelaide in the scope. She dips her feet in the water, studying her reflection on the surface. I imagine there must be parts of herself she is still discovering. I wonder what it would be like to look in a mirror and find someone foreign to you.

As the breeze hustles on by, it brings with it a sinister thought.

Do you think the Maiden's blood is special?

I clear my head with two sharp whistles. Adelaide searches for me before waving back. Both of us settle into our spots while we allow the minutes that follow to stretch on and on. My tense muscles quiver in anticipation as I react to each noise that sounds off near me; to each squirrel that causes enough ruckus to make me think a herd of deer is stomping through the underbrush.

Watching Adelaide constantly, I notice several birds fluttering down to rest on her open hand and shoulders. I can only assume she is so in tune with nature that they sense safety in her presence. She speaks to them like she had the doe, her face beaming with joy. I push away the past few days, and I think back to the last time I was as happy. When there was so much joy in me, it cracked my frown into a smile.

No matter how vigorously I try to keep my mind from Jay, it returns there. Jay and I used to be inseparable as kids. Back then, there were no complications with the guild, Hails and Alders, or Norsewood. We were just kids, exploring the world side by side.

That is what you could do, my thoughts tell me. *Resurrect Jay and escape. Leave everything else behind.*

It is impossible to keep that single thought, that single wish, from latching onto me. The what-if. What if Jay could be resurrected? What if I could make it right this time? *What if what if what if.*

A howl tears through the Forest.

I swing my rifle around, scanning for any movement. The wind seems to also stop in anticipation. Each breath I take is shallow enough that I can keep my body as still as possible. Then—

A flash of brown and pink cuts across my vision.

I fire once but miss. Dirt springs into the air as the feral races along the Forest floor.

I find the feral again, but he is fast and nimble. After sighting the Maiden, his gait has become frantic and sporadic. I press my eye to the scope, aim several yards ahead of the beast, and wait until I see—

Wham, my second bullet sinks deep into the feral's right thigh, dropping him in a tangle of limbs and momentum.

I drop from the branch; my feet unsteady as my weight comes crashing down. I rush to Adelaide's side and throw my pack at her feet as I place myself in front of her. The feral crawls and hisses its way toward us, taking fistfuls of dirt as it drags its body closer to the Maiden. Dried gore clings to the monster's horns like velvet.

"We have to hurry," I say, loading another bullet into my gun's chamber. "Noise travels in the Forest."

I aim again, and the gun explodes in my hands.

The feral falls onto its chest as the bullet clips his thigh. Both of his legs are too damaged for him to walk anymore, but he is still relentless in his pursuit.

I raise the rifle again, but Adelaide's hand stops me. Between one blink and the next, a haze drops from me as her palm rests against my shoulder. Her eyes travel the barrel of the gun, and it is impossible not to feel a fraction of shame.

I swallow down the desire to tell her that this is needed. That ferals are evil. That guns can do more than just kill. But how can I convince her of a truth I don't even fully believe?

"I think I can manage from here," she tells me as she peels her skin from my shoulder.

I set my rifle onto my back. "We have to immobilize him further. He is still dangerous."

I approach the male feral, taking my bow from my quiver. As I near, the creature lashes out ruthlessly, claws and teeth wanting to push me away, so they can find the Maiden. I fire an arrow into both the feral's forearms, pinning it to the dirt. While it still struggles, the beast no longer has the energy to break free.

I turn back to Adelaide, but she does not get close to the feral.

I bite my lip at the guilt that swells around her. "He won't hurt you. You are safe to do...whatever you have to do," I tell her.

She does not respond. Does not move.

The feral, with a face more beast than human, clacks its fangs at the Maiden, screaming and frothing like something possessed.

"We don't have all day. Act now or I'll put it out of its misery," I command, adding a steel edge to my words.

Finally, Adelaide drifts forward, afraid of me, and afraid of the feral. Her steps calculated and measured, ready to leap to safety if the fiend gains a second wind. Yet, with the bullet wounds and arrows holding it down, the feral can only scream horrendously.

I study the Forest, my anxiety snapping at my heels. "We have to hurry." Tales from the other hunters ripple through my mind. Stories about ferals that responded to the call of the wounded for an easy kill.

Propelled by my request, she reaches for the beast. Her pale hand brushes its cheeks. Adelaide holds onto the feral as it screeches and jerks about. I hold my breath, fingers curling around the hilt of my knife.

And that is how we stay. Both of us trapped in anticipation.

Then, Adelaide retracts her hand. "Nothing is happening. I don't think—I'm not sure anything is going to happen."

"What did you do the first time?" While I wait for her answer, I begin to doubt the significance of the Maiden. What if the color of her fur was the only thing validating her status as a legend? "Do you have to…kiss them or anything?"

Adelaide's eyes open in shock. "That does not sound pleasurable." Shaking her head, she says, "No. I just touched him. That was it."

"Try again," I say, pointing to the feral.

Uncertainty hangs over her shoulders. "I don't think I can—"

The feral sinks its fangs into Adelaide's flesh and she screams as blood gushes down the feral's snout. I stab at the feral, the dagger lodging itself into the beast's jaw. I leap onto its back and throw my hands into the feral's maw to pry it open. Adelaide, bent over, has her nails dug into the feral's face, tears streaming down her cheek as she also tries to force herself free.

I raise the knife into the air with the intent of delivering a final blow, but before I can, a blinding light flares from Adelaide's hand.

Like a trap springing open, the feral's jaw releases Adelaide. As the girl falls backward, the feral freezes up, body as rigid as wood. I crawl from the feral's back and collect Adelaide's bleeding calf in my hands while tearing a section of my shirt off. She fusses with me, trying to distract me, yet my hands move automatically.

When the feral screams with a volume reserved for life-ending agony, both Adelaide and I stare in shock. As it thrashes against the arrows, the feral's body starts to spasm, limbs breaking and contorting.

"What's happening to him?" Adelaide asks in a panic, her golden eyes stretched so large that they look like sparkling coins. "Did I kill him?"

I don't have time to answer before a single flower bursts out of the feral's pelt.

From the gun wounds come yellow-tinted buds, unraveling with unnatural speed. The bulb unfolds with snow-white petals, the color pulsating with life. Both his antlers crack at the base, wobbling once before falling to the ground without struggle. Claws revert back into thin fingers. Hooves break way to feet with five toes each.

I watch in horror and awe as the feral's throat convulses and throbs as something works its way free from inside. The jaw spreads wide open, as if the feral desires to consume the entire world, and a flower covered in blood spurts forth. It is larger than the others and glows with the intensity of the sun.

"Your knife," Adelaide demands, holding out her hand. Dumbfounded, I hand it over to her. She approaches the feral, standing up on her toes so that she can slide the blade along the stem of the flower. With a snap, she pulls the plant free. The smaller lilies start to drop to the ground, withering as they fall.

Adelaide turns the feral onto his back and pushes away his long hair to reveal his face. He is no longer part beast, part man. Now he looks only human, his body no different from mine.

Well, he is luckier in some other areas than I am. I avert my gaze and shake off my blush.

I lean over Adelaide, merely observing as she uses the edge of her dress to wipe free the muck from his jaw, chin, nose, until all I can see is—

"Shepperd?" I ask, shock numbing me.

The man looks to me with two golden eyes and no recognition. He parts his red lips, but no noise comes forth. His pupils swing from Adelaide then back to me, then back to Adelaide.

This isn't possible.

Shepperd isn't a fianna.

He's a man from Norsewood.

Adelaide

THE RELIEF THAT takes hold of me is unbearable. Water starts to pool in my eyes, but I blink fast enough to scatter the collection. The fianna before me already seems frightened enough without further emotions getting in the way.

I help the fianna sit up, hearing Finn speaking, but not understanding his words in the height of my joy. The fianna flexes his hands, inspecting his fingers, then his feet, and then finally he looks to me. The fianna male hesitates a moment before reaching for my skin.

Finn's fist smashes into the side of the fianna's face.

He pulls me to my feet, rather roughly, and places himself before me, his body leveled for a fight. The fianna male moans as he rolls onto his side, curling himself up into a tight ball.

"Finn! What are you doing?" I shout, confusion stronger than anger.

"What the hell is happening?" Finn lashes out again, his boot connecting with the fianna's exposed ribs.

"Finn!" I pull at him, dragging him back. His eyes are not with me but furiously locked onto the fianna. "What is wrong?"

"Stay away from him," Finn snarls. "He is a killer." He looks at me for just a moment. "What did you do? What kind of game are you playing at?"

I shake my head, bewildered. "Finn, I have no idea what you're talking about. Everything that happened was the same as when I saved Caleb. The flower and everything."

"This isn't possible," Finn says. He stands up straight, his shoulders still bunched up. "We need to tie him up." He moves for his pack. "You have to stay away from him, Adelaide. He isn't safe."

"Stop!" The volume of my voice causes Finn to stumble. He looks to the knife still in my hands, the knife that is now pointed at him. Does he know I could never harm him? That holding this knife means nothing to me, but a world to him? "Tell me what is happening, Finn. Please."

The fianna continues to rock in agony.

Squeezing his hands into fists several times, Finn seems to work out a fraction of his frustration. When he speaks, it is controlled. "Back when I was a kid, eight or so, there was this infamous hunter in the guild. He had trained me how to shoot, how to curse, how to chug a beer...but when I got old enough to understand why he was in the guild, I wanted nothing to do with him." Finn licks his lips. "He abused his wife, potentially worse. Then, only a few years ago, he killed three women and was hung for his crimes. There are only a few sins even the hunters don't accept." Finn stares at the fianna with a hatred I fear will catch the Forest on fire. "His name was Shepperd. And he looked a hell of a lot like you do."

"He was killed?" I ask. A cold dread clamps onto me. "And his body?"

"He can't be the same. I watched his body burn."

I stare at him in horror.

"It can't be him," Finn deduces. "I mean, the eyes, the face...it's not an identical image. But close enough."

"I'm...I don't know who I am..." the fianna stammers from the dirt. He tries to stand, but he does not have his body under control yet. I do not look to Finn as I rush to his side, letting the fianna lean against me for support. Even when his two feet are flat on the ground, he shakes. "I don't know where I am." Tears and terror hold his face captive as he says, "I don't..."

I throw Finn's knife further away from myself and closer to him. "Everything is okay now. Just relax." While I coax the fianna, I look to Finn. This male should not have to endure such brutality from Finn. Right now, he needs more than a fist to help him. "You were a witness to this," I jab at Finn, the anger feeling good. "This fianna proves that I am the Maiden."

"You don't understand." He shakes his head.

"How do I not?"

"We can't take him back into Norsewood!" Finn shouts. "It will cause a panic."

"I don't care how the feeble minds of humans will react," I snap.

Finn closes his eyes and collects a mighty breath. He slithers from his coat and tosses the material to me. I pick it out of the dirt and drape it over the fianna male. He huddles underneath the layers, shivering in appreciation, eyes fluttering shut.

When Finn speaks again, his words tremble less. "All right. Let's take him back. I'm..." He looks off into the distance. "You watch him. I'll keep a lookout."

"I don't know..." the fianna male rumbles from my side, clenching his head. "This is not my world."

"It is now," I say gently. "There will be a lot you don't understand, but that is okay." I give him a smile, hoping it might buoy his spirit. "I will keep you safe."

Again, the fianna male doubles over in pain. His fingers press so mightily against his skull that I fear they'll break through the bone and dig out whatever lies beneath. "But...you don't understand. This isn't..."

"This is not what?" I ask.

When the male looks back up at me, when his eyes find mine, a frown crosses his lips.

Only then, do I see the dark veins slithering through his brow.

His eyes darken, his fingers twitch. A transformation has begun.

"You do not understand that you—"

With a sound of a pebble dropping into water, an arrow slices through the fianna's neck. I scream as the body lurches forward, the fianna's hands clawing at its throat to try to pry the metal away. I drop to my knees and press my hands around the arrow. Despite how hard I pray, the blood does not stop flowing.

The fianna stops moving beneath my hands.

Looking over my shoulder, I see a human female stalking close by. She moves like a cougar, her body rippling with each precise step. Even without her pale golden hair as a hint, I would have recognized her instantly from her face alone.

I see the mark of the guild on her coat. I see her furs and her devilish grin.

"Hazel? What the hell?" Finn roars. He does not have his weapon poised, but his words seem powerful enough. "Are you insane?"

"I was saving you," she explains. She holds her bow before her like she means to use it again. "Look at all this blood! You nearly got mauled to death."

Finn growls. "I had everything under control."

Hazel frowns, but her overexaggerated pouting proves her sympathy is a sham. "I'm sorry. I must have made a mistake. But, don't we all, Finny? Sometimes our mistakes are deadly, aren't they?"

Finn does not respond.

Hazel turns to me. "I'm sorry that you're having so much trouble with the council, Maiden." Her tone is anything but apologetic. "Those silly old men don't know courtesy. Old age makes them rather cranky. I, personally, think you are just as magical as you say you are."

Finn calls her a name I don't know, but it is heavy.

"If I can be of any help to you two, let me know." Hazel presses her lips out like a pouting child. "I would do anything for you. Really."

"You killed him," I say, my thoughts whirling.

"Saved you. I don't know how many times I need to explain that difference for you, but I'll excuse it due to your...newness to humanity," Hazel finishes in a sneer. "I know that it can be hard understanding simple words sometimes. But really, I should be going now. I'm sure you would like to tend to the body, Maiden?"

The blood of the feral is cold now, sinking into my body until I am positive that is what prevents me from lashing out at this fiend with golden hair. I see, in death, a final flower dotting the feral's skin.

"Honestly, from one girl to another, I would look at possibly upgrading your guardian. Finn doesn't have the most colorful history when it comes to protecting— "

Finn has his gun out before I can even blink. He fires a single bullet at Hazel. Bark and dirt scatter, and the laughter of a maddened girl sings through the leaves as Hazel vanishes as effortlessly as morning mist.

He drops his weapon and sinks to the ground, his knees soaking in the blood of the fianna.

I'm not sure how, but I pull Finn to me and tuck his head against my shoulder. For several impossible moments, Finn does not move.

So, I stay there, holding two vastly different bodies.

Finn

"YOU SHOT AT her," Adelaide concludes as we push dirt over the corpse of the fianna.

The sky is dark blue, the birds have started losing motivation to call back and forth, and the finer details of the Maiden's face are slipping away. Her statement prods at me uncomfortably, but I have nothing to lose with my connection to Adelaide.

I pat down the dirt, watching dust clouds billowing away. "That is what guns do. You point them and they kill things."

Adelaide sits back, her filthy hands sprawled along her thighs, the combination of mud and blood almost natural looking. "You didn't try to hit her."

I punch the soil, my agitation spiking. The physical exertion draining my fury. "I did."

"That feral, though. You hit him while he was running. That's..." Adelaide trips up over the words, not sure she should complement my skill or be terrified of it. "That girl was standing still."

Heat spikes in my cheeks when she makes her observation.

"You missed her on purpose." She rests a white flower, like those that blossomed along the feral's skin, on the grave, and plants its roots into the soil. When I look into her eyes, no condemnation fills them, but a genuine desire to understand the unknown.

Yet, I find that I cannot easily describe the entanglement I am in with Hazel and Garth.

"You're right," I fib. "I tried to miss." Because, in the end, I don't want her to realize how much of my sanity is vanishing. That between one thought and the next, I aimed a gun at a girl without hesitation. "Tomorrow, we need to get into the Forest early. Before the sun rises. I won't even stop in town. Hazel will be looking for us again, I'm positive."

"Why?" she asks, so I offer her a little information.

"The leader of the hunters, Garth, is behind it, I'm sure. I can imagine that he has given her direct orders to make this whole ordeal difficult." But why Garth would do such a thing is lost within multiple possibilities. Does he want to see me struggle or to see the Maiden fail?

"I'm sure that he means you no harm."

Adelaide's head is tilted at the scaling moon, golden eyes collecting the nightglow. Doing the same, I find myself struck by the otherworldliness of the moon. At how, if I were human for the first time, I would assume it was magical. "You and he are the same."

I hold my breath, aware of how that statement causes each inhale to hurt a little too much.

"Both hunters, no?" she asks, eyes full of stars.

I let out a strangled sigh. "We are both hunters, yes." I pick at the blades of grass between my legs, distracting myself.

"May I ask you something?"

I look back at the Maiden, but her head has not yet left the sky. I don't blame her. Each dot looks close enough to touch. All you had to do was reach up and your fingers could brush through them like silk.

The gentle way she speaks reminds me of Jay, how whenever his feelings took on the manifestation of words, they were hushed. Being vulnerable was normally a quiet act. So, unlike the times with Jay when I would tease or belittle him for being candid, I tell Adelaide, "Of course, you can," because I wish Jay could ask one more time for me to just listen.

"Do you believe?" She asks. "In the Stag? Or...any god?"

I start ripping at the grass, my mind whirling. "If I'm being honest, I hope a higher power doesn't exist." Because if a benevolent is being watching over me, it isn't doing that a great job. "With so much darkness, shouldn't just a sliver of light be prominent? Yet here we are. Ripping flowers from the throats of beasts and being hunted by man."

Adelaide, finally, looks to me. "You've thought a lot about this, haven't you?"

I shrug, playing it off as minuscule. "All I'm saying is that if there is a god that allows all of this—" I point to the grave and the blood on Adelaide's skin "—then I'm not sure he's any god of mine."

Adelaide, as if ashamed for the lack of presence from her creator, hangs her head. "I'm sorry for all that you have endured."

The air around me freezes, and time comes to a messy halt. "What do you mean?" I ask.

"I'm sorry that the one who gave you hope was torn from you."

I flinch, taken aback. "I'm sorry, but my grief has nothing to do with your god."

"It has everything to do with him," she seethes. "You had hope before the grief. Doesn't that mean something?"

I stand, dusting the grass from my pants. "I think, by now, you know the way back to town." I don't look back as I pick up my pack and leave her to sit amongst the bloodstained dirt.

I SIGH IN relief when I get home, for the house looks relatively normal. I am grateful, because I know I don't have the patience for one of Pa's moods. None of the furniture is mismatched, and the clutter that settles in each room is undisturbed. I take off my boots and stoke the fire back to life, cursing that the house is so damn cold. I fold up blankets, put books away, and take dirty dishes to the kitchen sink. I compile Pa's feverish notes together on the dinner table, not even bothering to decipher the words clearly meant for another mind.

I let myself imagine—for just a moment, and not for the first time—a mother in these walls. I never knew the woman who gave birth to me, and even calling her "mom" feels false. She was only ever a weakness to Pa. But that did not prevent me from envisioning what she would look like dancing in the living room to her favorite songs. I picture her to be a strong and independent woman who still loves all the household chores. She is the picture of love and caring as she gives Pa a kiss on his forehead while she holds me tightly.

She would've held me while I cried for Jay. She would have told me that not everything would work out, because she would not lie to cheer me up. She would tell me I had the power to make it better, to overcome anything.

Yet, this house is but a cage for a madman. Love vacant. And any woman who could love Pa must've had a special kind of madness in her bosom.

I finish up the last clay cup when I hear the basement door behind me creak open. I turn, expecting to find Pa, but instead I see that the wood is slightly ajar. A sliver of darkness exposed to the kitchen.

I drape the towel and slide across the tile. I nudge the door open until a cold breeze crashes onto my legs and face. A chill crawls across the kitchen and throughout the house menacingly. Caution prickles at me, for I have seen the sublevel to this house once and it haunted my dreams as a child. Pa had bought the property and moved us here within a day and most of his possessions went beneath the floorboards. For a week, he had locked himself in the basement and only surfaced to eat and verify that I was still alive.

I take the first few steps down the stairs.

Once I reach the bottom, I can only see one corner of the basement where a lantern sits on a desk. I move forward, making sure I don't run into anything on my way over. After I trip twice, I pick up the lantern on the desk and notice small clouds of fog hanging around me with each exhale. The cold presses in from all angles. I scan over the books and pictures, but I don't find anything interesting. All of it looks like Pa's usual fixations.

I swirl the light around, continuing deeper on the ground level. I find dusty and broken furniture, boxes stuffed with old clothes, and spoiled looking cans of vegetables and fruits. Eventually, I reach the end of the basement. I turn left and right, yet see nothing abnormal down here.

It was just a—

The light catches the image of a foot.

I hold the lantern up high as I take in a large countertop with a corpse decorating the top. The body is all bones and paper-thin skin. Her closed eyes are sunk so far into her skull that I doubt they exist anymore. Her fingers which are sprawled across her chest are as brittle as straw. A simple white dress swallows her body, hiding the rest of the skeletal form. Packed tightly around her frame are shards of ice, sharp edges resting against pointy limbs.

"Finn?"

I spin at the sound of Pa's voice. He stands at the edge of the lantern's glow, only half of his face visible. Cloaked in shadows, Pa could've passed for a ghost.

"What are you doing down here?" His tone is accusing, and he rubs at his eyes groggily. Despite his thick cloak, his teeth chatter against each other.

"The door was open. And I was just making sure you were okay," I tell him, watching how the lamp bobs in tune with the shaking of my hand.

"You can't be down here, you know that." Pa takes a few steps, getting closer to me. "I don't want you to ever be afraid of her." Even though it causes my skin to crawl, I can hear the endearment in his tone. "Please, don't come down here. That is all I have ever asked of you."

"I'm sorry," I tell him, hoping to calm him. Any emotion, even those that aren't violent in nature, are not safe within Pa. "I'm gonna go back upstairs now. Did you eat dinner? I can make you something."

"Why did you come down here, Finn?" Pa whines. "I thought I was very clear. We need to keep—" Pa's eyes widen in disbelief. "He sent you. Didn't he?"

My heart plummets and fear pulses through me faster than blood. "Who are you talking about?"

"Dammit, Finn," Pa snaps. He takes a step closer to me, the rest of his figure slithering into the light. Clenched in his fist is a knife. "So, you do everything Garth asks of you now? He's taken my own son from me, huh?"

"Pa." I hold up my free hand to console him. "That is not the case. You need to let me—"

With a swing of his arm, a fire blazes across my palm. The lantern falls onto the cement floor and shatters into a thousand pieces. I fall back, scrambling on the ground until my back is pressed against a wall. The oil continues to burn on the ground, showing me Pa several feet away, stumbling and crying in bright anger.

"I won't let him steal you away, boy."

Another light explodes in the darkness as Pa ignites a second torch. His face is highlighted in pain as he finds me crouched in the dark. He lunges knife first, but I am able to dodge his clumsy strike. I knock his arm away, and the knife clamors further into the room. I pivot behind Pa and press my arm against his throat, strangling him as he swings at me with the lantern and his free hand. He sobs over and over, but I can barely hear the sound over the roar in my ears.

Eventually, the fight leaves him, and I release his body. We both collapse onto the floor, Pa's tears and my blood dripping on the floor.

He gasps for new air to fill his lungs. "I'm so sorry, Finn. I'm so sorry. I don't know what came over me. I don't know..."

"It's not your fault."

He sobs like his chest has broken open. Like all that remains of him is just tears and anguish.

"Please, please, save her. That is all I have ever wanted."

I don't respond, my thoughts lost in all of the things I couldn't protect.

"Please."

Adelaide

I WALK INTO the inn with a pressure in my chest. I replay the conversation between Finn and me around and around. I'm embarrassed that I could even doubt his devotion to the Stag when my own faith felt weak.

The woman at the front desk offers me no smile, only a tight nod. The town's leaders did not offer compensation for the fianna-occupied rooms at the inn but made it mandatory for the owners to open up their business. It's rare, but a few humans have welcomed the fianna like old friends coming for a visit, and the gesture thaws my heart considerably.

If I deny the council, the fianna will no longer have beds to rest in or homes to keep them warm. Just the trees above us. The moss at our feet. With no one to protect us.

When I reach my room, I hear grunting and moans of pain. As the door slides open, I see Caleb bent over, hands tangled in his hair as a counseling Anna rubs his back gently. Her lips are moving, but I do not hear the words she offers him. She wipes at his eyes and her hands come back bloody.

I see the stubs of claws where his nails should be, daggers at the tips of his fingers.

"Anna," I say, my voice hushed.

Leaping at the noise, Anna turns to me and centers herself before Caleb, blocking me from the image behind her. "Adelaide," Anna starts, her voice shaky. She tosses a blanket over Caleb's shoulders. "Could you find Willow for me? I think she is—"

"What is happening?" I ask. Caleb pivots his head toward me, his eyes a murky mixture of gold and black. He looks like the Caleb I found in the Forest.

My knees wobble, and I reach for the wall. "Anna...what is happening?"

"Nothing," Anna tells me, her hands coated in blood not her own. "I just need to talk to Willow. Caleb is...unwell."

Caleb parts his lips to speak, but all I can process are his teeth, keen as needles, poking out of his gums. I can see that each time he closes his jaw, the tips sink into soft flesh. Finding a discarded blanket, Caleb stuffs the material into his mouth and clamps down, attempting to alleviate the pain.

"I saved him," I say out loud, not really to Anna, not really to anyone. "He's cured. He can't look like this..."

I am the Maiden, I tell myself. *I can do this.*

But, my mind snaps in response, *what if the change isn't permanent? Only a temporary bandage.*

"Let me try again," I tell Anna. "If I did it once, I can do it again."

"Caleb is fine, and you shouldn't worry yourself over this," Anna states. "Just go get Willow."

"What can that human do that I can't?" I ask, a slice of jealousy cutting through me. I move across the room and take the burlap bag off the table. I peek into it and see the lilies huddled together like a mound of snow. "These flowers, they might be able to—"

"Please, Adelaide." The way she says my name, Anna looks as fragile as a newborn robin. "Right now, he's human, so he needs a human's help."

"But Caleb isn't human," I rebuke, pride stuck in my throat. He is better than human. "Can we induce a shift? Maybe in his natural—?"

"I will not lose him again," Anna snaps. Her hair clings to her sweaty skin. Her breathing is just as shallow as Caleb's. "I want him to hold my hand down the street...I want him to take me to the ocean again. I want..."

My hands tighten around the bag. "What? What do you want? This isn't our world, Anna. We don't get the lives they do."

She is silent under my wrath, and I wish that was enough to calm me.

But it isn't.

"The fianna is convinced being human is a gift. That it's the best thing that has ever happened to us. But I'm starting to think it's a curse."

I snatch my bag of lilies and slam the door behind me, hard enough that I hear the echoes of it even as I leave the building.

THE EVENING WARMTH invites humans to linger outdoors. They cluster around tables and open doorways, their conversations as light as the breeze. At first, I ignore each greeting and each human. I let my legs work off the annoyance that clogs my thoughts. I want to find Willow's home on my own, but each building appears exactly the same to me. Eventually, I break and ask a human woman who points me toward the edge of Norsewood, warning me to beware the "witch."

The hut that Willow deems her home nestles by itself, making space for a garden so unruly it rivals the Forest. The other houses are built upward, while Willow's looks more like a bubble. I knock on the front door twice and wait in silence for her to open. When I knock for the third time, the door pops open at the contact.

"Hello?" I ask into the darkness. "Willow, are you—?"

I scream as a furry body streaks out from behind the door. A fat cat flashes me a subtle blink before slinking off into Norsewood with what looks like no intention of returning.

"I really hope she didn't like that animal."

I step into the cottage to find no one is present. The space is crowded with an unmade bed, messy countertops, and a fireplace with ashes that have long gone cold. Willow could easily be stuffed beneath all the clutter, but after whispering her name a few more times, the cottage remains stagnant. I snoop for only a little before I realize nothing within this woman's home is going to make sense to me.

Turning to leave, I trip over a book cast aside. The fall is a harmless one, my hands catching on the edge of her desk before I can collapse. The sack of lilies tumbles onto the hardwood flooring, several spilling around me. As I stuff the flowers away, a flicker catches my eye at the bottom of the sack.

One of the flowers shimmers ever so faintly.

My hand grasps the plant carefully once it is free. The petals, like slivers of stars, cast away the shadows of the woman's home.

Yet, like a flame whisked out, the lily's light vanishes in an instant, suffocating me in the darkness.

"What was that?" I ask no one. I lift the flower into the air, hover it above the ground, and move it everywhere else, hoping the light fills the petals once more. It is only when the plant is pointed in the direction of the streets of Norsewood that it lights up once more.

As I spin, the light dims and flourishes depending on which direction it faces. I race after the glow, through the streets, down alleyways, until I stand beneath the entrance to Norsewood.

Before I can puzzle on it, my eyes catch the tops of the trees from the Forest.

And it clicks.

Once I make it to the fields, the flower continues to light my path, fiercer than ever. Livestock make noises of fright as I pass by like a ghost with a lantern full of burning souls. A few sheep chase me to the ends of their fences, unsure if I am their shepherd or an unruly spirit.

With my first step into the Forest, the lily pulses approvingly. I consider the danger of entering the Forest at night, of the creatures that wait like extensions of the darkness.

"You should turn back," I tell myself out loud, wanting my heart to hear the logic my mind readily spits out. "This isn't smart. This isn't safe."

Before logic could reign supreme, another lily springs up to my right. Settled on the surface of a pond like a fowl, the light that is cast off the plant illuminates the entire pool of water. I reach for the flower, wishing to collect it like all the others.

In the corner of my eye, an endless and dense array of flowers creates a path through the trees. I couldn't possibly claim them all, so instead, I rush along the trail they weave. I see animals of various shapes and sizes along the edge of the flowers, watching over my progression through the Forest with awe and bewilderment.

Suddenly, the trees disappear, between one step and the next, giving way to a strange oval-shaped clearing. A field, impossibly long, spreads before me with lilies packed so densely together that I debate if I am on the tops of clouds. I can't move, afraid to step on any of the lilies.

I look further into the field to find a gigantic tree sitting on a small island, surrounded by the brightest blue waters.

A thuggish urge lulls me forward, begging me to unleash everything—

A rustling nearby startles me.

To my left, a woman is bent over the lilies, tugging at the leaves, testing the roots, and watering each flower individually with a hollow rock. A golden dust clings to her skin from the contact. Her pale hair shines in the glow, her golden eyes filled with a similar fire.

I am frozen until the fianna says, "Beautiful, aren't they?" As she straightens her back, stretching out her muscles, my heart starts to quiver in confusion.

She and I share the same face.

"Who are you?" I ask the girl that is me. The girl whose face is a mirror to myself.

"I am the Maiden," she tells me with a smile as bright as the flowers. Her hair, cut a little shorter to her chin, is the only difference between the two of us. "I tend to this garden. May I ask who you are?"

"I am also the Maiden," I answer hollowly, unsure I have the correct answer.

The fianna grins, nodding with a spark of joy. "Of course, you are. I apologize for being rude!"

The fianna wears her skin—my skin—so much better. Without a shred of doubt or confusion, she stands tall, shoulders high. It is only within her confidence that I can say she—and I—are beautiful.

"You must be lost," she tells me as she tilts her cupped hands to the flowers at her feet. An endless supply of water pours from her palms, baffling me. "You are meant to be out there. This is your season, young Maiden."

I watch, for several moments, memorized in all that she is doing. In all that she is. I find that my finger traces my lips gently as I wonder if I could ever grin so prettily.

As she approaches me, I notice that the lilies move from her path, leaning so they do not find themselves beneath her bare feet. When she stands still before me, several of the flowers nuzzle against her legs. "Are those flowers?" she asks, pointing to the bag still in my hands.

I nod, unable to do much more.

"Oh, dear, do not worry over them. No matter where the lilies bloom out there—" she indicates with a finger, outside of the field and into the Forest "—they grow here as well. You carry but a fragment of what they are here. Here, they can grow safely."

I hold out the bag, and the Maiden, the girl who is me, takes them softly. Everything about her is rounded and delicate. "Why do they grow on the ferals?" I ask. "The lilies."

"Because the flowers are within them. At the center of them. Of you. Of them. Most importantly, in you and him," the Maiden tells me.

I blink.

"Look for yourself." She points to the ground and the lilies part, their roots slithering from the dirt, until only a single flower remains by my feet. "See what slumbers beneath."

I oblige, dropping to the ground so that I may give the stem of the lily a tug. I put my fingers in the dirt and start to scrape away the layers as easily as someone would peel back blankets in the morning. The roots, thick and corded like ropes, work with me, crawling and shifting to unravel themselves for me. I keep digging, falling into the mind-numbing task, only coming to a halt when my fingers press into something...soft.

I glance at the girl who sits close by, braiding blades of grass together. Closing her eyes, she nods for me to continue.

With a single touch, the roots continue to aid me. They untangle and pry the object from the soil. The midnight dirt sifts until all I can see is—

I scream, falling backward. I kick away from the hole, panic fueling me.

The fianna female peers into the ditch, alarm etched into her own face. "Why are you frightened?"

I point, my hand shaking violently. "Why is he in the ground?" I ask, pointing into the dirt.

Toward the shape of a body buried beneath the grass and flowers.

I yelp as another figure passes me, approaching from behind. At first, I see four legs as white as the moon. As the doe continues to move, I notice arrows and scars dotting her pelt like the dots on a fawn. Effortlessly, and magnificently, the doe's body shifts and buckles until a girl stands before me. A process I know as painful displayed in such elegance. Instead of patches of fur cascading down her naked form, white petals and golden dust ripple down her body.

She, like the other, is an exact replica of me. I notice, with a start, that one of her golden eyes is missing, a vicious scar left behind as a story.

"We all die. We are all dead," the new arrival spits at me. She is not as kind as the other, her words alone spewing danger. "We all grow, we all wither. The timing is irrelevant."

My spine seizes up, and a shriek leaves my lips. With a crack, the bones in my arms snap and break by themselves. The agony is too overwhelming to be able to contain the screams that beg for an audience. I fight with my body, demanding it to stay in one shape, but I know I am losing.

Control disappears when my spine snaps in two.

I see the feet of the nude fianna as she approaches me, her single eye gathering all that I am. She judges my unraveling as if it wasn't as graceful as her own. "Do you not remember what they did to me?" she asks. She leans down so that I can see her easier. The scars traveled from one form to another, the arrows burrowed beneath layers of muscle. Each movement brings forth a stream of blood. "If not, you will soon."

I look to the other Maiden for aid, but I can no longer see her amongst the lilies.

"Begin again, begin again," she sings to me, sliding her hand down my neck, smearing red along my inconsistent form. Her other palm grips one of her many arrows and yanks it from her flesh with a shredding sound. She poises the shaft above me, the metal tip prodding along my ribcage. "Begin."

The fianna brings the metal down, piercing me through the heart until a scream echoing through the leaves is all that remains of me.

Finn

A LOUD THUD throws me from my slumber. I find myself in the living room, my neck and back sore from sleeping on the floor. My eyes fixate on a red stain where my cut had once been. I touch my skin, finding the tender edges of the knife wound.

Boom, boom, boom.

The noise vibrates through the entirety of the house, strong and boisterous. I stand up, my joints popping like logs in a fire. I listen, wondering if Pa has escaped his room and is causing chaos. I had carried him up to his bed and strapped him down to the mattress, unsure what he would do if left unattended.

It's strange, restraining your own father like some rabid dog.

I had been staring at the ceiling in my bedroom until around midnight when Pa awoke in a fury. With enough screaming and cursing, I escaped downstairs, away from his curved and jagged words.

Boom, boom, boom.

I slide three books from the shelf, revealing Pa's most beloved pistol behind the volumes. I open the chamber, count four bullets, and shove a fistful more into my pockets. Only then do I realize that I wear nothing but my underwear as the bullets slide down bare skin and bounce around my feet.

I'm no expert, but don't you need pants for this?

I remember Jay, what it felt like to have him standing in this room, and before I know it, the pain robs me of the ability to move. I close my eyes and hear him laughing by the hearth. I can feel the press of his hand against my face right before he—

He died.

After fully clothing my person, I walk onto the front lawn, scanning the area. I wait until I hear the noise bouncing from the side of the house. I swing around the corner, seeing the Forest, the shed, and an enormous stag slamming his head against the house.

I worry for a moment that it is a feral, despite him not being split between two forms. Yet, his fur is richly brown, and his antlers thick and spread out wide while spiderwebs and foliage hang from them like decorations. Rearing up on its hind legs, the stag brings his head down onto the wall with a mighty thud. He does it twice more, the force chipping at the wood.

I cock the pistol, ready to fire into the air as a distraction when the stag turns to me. His humanlike alertness is unsettling as he takes in all of me.

His golden eyes look from the pistol to my hand, to my face, figuring out how all those components fit together, and what it spells for him. Even though I know he is fianna, for his eyes give him away, a unique wonder radiates off him. The mere sight of me should have scared off the beast, but he lingers, his front hooves pawing at the grass with impatience.

The stag looks away from me and focuses on the house. He makes a sound deep in his throat and edges to the window, peering inside. Another rumble comes from within the animal as he scrutinizes my kitchen, this one causing his entire frame to quiver. When he backs up, I expect him to wander back into the Forest with a cocky flick of his tail and no regard for the damage left behind.

Instead, he rears up and slams back down into the house once more.

"Hey!" I shout, aiming the pistol at his chest threateningly. "Kindly stop being an ass. I'll be the one who has to fix that."

The mouth of the buck opens, and for a strange moment, I think he is going to speak to me, because at this point in my life, I would have believed in nothing less.

But instead, a scream sounds off in the Forest.

I swivel in the direction of the leaves, pistol poised with the safety still on. I am about to pass off the shriek as an odd bird until I see a girl running through the trees, as swift as any fox. Behind her trail at least two ferals, snapping their jaws audibly.

I look to my right to see that the buck no longer stands there, the dent he left behind the only proof he ever existed.

As another cry sings through the air, I break into the Forest.

I race as quick as I can, but every glimpse of the girl is further off, always a few more trees ahead of me. The next time I see her, she is no longer on two legs, but four. The color of her fur gives her away.

Adelaide, my mind tells me.

I gain on her, noticing that she limps along the Forest floor. The ferals that prance around the doe toy with her, slashing at her thighs, biting her shallowly.

"Hey!" I shout, but to no avail. The ferals continue to lumber around her, entranced in a dance. "Hey! Over here!" No matter how much my voice carries through the green, the ferals pay me no mind.

I'm exhausted by the time I am close enough to fire directly into the first unsuspecting beast. But even from this distance, the shot goes wide and clips the feral in the shoulder. He recoils and lands against a fallen log.

The other feral forgets Adelaide, leaping over her back and charging me like a bull. I barely have enough time to reload before I have to jump to the right to dodge the bulk of the feral. She collides with a sapling, but it takes her mere seconds to straighten herself to rush me once more. I hold out my arm, aim, and pull the trigger.

Click.

The bullet jams in the chamber.

The feral collides with me in the space of those seconds in between. I throw up my forearm, catching the feral's claws within my flesh. I yelp at the stinging pain and lash out with the pistol like a club. Once the handle smacks the feral in the cheek, she roars and spits out blood and a few teeth. Using the force in her hind legs, she pounces on me like a mountain lion, her hands pulling me down with her. On my back, I brace my gun against her throat while she snaps her teeth.

Struggling with her, I am able to free the knife at my belt. I use whatever disadvantaged strength I can muster and give her a push, then pull my knife between our bodies. When she falls back onto me, the blade eats her skin up like a wolf as her struggles bury the knife deep into her gut.

Rolling the body off, I locate Adelaide stumbling through a thick patch of ferns.

A hell-bent scream silences the birds in the treetops. Several ferals are darting through the trees with such potency that they might as well have been slipping from the bark or sprouting from the dirt itself.

When I reach her, I press up against Adelaide's flank and place my palms against her pelt, trying to steady her with breathless words and coos. This close to Adelaide, I contemplate if I have ever realized the *size* of the fianna in their true forms. With a figure that rivals a smaller horse, I worry her pain will cause her to be defensive with every inch of her mass.

I spin and squint, aim, and smoke fills the air as another feral drops like a stone. His body rolls and causes another to trip. Adelaide continues to lurch right and left, prancing despite her wound, just wanting distance.

Guns are loud, my mind urges. *Ferals don't hunt by noise, but you'll bring any that are close enough.*

With the closest ferals dead, I wrap my arms around Adelaide's neck and attempt to lure her to a nearby creek. I hope the steep slopes will offer us cover while the rushing water masks our scents. Yet, no matter how much strength I summon to corral her, Adelaide proves that she is more powerful and stubborn.

"Seems a waste to be human when you can be this blasted strong," I shout at her. She rears her head back and her skull cracks against my jaw, forcing me to lose my grip on her while I see stars. I grab a fistful of her ear and yank her back down to eye level like I would an arrogant horse. I hold her head between my hands and force her to focus on me. Her eyes collect everything while her ears absorb each sound.

But once her eyes lock with mine, she stills.

"I'm here," I tell her, trying to be soothing like a lullaby. "I got you."

With a shudder, Adelaide's legs crumble, and her long neck bends at the wrong angle as she tilts downwards. An agony-induced whine leaves her mouth as she tumbles to the Forest floor. I aim, fire, and hit an approaching feral in his thigh. Loading one more bullet, I see Adelaide's white pelt ripping like thin paper. Her skeleton dissembling like a collapsing building.

The ferals are relentless as her blood baptizes the Forest floor.

I try to get a hold of Adelaide, but her body is shifting, each piece changing to become another. I drench my hands in her blood, but finally I grab some part of her that settles. I heave and grunt as her weight melts away for slimmer muscles. Eventually, I pull a girl of red and white petals from the carcass of a doe.

I reach the edge of the creek, scanning the best way to descend the—

A feral cracks against my side, pitching the three of us over the ledge. I roll, roots and rocks digging into my body as I pass. My body lands ungracefully on the bank and I scramble to find Adelaide several feet away. After I pull her into my arms, I jump into the water and hold my breath as it rushes over my head.

I go underneath, shock numbing all my senses. My boots touch the rocky bottom, and I bunch up my heavy legs to push back to the top. I surface with a gasp. Inches from me, I see that the feral has followed me into the stream, thrashing and shrieking as it drowns. I lash out, slashing my knife through the water and slamming it onto whatever part of him I hit. With the knife as a hook, I wrench the beast closer and grab a fistful of his fur and hold him underwater until he stops struggling. He bobs to the surface once I release him.

I reach for Adelaide who floats along the current like a leaf, her face tilted to the treetops. My limbs disobey me, seizing up while I pull her close to my chest.

"You need to wake up!" I yell, the cold making each word a battle. Two ferals have crawled down the slope and pace at the edge of the water, unsure of how to strike.

One of the ferals steps into the water, wobbling as it fights the undercurrent.

With a thud, an arrow slices from the feral's chest and out the other end. He topples backward, his blood staining the pebbles. The other feral turns around, shocked, but it has barely enough time to consider fleeing before an arrow pierces its right thigh. In the blink of an eye, another arrow smacks into its forehead.

"Get out of the water!" a voice screams. I look up the creek to see a younger man with a bow held taut in his hands, thigh deep in the water. His black hair is pulled back in a knot, the feathers of his arrows tickling his neck. "My charity is only good for so long."

I drag both Adelaide and myself from the icy current, but my limbs are too sluggish to work properly. I slip on the stones, and Adelaide crashes to the ground.

"Take her," I say, but I don't think a noise actually leaves my lips. "Take her."

The boy lands beside me, his boots crunching in the gravel. He pulls me to my feet and slaps me gently on the cheek twice. "I know it might be tempting to just hang around here like an icicle, but I suggest you go. And now, preferably."

The boy removes his jacket and wraps it around Adelaide's naked body. He picks her off the ground and hands her to me, and I'm surprised that she is as light as a feather. Petals stick to her like feathers on a crow. I turn to thank the boy, but he is gone, slipping back into the Forest with enough grace to make a fianna jealous.

I flee as fast as possible. Each time I stumble, Adelaide is thrown from my arms and across the ground, limp as a rug. Each time I must scoop her back into my arms, I wonder when she will be too heavy for my fleeting energy.

I allow myself a few moments to just breathe, holding Adelaide to my chest. "I got you, I got you, I got you."

When my soggy boots step onto grass, my entire body gives out. Adelaide and I roll through the weeds until I'm facing the blue sky without a single breath in me remaining. I look over and see Adelaide close by, but too far for these dead hands.

I'm sorry, I think. *I don't know if I can do this.*

Despite the sunset radiantly burning sunset, I can't feel a damn thing.

I moan as I push myself up until I am sitting. I crawl over to Adelaide and pull the boy's coat tighter against her. I have to get her someplace, and soon. But I know I can't make it back to town, to a local farmhouse.

"I'm sorry," I tell her.

For I know exactly where we shall go.

Adelaide

I OPEN MY eyes and see a thriving fire. I panic at first, sure that the warmth I feel is because it is I who burns so bright, that the fire licks my skin greedily. But after a calmed moment, I can see the fire lies safely within a hearth, and my legs are wrapped within a...blanket.

With a startle, I find that another body is coiled around mine. I turn to see Finn, his shoulders rising and falling with each breath and his eyes drooped in slumber. My forehead hovers over his bare chest while his right arm is draped along my ribs like a wing.

Finn stirs but does not wake. I watch as his eyelids flutter as he dreams, how his parted lips expose two crooked teeth. I focus on all these small details to distract myself from how much our bodies press against one another.

When Finn opens his eyes, mine are right there, staring at him. With a yelp, he pushes against me, separating the contact between us.

After collecting himself and evening his breathing, Finn runs a hand through his hair and asks, "How are you?"

"Cold," I tell him as I sit up, pulling the blanket around me like a hide.

"I'm sorry," he says. "About being that close. You weren't awake for me to ask and your body was going into shock. I thought the more body heat, the better...?"

I swallow, blushing in sync with the boy. "I'm grateful," I tell him.

Finn huffs a sigh of relief as he crosses his arms across his stomach, hiding his skin. "You were in the Forest. As a doe." Each pause between words is filled with the crackling of smoldering logs. "Ferals were attacking you. And then I threw you into a creek."

Dread squeezes at my heart. I had known that this human consciousness was new, that it did not exist within my true form, but the actuality of the fact is pressing into me. I know that I am a doe, a creature of nature, the...void from the past few hours is terrifying. The longer I remain human, the more solidified the two parts of me become.

Two halves but no whole.

"I'm sure you want to get going," Finn tells me, his words quick and short. "Your guardians are probably worried."

I think of Caleb and his claws. Of Anna and her fears. Right now, I imagine they have plenty of other things to occupy themselves over.

"Let me grab you some clothes." Finn stands. With cheeks aflame, I realize Finn is covered only by his briefs. But it does not seem to be something he has considered. "Did you want any water...or food?"

I shake my head, looking at the flames. "No, I'm all right. Thank you."

Finn hesitates for a moment before nodding and slipping off behind me.

Time stretches and cracks while Finn is gone. Minutes stretch into an eternity as I inspect my skin and flex my muscles. I want to revel in my blemish-free limbs, but all I can imagine is how my fur must rest right beneath this skin, waiting to rupture.

I dig my fingernails into my thighs, wondering how difficult it would be to force myself to shift. To revert to my true form.

Or, how grueling would it be to stop myself from changing?

I hear footsteps behind me. I rise, pulling the blanket against me as I turn to greet Finn—

Yet, it is a man who stands before me, not a boy.

He stands a head taller than I, with a slender frame that slips in and out of shadows as he approaches me. His eyes, colorless, focus on me with an intensity that belongs to beasts, not men. Paralyzed in fright, I do nothing as the man lifts a hand to rest against my cheek.

"You look like her," he tells me, his voice gritty like lightning. "You must be the Maiden. In my house. With the blood of the Stag." He slides his thumb across my skin and rests it beneath my right eye. He presses his finger against me as he says, "I remember you with a scar. And only one eye."

He raises his entire hand until the right side of my face is hidden.

I shake in uncontrollable terror as I remember the girl in the field of lilies.

"Pa."

The man before me does not move, but I find it within myself to pull away enough to see Finn standing at the bottom of steps, a random assortment of clothing discarded around his feet.

The man lowers his hand back to his side, cocking his head while he grins at me. "Finn, you did not mention we had a guest in the house. And one of such nobility."

"Adelaide," Finn growls. "You need to leave."

I can do nothing but shake.

"We don't want to be rude." The man laughs once and then shakes his head in pity. "My son is a troubled boy. Do you know that?" he asks me. "Did he tell you all of my secrets? Did he tell any of his own? He tied me to a bed, that little devil."

Finn pushes past his father and locks his hand around my wrist as he pulls me from the room. Once we are outside, my toes buried in the grass, I tell Finn, "I'm sorry, I didn't know what to—"

"You need to leave now," Finn interjects. The shy and stumbling boy from the fire is gone. Finn's lips are solid while he holds his shoulder high.

"Finn, are you—?"

"Please," he snaps. "Please, just go."

"I'm sorry," I say one more time, not sure exactly what I'm trying to express. All I want to do is ease the tension in my own chest.

Finn does not reply.

The front door to Finn's home creaks open, releasing Finn's father. The man stands on the porch, arms crossed, and a ruthless smile dug across his face like a knife wound.

Finn doesn't need to utter another word before I am racing down a dirt path, blanket flapping in the air behind me.

Finn

WHEN I WAKE, Pa is already in the basement. Normally, when he is lost within his lair, he is as silent as a mouse, scurrying through the house with only a mess to show he was even there.

But not today. Pa is making enough noise in the basement that I would believe the man coaxed bulls down the steps. Pressing my ear to the old door, I hear Pa rambling to himself as though he were putting on a stage production and playing the entire cast. I grab one of the kitchen chairs and prop it against the doorknob. It won't keep him contained for long, but hopefully it will give me enough time to get to town and back.

Once I deem the kitchen clean, I swing into the living room and I see the blankets that have remained on the floor beside the hearth. As I start to fold them back up, I think about Jay. I wonder what he would have thought of Adelaide. Jay's personality would have meshed well with the Maiden's.

"You would have liked her," I decide.

When I get to Norsewood, the hunters are pacing up and down the streets, passing the persistent merchants with stern faces, ignoring the jabs made at their station. With even the presence of the hunters, there seem to be fewer children playing, and less friendly chatter flying about.

The fianna are the rarest of all. If I get a glimpse of golden eyes, it's fleeting. Disappearing as quickly as a sparrow through the trees.

I cut through the streets, making my goal to not be detected by the hunters. It is strange to feel like an outcast amongst the outcasts of Norsewood. The guild was a pack of wolves that I had once belonged to. Now, the alpha was bearing down on me, forcing me into a fight that I wasn't strong enough to win. But, oh, how I wanted to be. I didn't want the throne of the hunters though. I wanted the title of usurper.

I see a flash of blonde in the crowds, and with irrational paranoia, I dart into an alley littered with children's chalk drawings.

On the opposing end of the alley, blocking the exit is a bored Noah. Arms crossed with a hatchet slung across his shoulders aggressively. I step backward, away from a fight I'm ill equipped for.

"Ever the sneaky sneak, Finny," Hazel announces from behind. I look over my shoulder to see her isolating grin, as if I was a rodent between two tomcats. "You might not have noticed, but the hunters are a little more welcomed in Norsewood as of late."

"What do you want?" I ask Hazel specifically, knowing Noah has no say on where he ends up. "I'm sure Noah didn't come to tell me how much he loves me?" He does not look amused or even slightly fazed. "I've always had a thing for strong, muscular men—"

"We all know that isn't your type," Hazel squawks out with laughter. "Speaking of which, where is ol' Jay boy? He hasn't been in the lodge in a long time." Hazel plays with the ends of her straw-colored hair with a look of bewilderment. "He isn't lost, is he?"

My throat closes up. I want to snap back, to allow venom to lace my words. I mostly want Jay's death to stop ripping my heart apart. It is a weakness that is written across my forehead and the ruthless creatures like Hazel read it aloud as if it's a harmless nursery rhyme.

"What do you want?" I ask, my voice defeated and hushed, but I can't manage anything else. Hazel knows she won, and the only thing I have left to do is keep my dignity.

"Just checking up on you, Finn!" Hazel scoots against me, wrapping her arms around me elegantly and almost tenderly. She lays her head on my shoulder. I stiffen as Noah moves closer too. A hug from him would be much less kind.

My arms twitch at the realization that I could strangle her. I would be killed shortly after by Noah, but sending Hazel into the darkest regions of Hell would see me rewarded with the highest throne in the afterlife, I'm sure.

"We're here to help. We are brothers in arms, Finny." Hazel slides away with the grace of a swan.

"Your idea of helping is vastly different than mine."

Hazel sneers. "What if you're looking at it from the wrong angle?"

"You killed that fianna. Purposefully—"

"You do seem rather pathetic." Hazel taps her finger to her chin, ignoring my statement, ignoring her sins. "How do you not need assistance when you let your old partner die at your—"

Red hot rage erupts through me. It bursts through my fingers and causes me to strike at Hazel, but Noah is ready for the assault. He flings me backward like I'm a pebble. My back meets a sturdy wall and the air is forced to enter my lungs through a narrow throat.

"You're a bitch," I spit at her. "So flattering that Garth has personally assigned the two of you to babysit me."

"Garth is not stupid. He knows he made himself an enemy to the Hail family. Renowned hunters and madmen. He is very aware that you may put a bullet through his heart. He must have loyal confidants." Hazel flicks her hair dramatically. An act too playful for a woman who deals with blood and bones. "And you do seem a little reckless lately."

"What's he offering you?" I ask like I could possibly outbid him. That I could even sway the loyalty of a demon.

Hazel's eyes glisten. "I'm on your side, Finny. Everything we do, we do for you." She places a hand on my cheek, and when I go to pull away, her nails dig into my earlobe. "What we do, we do for the good of all the hunters and Norsewood. Stop pretending you're the only person who has problems."

And without another snap or nip, they slip back into the crowd and vanish.

I stand up, allowing myself a few minutes to cool down before I go back into the fold myself, no longer caring what eyes fall upon me.

With the sun well positioned in the middle of the sky, the citizens find the bravery to begin making the loudest of bargains and laughing the hardest. Every inch of the streets is alive, flourishing, and full of happiness I feel excluded from. It is now, more than ever, that I want to walk down these pathways and be greeted like a citizen, to have someone elderly and wise tell me how much I've grown, or to have someone ask how my father fares despite knowing for themselves the answer.

I find a bench between two vendors, placing myself in the middle of the madness. As I wait, I drown in familiar faces I have known my entire life, in stories and tales I've heard at least three times before, and the ease with which these people smile.

I see a bold fianna woman shifting through the crowd, her golden eyes constantly looking back at the human woman behind her. They talk and joke like old friends while searching for the best cut flowers, and their simple interaction warms a distant part of me.

"Deliane's bakery just started making her festive buns. I think you need—" a woman tells her partner as they shuffle past.

"Like Blaster could win in a race against Cutter! You couldn't even—" two grumpy old goats of men argue as they rock back and forth on their chairs.

"Isn't doing too well. Ever since old Luth died, that boy has had to work himself to the bone," a sturdy man tells his wife.

"Damn fianna stinkin' up the town. I could only imagine—" says a bold and arrogant boy who has yet to form his own opinion that didn't originate from the hatred of the citizens.

I get up, and I leave Norsewood when I've heard everything I need before my mind clicks the pieces together.

"HOW DID YOU find me?" the boy asks me.

I lean against the fence that proclaims the start of Luth property. I thought my arrival had gone unnoticed, for the boy was relentless as he worked in the garden, but maybe he had known I was here all along. Turning to me, he swipes at his sweaty brow, pulling his black hair away from hard lines of his face.

I clear my throat. "Your father just recently died." I say the statement out loud before I consider it. The words don't seem polite. Even amongst others my own age, I am awkward and uncomfortable. I had grown up playing with Jay, and Jay alone. Who wanted extra friends when one encompassed everything I needed? "I don't see you around town much. I had almost forgotten Luth had a son."

The boy leans on the hoe, eyes squinted at me. "Don't worry, Dad always said I wasn't very pretty. I think he hid me in the barn so I didn't scare people off." I blink in confusion. He clarifies with, "I didn't leave the farm very often," in an effort to explain why he is unfamiliar to me.

I roll my eyes. "A little dramatic, no?" The boy just shrugs. "You clearly know my name." Hails need no introduction. "What's yours?"

"They never named me. They called me 'it.'" I do not smile, do not laugh, but let my irritation bleed through my silence. Finally, he gives me, "Marshall. Marshall Luth."

"I should thank you. You saved my life. And the Maiden's," I add. "I doubt I need to express the severity of that."

Marshall dismisses me and continues to work at the fields. "Damsels in distress and shit."

"You're good with that bow," I comment. "Yet you're not a hunter. Entering the Forest without the permission of the guild is basically blasphemous."

Marshall grunts as a chicken tiptoes up to him. He leans down, snatches up the bird, and holds it in his arms lovingly. "I hope you're not trying to recruit me. I have such a raving reputation that I would hate to tarnish it by joining your band of sisters."

This boy is exhausting, I conclude. He is the kind of person who drains me. "Who taught you to shoot like that?"

"My dad," he tells me. I notice how in control of his emotions he is, how easily he maneuvers around a wound I imagine is still fresh. "He always said that hunting should be mandatory for all to learn. Protecting people was to be a source of pride, and so on and so forth. He liked to talk a lot. It was a trait I didn't really pick up from him."

I raise a single brow.

Marshall throws his hen into the air. Panicked shrieks and feathers dance in the space between us. "When I go into the Forest, I can remember him easier. Most of him is just memories now. You know that well, I'm sure."

There is no bite in his comment, no sense of maliciousness from Marshall. Just a connection through shared pain.

"Your father was a good man," I tell him because it is a rare thing. Most men of Norsewood are not brutal or violent, but they are "men." They do not show affection to their children and expect too much from their wives. But Luth, who was never called by his first name, was an honorable human. His love covered like a blanket.

I cut the pouch from my belt and toss it to Marshall.

"What is this?"

"Coin. Just take it."

"Does it look like I need your charity?" Marshall demands.

"Just a little," I tell him. I put my hands in my pockets and study his reddened face. "But this isn't pity. This is thanks. You didn't have to save me, but you did."

The common youth of Norsewood save their money for future homes, for the blade that glistens seductively, to marry the love of their lives, but I have nothing. There was never a future like that for me, and there continues to be none. If anything, I'll inherit the farmhouse and Pa's madness. None of which needs money.

"Why are you helping her?" Marshall asks boldly. "The Maiden. If I can be blunt, you don't seem like the type that gains much from helping others."

"You're right, I don't," I say as I start to leave the way I came.

"Then why? Why help her?" he shouts after me.

"Because he'd want me to."

Adelaide

AT DAWN, I'M perched at the window, watching cats tiptoe across rooftops like sneaky thieves. I coax them to come to me, using treats fashioned from baked goods Anna has been collecting. Yet, they only glare at me in distaste.

"Adelaide?"

I give a tiny yelp at the sound of Anna saying my name, damning the last chance I had to convince an orange tabby that I am of no harm.

"I didn't mean to frighten you," she tells me with her tangled hair looking as restless as her.

Last night, when I returned to our cramped quarters, Anna had inquired about Willow first, her concern focused on the human female. It was only when I told her of Willow's absence that her worry shifted to me.

"I was thinking about how you and Caleb described being human. The joy and peace you told me to expect." I pick at the windows with my nails, scratching at hardened stains. "It's almost like you made it up. Nothing about this world is joyous."

Anna brushes the hair from my face, and I hate how it is different than before. "Once Caleb feels better, you'll see I did not fib." I see the bruise that stretches from her cheekbone to the bridge of her nose.

"I have more to worry over than just Caleb," I say, my words carrying a surprising weight.

I'm angry, I realize. "While the rest of the fianna hide in this accursed town, I'm out in the Forest being hunted, getting shot at—"

I see Anna's face in the corner of my eye and it brings me to a halt. Instead, I gaze out of the window at the milling humans below. I can determine, without further proof, that none of them are my people. The fianna keep to the inn or the humans' homes. Too afraid to be courageous. "I'll find him," I say. "I'll find the Stag, and I will fix all of this. Caleb, the ferals, even us."

"But you're not sick. You don't need to be cured of anything."

I sprawl my five fingers against the glass. "This," I tell her, indicating my hand, "this is what ails us. Being human is no blessing."

Anna's fists clench at her blue dress. "How can you say that with all the great things—"

"I haven't seen any greatness," I blurt. "Not from man and not from this body." Before she can reply, try to convince me that I should revel in this time as a human female, I stand up and cross the room for my boots. Borrowed boots.

"You will miss being human," Anna speaks out loud, but more to herself. She stares at her lap, her eyes distant. "The memories, the sensation of a hand holding your own, and the—"

"I won't miss something that was never meant to be mine." I close the door behind me with a solidifying thud. I stay there, for a moment, and wonder if I should turn back, if I should go and apologize to Anna.

But I don't. I leave her with my words.

WHEN THE COUNCIL had originally given Caleb, Anna, and me a bundle of their currency, I childishly thought we were rich. Only now, as the humans scoff at petty change do I realize I was given minimal funds.

At my final attempt to purchase food, the man gives me a belittling lecture on Norsewood morals that I automatically tune out. Can one be judgmental and hypocritical?

"I'll take two of those apples and whatever else she wants." I turn to see Finn tucking two of the reddest fruits into his pack. I don't ask for further details while I grab a third. He flicks the man a pale-looking coin before moving to another stand. "What else do you need? You don't have a jacket, do you?"

I shake my head, unsure of how to answer. His tone is soft, and it confuses me. It is strange how, after dealing with a handful of Norsewood citizens, I can conclude that Finn, of all humans, seems kinder. Gentler.

Finn leads me into a brightly colored shop and speaks curtly to the girl behind the counter, who scampers into the bowels of the store to fulfill his request. When she returns, she hands me a light coat with fur lining the hood. I hold the clothing carefully, a sick twist rising in my stomach.

"I can promise you that the fur was not from the Forest," the girl tells me, her attentiveness a breath of fresh air. "Please, try it on!"

"You don't have to do this," I tell Finn once the girl scuttles off. I look into his pale gray eyes, telling myself to reject his generosity.

I don't need his help.

"I want to. I was an ass," he says, as though he were talking about the temperature and not his actions. "Would this make us even?" He points to the coat.

I turn to the side, inspecting each angle in the store's mirror. As I twirl, I make sure the shopkeeper is nowhere to be seen. "It is very ugly."

Finn chokes out a laugh before he can cover up his mouth with the back of his hand. "Yeah, it is, isn't it?" He twists his mouth to the side, concentrating. "I think you need a little lighter one."

And Finn dives into the folds of fabric, and I spin in numerous colors and fits, giggling the entire time. Finn seems, oddly, to be enjoying himself in the collision of dyes and fits. I realize, sluggishly, that there are no guns here. No blades, and no blood.

Just a boy smiling and a girl laughing.

When I pick out a casual coat, I do not let Finn bully me into a more expensive style.

We are still in good spirits when our feet slap the cobble streets.

Yet, as soon as we turn the street, Willow appears before us, a gray cloak hugging her figure tightly. She looks about herself nervously, her gray hair poking from the shaded hood. "Follow me." She doesn't wait for a response before vanishing like a wispy cloud. Finn offers up an effortless sigh before following her.

Willow leads us to the outer rim of the city and closer to her home. Her frayed hair displays her panic more than her face. "Where have you been? It was impossible to find either of you!"

"I tried looking for you yesterday," I say in defense. "Anna was looking for you. I stopped by your cottage."

And there's a good chance I released your pet.

"Is she ill?" Willow inquires.

I clench my teeth together, not sure how exposed I want to be before Finn. "Caleb is feeling under the weather. She wanted to know if you had herbs for him. She would really like for you visit him in person," I say with what I hope is urgency.

Willow nods, biting at her lip. "I will make sure I swing by the inn. But most importantly, how goes the search? Have you found anything?"

"Well, we—"

Finn quickly cuts me off by telling Willow, "We haven't found much. We don't know what to go off of but legends that are told over campfires. If you have any concrete leads, we'd take them graciously."

I give Finn a frown. Does he not trust Willow? I try again to tell Willow of the fianna and the huntress who thwarts our every move, but again, he cuts me off, "Is there anything we can assist you with, Willow?"

"I'm beginning to worry," she admits, and I find her concern also alarming. This woman seemed unshakable even before the council of man. "I was at the town hall when I happened upon a meeting that seemed to be taking place in private."

"'Happened upon?'" Finn asks, crossing his arms in the process.

"I don't need to explain my actions to you, boy," she bites back. "Regardless of how I saw it, I witnessed Garth meeting with the council by himself."

Finn shrugs. "And? Maybe Garth and those bastards play cards."

Willow rolls her eyes and I find myself matching the motion. Finn can be very taxing at times. His humor, often at the expense of others, can only be taken in tiny segments. "Granted, I didn't have a lot of time, but I heard them discussing a great deal of things."

I press a hand against Finn's arm before he can respond, attempting to silence him. "What did they speak of?"

Willow's eyes find mine and I immediately shiver. "They spoke on the inevitability that you will fail, Maiden."

I step back, placing a hand to my chest as my heart hammers against my collarbone. "Why—the nerve—"

It is Finn's turn to rest a palm against my shoulder, bringing my anger to a halt. "This is no surprise. The hunters don't believe in the legends of the fianna. It is only natural that they would have a backup plan."

"But I'm not going to fail," I say to both Willow and Finn, but it goes unheard.

"You even think like them," Willow retaliates, striking at Finn.

But the boy seems immovable. "It is only logical."

She shakes her head. "You don't understand. The lengths they mean to go to prevent the ferals from rising are horrid. If you would just listen to me instead of being your smartass self—"

"Willow. That is enough."

All three of us turn to see the lead hunter, Garth, standing under the town's entrance. He is flanked by two hunters who look just as stern as him. Their tunics are embellished with bones, some resting on the shoulders while others are sewn onto the chest like actual ribs.

"If I heard correctly, you were eavesdropping on a classified meeting. That is a very naughty thing, Willow." Garth cocks his head to the side. "Women can be such gossips."

I swallow.

"I'm more amused you are heeling to the council," Willow snarls, her original fire flaring back inside her chest.

Yet, I question if her brave words can be followed through with braver actions. "To think you would follow the lead from the very ones who shun you."

Garth plays with his beard, a grin sprawling across his features. "I am not one to turn down an opportunity, Willow. You should know that." He rolls his shoulders and winks at Finn. "I hope it won't inconvenience you both, but the council would like to talk to the Maiden and her escort tonight. They ask that all present studies to be brought with you."

"We don't have the time for that," Finn tells the man. "You will have to give them our deepest apologies."

Garth's face shifts until he looks surprised, but mockingly so. "Goodness, I should be the one to apologize to you." With a snap of his fingers, the two hunters at his side walk past him until they hold Willow between them. "It really isn't an option. The meeting will happen. And you will be there."

We both stare in horror as Willow is dragged away from us, not an ounce of fight in her. She looks over her shoulder once at us with a sadness that causes my heart to squeeze.

"Misunderstandings are such ugly affairs." Garth moves until he stands inches from Finn and raises his hand to lift the boy's chin. "We wouldn't want people getting the wrong information, now, would we?" Garth seems to speak only to Finn, but his menace brushes me.

When Finn takes hold of my hand, I don't fight him as he peels us away from the town.

Finn

TODAY, THE FOREST is stagnant. The colors don't pop, the musical tone of the birds' cries is muted, and there isn't a breeze to be felt. A shrill tone of insects rumbling back and forth naturally fills up the pockets of silence.

For not the first time, I consider what might exist beyond this Forest. That there might be a distance that even Hazel wouldn't go to find me.

"Finn," Adelaide says, out of breath as she struggles to keep up with me. "Can we please slow down?" She groans as a passing branch slices a red line across her forearm.

I stop, realizing that my own chest heaves with exertion. Adelaide wraps her arms around her stomach, clenching her rips tenderly.

"What is the significance of the lilies?" Because we must start someplace. "Are they magical? Are they...?"

"I don't know," she tells me with a sorrowful frown. "They bloom from the ferals. Like they do from the ground. Why they do or what they are is lost to me." She pulls back her hair and I see every line of her jaw, her unnatural eyes. "They seem like normal flowers."

I sit down on a stump, dragging my fingers through my scalp. Shortly after, Adelaide sits with her back to mine, the same sense of defeat rippling off her. Just the minor brush conveys more than our words can.

"Do you think Willow is safe?" Adelaide asks.

I shrug. "I'm sure she can talk her way out of a situation."

Adelaide pitches a stone into the weeds. "What do you know about past Maidens?"

"I know what has been told in stories, what little is recorded in the human studies."

"And?"

I sigh. "Last Maiden was over a hundred years ago. It was during a time when the town attempted to cut back some of the Forest. Ferals came, killed 'em all. Back then, the guild and the town weren't on such—" I think of the proper word "—friendly terms. The hunters watched as people died left and right. Then, during the season of the fianna, it is said a beautiful girl walked into Norsewood, the sun shining on her like a diamond, and she declared she was 'the Maiden of the Stag.' Or so goes the stories."

"Hmm. To be remembered as beautiful," was all Adelaide said at first. "Anything else?"

"It is only ever told that she arrived, disappeared, and took the ferals with her. Don't you have any insider information?" I don't want to point out that this is kind of her thing.

Adelaide picks at the bark by her thigh, her fingers restlessly reconstructing the Forest. "I wish I did. Instead, I'm useless."

"Do you believe in your own god, Adelaide?"

The girl turns to me, narrowing her eyes.

"You asked me if I believed in him. I gave you my reasonings for why I don't..." I bite my lip. "I gave you reasons for why I may be skeptical. But what about you?"

Adelaide can only hold my gaze for a fraction of a moment before she returns to supervising her fingers scratching at the wood.

At first, I doubt that she will answer. That there are no parts of her which deny a higher power. That all she breathes is her faith. Yet, when she does speak, the entire Forest seems to lean in to catch her words.

"I don't doubt the Stag exists. Maybe I haven't been human long enough to think any other way, but I can't look at the world around me and not see something more." Adelaide stills. "But that doesn't mean I don't wonder where he is. Is it possible..." I see the doubt threatening to silence her, but she is stronger than her fears. "Maybe there once was a god. Maybe he created all of this," she considers while throwing twigs into the weeds, "and went to create something else. Somewhere else."

"Why would you think that?"

"Because I need him. If he were here, in the Forest, he would have found me by now, right?" Her eyes find mine, begging for an answer I don't believe I can give. When she opens her lips, I expect another truth to fall from them. Another proclamation that will evolve the girl I see before me. "May I be bold?"

I almost tell her, "Of course, why wouldn't you be able to?" but then I realize she means to ask me another question. And after the last *personable* conversation we had, I can understand her worry. I nod my consent because I don't trust my words.

"Your friend, Jay, he died, didn't he?"

When the air flees from my lungs, the birds sing even higher, as if the wind stolen from me was sucked up into their breasts.

"He died, and you blame me, don't you?"

A flash of fury brushes past my heart, but I try to dodge it. I can't let it take hold of me. Instead, I close my eyes and tell her, "I do not."

"You lie to me."

I ball my fingers up into fists so tiny I worry I'll break my knuckles. "You didn't cause this. All of this is beyond you. If anything, it is your god that—"

My eyes fly open, finding her face tilted, studying me. A bug crawls up a strand of her hair while we watch one another.

"I draw them in. They are attracted to me like bees to a flower."

"Why do you want me to hate you?" I ask, the honesty stinging.

"Because that would be easier," she admits. "The humans in your town only see one thing about me. It's simple. Easy to understand. But not you. I keep waiting to figure out what drives you. If it isn't resentment, then I don't know what it could be."

It is hate, I want to tell her, to confess the darkest reaches of my heart. *It is a hate bright enough that I worry everyone sees it written across my skin.*

"Amongst all the others, there is a legend about blood and resurrection. That the Stag can offer up—or lose—its blood as a boon. That it can cure anything. Even death." I know she watches me now, closer than ever, but I can't acknowledge her. "But that means nothing with Garth around."

Adelaide wants to respond, but I rise, trying to find the best way to bring this conversation to an end, to make sure I don't slam another figurative door in her face. I want to be better, to treat her right, but I don't have a good track record once my mouth is open.

"We have to keep looking for the Stag. Or...something." I watch a squirrel careen through the branches. "We can't give up."

She stands up, dusting off her rear when she asks, "You're doing it for him, aren't you?"

I take a step back, hoping even an inch of distance would cause her words to be less impactful. But it isn't. If only I was—

My boot catches, and I fall backward. My butt smashes against the Forest floor in a jarring jolt. Adelaide, trying to suppress her smile, holds out a hand for me, saying how clumsy I am. I reach for her aid while my other hand pushes off the ground—

And lands in a slick *mush*.

Wrist deep, my hand disappears into the corpse of a goat. Adelaide screams while the skeleton of the creature becomes evident to both of us. The stink, somehow undetected before, wafts into my nose until tears prick at my eyes from the intensity. Flies storm around me, vexed that I interrupted their buffet. The stomach, where my hand once rested, is torn up like a shredded teddy bear.

The only word that escapes past the hand pressed to Adelaide's mouth is "what?"

But the hum in my ears is much louder. Because when I stand back up, I see the goat is not alone. Numerous corpses are thrown about like a graveyard unearthed. Each creature has a lax rope tied around their throat, tethering their skeleton to the trees.

"How did they—?" Adelaide continues to try to speak, but each sentence is butchered when she must pry her eyes from the scene and catch her breath.

"These are traps," I tell her, numb. "All of them were bait."

"Finn," Adelaide starts, her hand brushing my shoulder. "What do you—?"

"You weren't the only thing pulling in the ferals."

Adelaide

I CAN'T CALM Finn down. He is as violent as a windstorm as he kicks and swears and he waves his gun carelessly. All I can do is study the carnage around me. Ferals rarely hunt for food, but typically for pleasure. Doesn't matter the species or level of difficulty; prey is prey.

Finn swirls around, screaming with abandon. "If I find out this was Hazel, I'll gut her, I'll—" His frustration manifests as he smashes his fist into a tree trunk. "I'll kill him."

"Finn, please calm down," I say, carefully selecting my words for he is dangerously close to ignoring all reason. Yet, his thoughts seem to be a whirlwind.

"No," he tells me. "This is Hazel. It has her stench all over it. Her or Garth. Both of them. They brought the ferals to the fianna village."

"The ferals come for me," I state. "The fault is mine."

Finn spits as he talks, all control of his mouth slipping away. "They do. But how close do they have to be? How far will they come to find you? How far can they smell?"

"You think the hunters are luring them in? That they killed these creatures to bring the ferals closer to the village?" I ask.

Meeting my eyes, Finn nods.

My heart skips. "And then I do the rest?"

He nods again.

A sickness turns my stomach into a knot. I focus on the air that I take in, on the noises of the Forest around me. "Caleb and Anna." My thoughts crash and break against one another. "We have to do something."

Finn pulls his rifle onto his lap and starts to clean at the metal with his shirt. "I am. I'm gonna kill 'em."

"You must be joking," I tell him. Yet, Finn does not stop. "You can't do that, Finn! You don't—"

"If they drew the ferals in, that means they also killed Jay!"

The crack of Finn's voice rivals that of thunder. With his lips pulled back and his teeth flashing, he is a boy posed for a skirmish. "If Garth is responsible for that, I'll kill him. I won't even hesitate. I won't—"

"You need to think straight!" I shout back at him, like two wolves howling at one another. Yet, the truth of his words, the conviction that rolls from Finn, causes my skin to prickle. "What will that solve?" I ask.

"Everything," he snaps. "Wouldn't you kill to protect those you care for?"

I can't answer him.

"Because if Garth dies, this will all end. You can't stand here and tell me you wouldn't kill for peace. If one life equaled hundreds."

My heart tells me I would never, but my mind demands otherwise. *If a single bullet could save my people, would I be willing to fire it?* "The ferals won't end. I have to find the Stag. That much can't be changed with violence," I tell him because it is the only thing I can cling to. The only thing that separates me from what I fear.

"You can't always believe in fairy tales," Finn says as he stands. He slides a bullet into the chamber and readies his weapon. As he snaps on the safety, he locks into silence.

Finn

NIGHT DESCENDS UPON us as we race back to Norsewood. The colors start to melt together until it is only purples and dark blues smearing past us.

And no matter how many times I think it, I cannot feel a shred of guilt in me that I plan on ending a man's life.

I want Adelaide to convince me I'm wrong, that there is another way to douse the fire in my heart. But she can't. She even knows it.

I am a bundle of fury and justice.

Rage is all I need right now.

"You need to think," she shouts before dipping beneath swinging branches. "You can't just strike without a plan."

"I have a plan," I snap.

"I mean, an intelligent one!"

We leave the trees behind and plant our feet in the fields cushioning Norsewood, and Adelaide stands beneath the moonlight like a goddess. Her golden hair whisks around her while her dress whips like a sail on the open seas. I want to tell her that she is beautiful, that she looks like the kind of deity I would pray to, yet I remain quiet. "If you don't think this through and you die, this will have been for nothing. You won't be able to save him."

"I didn't save him the first time," I say, the truth of it a dangerous thing to give life to.

The Maiden looks to me, her eyes devouring me. "Then don't fail again."

I try to tell her that I won't. That, this time, I am lethal. But all I can do is keep running.

WE CREST THE final hill and Norsewood explodes before me, brighter than usual. The streetlamps are swallowed within the blaze of another glow, thick and corded smoke soaring into the sky. People mill around a single cottage like ants from their hill.

"Is that...?" Adelaide begins, yet is unable to finish.

"A fire," I finish before we take off running.

We sprint along the edge of the town until we come face to face with the fire. Men and women slug buckets of well water back and forth, trying to battle the dominating flames. Yet, even as the water douses a section, the fire rises higher in another. They are not equipped to deal with this evolving disaster.

Two hunters stand idly by as the fire expands and retracts like a pulse. I see Rowan, his eyes cloudy as he stares into the flames, and I move to him. Gripping his tunic in my fist, I pull him so closely that one could mistake it for a tender embrace. "What happened here?" I ask, but he is too far away to hear me, his gaze lost in the flames. "Where is Willow?" I shout.

As I watch, her home crumbles into ash.

I shake him roughly, his head snapping back like a doll's. "Where is she?"

Rowan holds his eyes shut tightly, refusing to look at me. "She was sent back to her home. She was collecting her belongings, and then..." Rowan swallows. "A beam fell at the entrance. She didn't make it—"

I swing my fist into Rowan's face. My knuckles crunch into his nose. He drops to his knees, not an ounce of fight in him as he accepts the pain. I drop my belongings and dive forward to smash my boot into the door. The edges of my pants catch, but I keep kicking, kicking, kicking.

Adelaide is pulling me back, her hands struggling against me as I thrash. She shouts into my ear, but it's too noisy to focus on her.

The cottage's roof collapses into itself. Willow's home, isolated, keeps the fires away from all the other buildings. I stand still, Adelaide beside me, watching until there is no more resemblance of the cottage. Ash floats back down onto the streets like the first snowfall.

As the flames dwindle, a singular, remorseless figure comes into focus. Legs dangling from the edge of a roof, box of matches being tossed in the air, and a grin to best even devils.

Just like the smoke, Hazel disappears with the next evening breeze.

"THEY KILLED HER," Adelaide says.

I lead Adelaide to a vacant market stand. The two of us shake beneath the chipping wood and aroma of rotten fruit.

I rub at the pain blossoming in my brow. I can't say the actual death of Willow saddens me, and that alone bothers me. My gut clenches up at the fact that Garth's power expands so far in Norsewood.

"We have to get out of Norsewood for now. I know it probably isn't a good idea, but we can—"

Like the hand of a god, a fist drops out of nowhere to clench the edge of my tunic. With an *hmmpf*, I am thrown over the counter of the stand. Landing on the cobble streets, I look up to see Noah rolling his shoulders. Adelaide struggles as Hazel twists her arms behind her back.

Grime and soot rests against the huntress's skin like a blanket.

I get to my feet and position myself to attack Noah, because to hell with running. If I can knock aside Noah, I can try and get to—

Noah's boots eat up the dirt as he lunges for me. His fist sails toward me and I am able to knock the blow to the side, but Noah is prepared. He brings his knee into my gut. I barely have any time to react before Noah sweeps my legs out from under me.

It all ends with a boot pressed lightly against my heaving chest.

"Can't be late. Some really old hags wanna chat," Hazel says with a toothy grin. "You are really good at pissing off old men, Hail."

Adelaide

FINN AND I are taken to a windowless room that smells like it once housed countless pigs. Hazel deposits us like a couple of stubborn sheep needing penned. She slams the door shut and I give the knob an experimental tug despite knowing it will be locked. The room is barely big enough for us to move around each other. Finn has his back to the wall, leaving the cot in the corner for me.

"How's your stomach?" I ask.

Finn leans his head back, eyes closed to the light that hangs above him. His sweat and scratches nearly transform his face into someone else. "He hits pretty hard. A guy as big as him shouldn't be so agile."

"How can they keep us prisoner without anyone else questioning it?" I touch the wallpaper, picking at the peeling edges. "Does the town just look away?"

Finn stretches out on the floor, taking up all the remaining room. "You should try to get some rest."

"How can you relax? Do you even know where we are?"

"Town hall. No matter what you do right now, it won't change the fact that soon you will be standing before the council."

I lay on my side, keeping my eyes on Finn's face. "What if I shifted? Right in here? Think that would get us out?"

Finn smirks. "Yeah. But not before you squash me to death."

I throw the one pillow I have at Finn who catches it then places it beneath his head. "What does that mean?" I ask in mock anger.

"Tell me something, Maiden."

I rest my head against my arms. "Go ahead."

"If you were human—just human—what do you think your life would be like?" Finn's eyes peek at me from underneath his lids before hiding themselves again. "Pretend there is another town. Huge. Multiple towns. Endless places to discover. What would you be doing?"

I have never considered what my life would be if I wasn't the Maiden, or fianna, for that matter. I have never considered a life that wasn't mine. Honestly, it seems rather pointless, but I play along. "I think I would have a garden," I tell him. "Plant as many flowers as I could."

"To sell?"

"No." Because I don't envision that at all. "I don't think I would be around people. Even my own kind. I would want a house. In the trees. With just..." I try to picture it, to imagine a field of flowers, but each time I do, I see the lilies dripping with blood.

Finn blinks at me, waiting for me to finish my sentence, but I can't. Not after I've dismantled the illusion. "What about you?"

Propping himself up, Finn picks at his pants, pulling the threads until they further unravel the material. "That's a tough one. I'm not sure what my life would be like somewhere else." He raises his chin, for a moment, and our eyes connect. "No matter where I go, I always take me along."

My jaw tenses. "What does that mean?"

Finn lowers his head. "It means that new scenery won't change how I view myself. It means that no matter where I go, I won't be able to convince myself to not care what others think. I can't go far enough to be someone I'm not." His hands are still, his chest the only piece of him moving. "Living in Norsewood might not be so terrible if I could start fixing up myself."

I'm quiet for a good portion after Finn's statement. Long enough for the door to our room to fling open and reveal a dolled-up Hazel. Another nameless hunter fills up the doorway with weapons at the ready. Hazel, not expecting a fight, approaches Finn with only a grin. "You two have been summoned. Try to look presentable."

"I AM SORRY to hear that you still have no documentation of your pilgrimage, Maiden."

The oldest man in the council, Jal, glares at me through a thick lens of glass. Finn stands in his own little box. We are but a body's length from one another, but it's like a sea separates us. These men are skilled at isolating someone with words alone.

All around me are humans, humans, humans. I am the only fianna amongst them.

"I was not made aware there was a due date," I state.

Jal rolls his thin shoulders, the joints popping as he goes. "Of course not. Yet, with such a matter, time is of the utmost importance."

I must be smarter than them. "It saddens me that Willow has died," I begin, letting true sorrow show. "She was a great ally to the fianna."

One of the councilmen shifts uncomfortably. "She was."

I glance at Finn. "I am sorry to have been keeping information from the council, but Willow had been aiding Finn and me on our quest."

Jal cocks his head to the side doubtfully. "Why was she doing that?"

"You know as much as anyone that Willow strived for the peace of the fianna. She was helping me record my findings."

Jal taps his fingers against his desk. "I hope she was of aid to you."

"Very much," I say, nodding. It is strange, and terrifying to look that man in the face and know that he very well could have sentenced Willow to her demise. How aware is he that I am not stupid? "It is also unfortunate that Willow died in her home. Amongst all her studies."

Finn remains quiet, allowing me to weave this tale.

"Willow, after deciding Finn did not have attention to detail, took it upon herself to record and document all of our discoveries."

"That was not what was requested," the man furthest to the right snaps in agitation. "Finn Hail was meant to record your rituals. Not some—" He catches himself before continuing, "It was not Willow's duty." He points a meaty finger at Finn. "You can't just relinquish the responsibilities given to you, boy."

Finn shrugs, bored of it all.

"I understand that," I tell him. "And I apologize for involving another person into this. I was only trying to get the quickest results."

Jal clears his throat loudly enough that the attention of the room flashes back to him. He likes that, I realize. He eats up the attention. "I fail to see how this is important to the matters we discuss now. I asked you if you had any proof of your Maidenhood. If you follow in the lineage of past Maidens."

"The proof was in Willow's studies," Finn adds. "In her house."

"We lost all of it when her cottage burned," I finish.

Jal processes the information while a few of the councilmen mutter to each other. I can see the annoyance build up on his face. It makes me want to grin in satisfaction. "What information have we lost?"

"The cure to the ferals," I say, trying to wear my lie as convincingly as I can.

The crowd behind me gasps and whispers to each other. The councilmen look to one another, eyebrows raised and clearly confused. The council and the guild may have similar plans, but the citizens of Norsewood do not. I don't have to expose the madness behind their actions, I just have to best them.

I can do this.

I am strong enough.

"I would also like to thank the councilmen, and the citizens of Norsewood for housing my people," I state as loudly as I can. My voice rings through the space like thunder striking. "I am doing all that I can in the given time. I ask for more time, so that I may protect everyone. The people of Norsewood and the fianna. I mean to rid the world of the feral threat. Not for a little while. But permanently."

The councilmen talk amongst themselves while the people before them thrive and devour the lie I have fed them. That ferals may be no more. Not just a lapse in the cycle, but a permanent end to the fiends.

The councilmen pound on their desks, demanding silence from the people. Their voices die off, but their interest is thriving.

"Finn, we request that you recreate the information lost in the recent fire within a week. Meanwhile, we will continue to plan to put the safety of Norsewood before all else. And, Maiden," Jal zeroes in on me, but I refuse to acknowledge fear. "We wish you the best of luck."

I bow before I exit.

FINN HOLDS IT together until we are near the entrance of Norsewood before he laughs, a sound so pure and honest that a part of me hurts to just watch him smiling. He pulls me into a brief hug, his arms leaving behind their warmth once they are gone.

"That was brilliant."

A blush in my cheeks ignites at his admiration.

"A week," he says, the earlier joy slipping through the cracks. "We have a week."

"I need to figure something out," I confirm.

"We can capture more ferals. We could collect more lilies, we could—"

"We should find another place for the fianna," I say. Finn blinks at me, confused. "Find a place they will be safe. Not in Norsewood. Not in the village."

Finn crosses his arms. "You plan on running?"

I'm not sure if Finn intentionally adds heat to his words, but it's there. "The humans are clearly expecting me to fail. They want me to prove to them that god exists. I don't know if I can do that."

"But you're the Maiden."

"That doesn't mean anything," I say as the words tear through my throat and leave me empty. The lie that I was *special* or anything other than ordinary had filled up my body, holding me together, and now, with it gone, I am lifeless. "In a week, if I don't hand them a god, my people will be stranded. I need to have options."

Finn, in frequent consistency, surprises me. "Well, I don't think you should stop looking for him. For the Stag. But either way, we need to be back in the Forest. Be it looking for the Stag or finding a new place for the fianna, we need to be out there. I can pack supplies for an overnight trip. Stay in the fianna village and explore further into the woods."

I nod. "We have to."

Finn shifts his weight between his feet, shuffling uncomfortably. "Also..." He scratches at his neck while saying, "Don't give up hope. On finding your god. On finding a cure. Not yet. Once you stop believing, there will be no one else who does."

Saving me from replying, I hear, "Adelaide."

I turn. Anna is standing in the middle of the street, and regardless of the lanterns casting shadows over her, I still see the blotches of discolored skin that stretch from her eye to her cheek. Anna's fingers play with the end of her shirt, her body screaming nervousness.

"Did someone hit you?" Finn asks, taking a step forward.

Anna takes one backward.

"No. I just need to speak with the Maiden."

"Of course." I turn to Finn who hasn't stopped looking at Anna, sprung and ready to launch into action. "It's all right, Finn. I will find you tomorrow?"

Finn takes a moment but then nods. He walks away with a few glances over his shoulder.

Anna doesn't say a word as she turns and leads the way by several feet. I notice immediately that the distance between us is practically solid. It's not the same as when I first arrived in this town, hand in hand with Anna.

Now, it feels as if it doesn't matter how far I stretch. I couldn't reach her.

Anna hesitates outside the room, her hair looking like a bramble bush as she presses her forehead against the door. "I saw her hut." She wouldn't need to say anything else, but she does. "Is she dead? Did Willow die?"

I want to deny it at first, but Anna has never asked me to spare her from these hard truths. If anything, she has been human more times than I. She should know, by now, that not much joy can be had in this life. "Yes."

Anna closes her eyes, and I wait for tears, but not a single one falls. "She was our only supporter in this town. The only one who stood up for the fianna."

Deep breath, Adelaide. "I have been defending our kind since I've arrived in Norsewood. And I will continue to do so. What is it you wanted me to see?" I ask briskly.

Anna pushes off the door, collecting herself before saying, "Please, stay calm," she tells me, her wrist twisting and the door popping open. "I have everything under control."

I step around Anna and enter the room.

The furniture, once placed intentionally, is scattered around the room in pieces. The floors are torn and now wear deep gashes along the planks. Clothes and collected human niceties rest in haphazard piles. If this room didn't have a roof, I would assume a storm blew through these walls.

From the corner of my eye, I see a creature tethered to the pipes. With a cloth tied tightly around his mouth, muffling the sounds of snarls, I almost miss the bloody fangs. Black, lacy veins trail up and down his body like snakes. Even darker eyes gleam at me. Two twisted and malformed horns sprout from his brow like flowers. Fresh blood puddles where his wrists and ankles are rubbed raw from the ropes.

Anna shuts the door behind her, as if locking me into a trap.

"Caleb—" I start, but I can't think straight. He surges against his restraints, urging his muscles to tear free and...and what? Devour me? Kill me? I am stunned while I consider untying Caleb, needing to prove to myself he would never do that.

But he tried once.

"I don't know what to do anymore." Anna slides down the wall until she is sprawled out like a puddle on the floor. "You said you healed him. You said he would be okay."

My heart fades until I am sure it is hidden somewhere in my body, refusing to be hurt anymore. I reach out a hand to Caleb, stepping closer and closer until his hot exhales tickling my skin. His thrashing is ruthless the nearer I am to him.

I grip his throat, digging my nails into his flesh. And I wait.

For seconds.

Minutes.

I wait for another miracle.

"I can't lose him again," Anna sobs, her cries a declaration. Proof that even she no longer believes in me. That I am the Maiden.

I let go of Caleb and I stare at my human hands.

So human. So pathetically human.

"We can't let the humans find him. If the hunters see him...they'll..." Anna's lips stop moving while her eyes lose themselves in the ways Caleb bends and twists.

"They won't find him," I say, squaring off my shoulders. "That much I can promise you." I move behind Caleb, and while he tries to reach for me, I can knock away his limbs easily. "I have a week before the humans' plan comes to life. If it comes to it, we will take Caleb into the woods."

"And let him go?" Anna asks, shaking her head in disapproval.

"It's that or you watch him being filled with arrows." I stare directly at her, my face hardened, and my words clipped. "I would do anything to save him. And you."

Anna is silent but eventually nods.

"Now, get up. We need to secure him better." And when she stands, I know our night has just begun.

Finn

WHILE PA SCRIBBLES furiously into his journal, I slice up various fruits and vegetables, prepare a meal for Adelaide and myself. Pa, increasingly dogged, peppers me with questions about the Maiden. I have, and continue, to play off Adelaide being in this house as one of his many delusions. I can't say I'm proud of helping him fall further into his madness, but the alternative is even worse.

"You can still smell her," Pa murmurs as he writes. "I bet her blood smells even sweeter."

I shiver. "She left you some," I tell him, lying as I wrap up my food. "She left it on the counter, but you said it didn't work."

"Lies," Pa shouts. Yet, he doesn't sound like he's convinced. "She gave me nothing. She only takes. Years ago, she took. And she'll take again."

"She can't do that. She already left. Went back into the Forest."

"That can't be true." Pa's pen stabs the open pages. "She can't leave yet."

"She's a busy girl," I apologize, washing off the kitchen knife.

Pa sighs, waits, and then rises from the table. He shuffles all his pages together, humming under his breath as he works. When I turn the faucet, I hear a fragment of his tune.

"What are you saying?"

Pa raises his eyebrows. "Hmm? Oh, it is what she told me as my love died," he says, in his own way of explaining. "She told me 'begin again, begin again.'"

A tickle itches at the back of my mind. "What does that mean?"

"She'll be back." Pa walks to the basement. "She'll be back with her blood."

WHEN I ENTER the hunters' lodge, the deafening roar of man ceases as my boots touch the sticky wooden floor.

Conversations are put on hold, beer sloshes in stilled mugs that, seconds ago, were waved around like flags, and the hunters stare at me as though I were a ghost.

Within a blink, the noise explodes back into place, filling up the rafters and leaving no room for shyness. I walk through the unaligned and cramped tables, remembering when all this noise had been comforting.

I see Rowan for a moment, his face swollen. He does nothing to cover it up, and I try to convince myself to be proud of the scar I've given him, yet all I can muster up is shame.

The lodge, with its piles of unorganized equipment and dirty clothing, rivals the mess of a robin's nest. As I tiptoe through the junk, my body prepares itself for Garth. Even though he's the leader, Garth tends to spend his time far from the lodge.

I snag two backpacks and start to glean whatever seems useful from the collection on the ground.

When Rowan crouches into my vision, I do not stop loading up the packs, and he doesn't interfere. He simply bends down and picks up a mud-encrusted boot, sighing as he throws it onto another mound.

As he hands me a rolled-up blanket, I see his hands are wrapped several times in soiled bandages.

It doesn't register at first. I stare at his long fingers.

"I tried," he mutters in explanation. His skin is agitated and red, blisters bubbling up like pond scum. "I really did."

I can't say anything once his words form within my mind.

Rowan tightens up the strings of the nearest pack and hides it underneath a table. "After everyone is too drunk to remember anything, I'll place them outside. Behind the bush with the red berries."

I nod.

"I know Garth has you by the balls. Somehow." He rises to leave. "Just remember you're not the only one. I'll do anything to keep Garth from her."

Never has it occurred to me that Garth could have others ensnared like he does me. I look over my shoulder, wondering if the guild is filled with people whose lives are held captive.

I crack the joints in my thumbs, saying, "Sorry," along with the pops.

Rowan simply smiles, something bright and easy on his bruised features. "Also, I'm sorry...about Jay." He can't look at me when he offers up his condolences, but I know it's real. "I didn't know him as well as you did, but I do miss him." In a flash, Rowan has a full smile, his gaze hazy in memory. "He was a damn good card player."

"He liked playing with you," I comment. Because Rowan was the only hunter who Jay seemed partially fond of.

"You meant a lot to him. I hope you know that. You can pretend all you like that you're some fiend, but you were good to him. You made Jay a better person."

Emotion is too thick to speak through. I can't fathom how Jay could have become anything with the aid of me. What parts of me could he even take when there was no bad to himself?

Instead, I point to his face. "Did it hurt?"

"Like a bitch." He smirks.

"Good."

One day, when all of this goes to hell, I hope that Rowan's hands are not stained red. Because right now, I find myself kind of liking the hunter with the shy smile.

NORSEWOOD AT NIGHT is my favorite version of the town.

A different kind of crowd seems to collect outside their homes. The kids are tucked into their beds with stories of grand adventures and beautiful royalty, and the adults are finally gearing into relaxation. As the bonfires strike up in backyards, neighbors and friends sit in tight circles, laughing and passing the time with each other's company.

I leap from circle to illuminated circle, the lanterns hung above me casting blotches of visibility for me to travel by. Despite slipping through the light, I still feel like a phantom that could slither into the darkness without anyone knowing I had ever been there.

My feet stop before a house with blue shutters. It has been a long time since I've seen this building. The place where Pa once lived with his love, my mother.

I too lived here, for a brief season in my early life, but never long enough to have fond memories. To think that the Hail family once existed inside Norsewood seems like a fantasy. For just a moment, a torturous moment, I let myself imagine a Finn Hail who was raised with the other children of Norsewood. A boy with a mother who held her boy when he cried. A boy with a father who would do anything to protect his wife and child.

To me, despite the fianna and a legendary god, that kind of life seems like a myth.

"Finn?"

I look to my right to see Adelaide standing underneath the lantern's glow. Her hair is pulled back into a messy bun, and her golden eyes threaten to overflow. I snort at her outfit, which was clearly pieced together in a hurry. That, or she enjoys a combination of men's clothes that do not match. Either way, once the image settles, I can conclude that it all looks good on her.

"What are you doing here?" she asks innocently, yet somehow Adelaide, a foreigner, has more of a place in Norsewood than I lately. "Were you looking for me?"

I shake my head. "No, sorry. I was just heading home. I was at the lodge getting supplies for tomorrow."

"Oh...?" She leans her head slightly to the side. It isn't the first time I've noticed Adelaide's beauty, but tonight, it's elevated. If her eyes were any other color, she'd be the talk of the town, the prize for those hunting for love.

It is startling what little separates us.

I debate on telling her how she looks. "I used to live here," I say instead because, for an instant, I want her to know parts of me no one else does anymore so that I might remember me as more than a hunter. "When I was young, my father, mother, and I stayed in this house."

"That sounds like it was nice."

I nod. "My father has never been normal, not ever since he lost my mother. People tell me that he loved her fiercely. Almost otherworldly."

Adelaide inspects the house. "I hear love makes humans do miraculous things. What was it like to live here? In Norsewood?"

I shrug. "I was too young to properly remember it."

Adelaide smiles at me. "Tell me what you do recall."

I tap my boot on the street. "It's one of those things where I don't know if it's a memory or something told to you. Like, I remember her voice. Or at least, I think I do. I have this faint memory of her voice echoing and traveling through the house. No matter where I was, I could hear her song." I blink, realizing I haven't really explained life in Norsewood. But something else entirely.

Adelaide folds her hands together. "Do you miss her?"

I find myself wanting to lie to her, to try to make Adelaide think of me as human. "I don't. I never really knew her. I only know Pa." And he has long since distorted the image I once had of my mother. "The people of Norsewood believe that my father killed my mother."

Adelaide turns to me, and her eyes widen slightly in surprise. "Did he?"

I hang my head. "I don't think he did. He loved her too much. But it was Garth who spread the rumor. He used Pa's grief to dethrone him from the guild."

Adelaide touches the building, rolling a finger along the chipped paint. Despite the home being vacant for years, I'm worried someone will scold us for snooping. "He seemed like he knew me."

I had hoped Adelaide would forget my father's strange proclamations, but just like me, she seems haunted by it. "I think he is confusing you with someone else."

"He thought I was the one who killed his love."

A shiver, unwelcomed, ripples along my spine. After all these years, I still don't know for certain the fate that befell my mother, but Pa relentlessly searches for his own kind of justice.

"Did you ever consider that you might—?"

Before I can finish my sentence, the ground beneath my feet shakes so viciously that I am thrown to the streets while Norsewood comes tumbling down around me.

Adelaide

I COLLAPSE TO my knees as the world rumbles like thunderclouds. The lights sway in the air and the houses shudder for but a moment, but within one quick breath and the next, it stills itself. Finn helps me back up to my feet, eyeing the buildings with a fear that they might come toppling down on him.

"What do you think that—?" Finn starts to ask.

The ground rumbles once more, this time, with frightening power. I scream as both Finn and I crumple onto the streets. I hear the symphony of shattering of glass windows, broken potted plants, and collective shrieks rising into the sky. Finn pulls me underneath him as debris rains down around us.

With a final shudder, the sensation trickles away. People start to flood back into the open. The music of crying children and frightened dogs bounces against the walls.

"What was that?" Finn asks, looking around wildly. "Are you okay?"

My heart is the only thing still affected by the quakes. "I think so. It was just—"

My scream is stolen from me as a pungent force tears through my limbs. My legs seize up and my fingers start to crack and bend at incorrect angles, propelled on their own to take new shapes. Finn stands over me, unsure of what to do. When he finally scoops me up, the skin along my arms parts to give way to thick, white fur.

Finn struggles as my body spasms, the motion throwing him off balance. No matter where he places his arms and hands, a blossom of fire erupts from the contact.

"Just hold on," he commands as we begin to move. "Let's get you out of here." His voice contains the kind of control I need right now.

He manages to carry me to the first hill beside Norsewood and lays me on top of the grass as gently as possible. "Are you in pain?"

I clench my eyes tightly shut because everything burns. "Yes," I lie to him, because this feels a lot like a shift, like my body wanting to change forms.

"Is there anything I can do?" he asks as he glances back to Norsewood, curious what the disturbance was.

When I roll onto my stomach, Finn aids me in sitting up, wrapping his arms around me. He does not move away in disgust as my skin expands and slithers beneath his touch. He even holds back my hair as I vomit onto the grass, graciously averting his eyes at the sight. As I wipe at my lips and he continues to pepper me with questions on my well-being, a dim light simultaneously catches our attention.

At first, it is a sliver of a smolder in the Forest, tiny enough to be a bug. As it grows, the radiance increasing with each second, the light seems to be getting closer. By now, Finn and I are not the only ones who notice how the trees in the Forest seem to be glimmering. As both humans and fianna gather outside the town, the light shifts and evolves until it takes on a familiar shape.

The light extends, twists, and expands until a stag the size of a house stands at the edge of the Forest.

His fur is a mixture of gold and white, a color that looks alive. Along his spine sprout mushrooms and other wild vegetation, as though he was unearthed from the ground itself. His antlers sprawl above his head, not really horns, but branches from a tree. Flowers and leaves hang from the tips, birds flying back and forth in delight.

In the end, the eyes are what captivate me.

From a distance, his gaze searches for me, finds me, and captures me. His eyes are more like smoldering flames, like a fire burned within his skull as he exuded power, growth, and majesty.

Like an arrow slicing through me, I hear, *come to me.* The words echo around my mind like a song. At the hum of his tune, my veins respond, twisting in me like vises, my organs swelling and desiring to be in a bigger space.

Finn's arms tighten around me.

Stationed around the stag are several other deer that glow like him, as if he is the moon and they are his stars. All of them stand stoically, watching us, but never moving. For a moment, I imagine they are simply trees. Odd plants that are a trick of the eye.

A lone woman walks from Norsewood and into the fields, swaying like a newborn. Her body, which twitches like mine, falls forward seamlessly onto four hooves. Unlike me, this woman leaps through her forms with no hesitation. She races across the green like a bullet as several other fianna answer the call of the Forest.

My kneecaps snap backward, my bones grinding against each other. Finn can't hide how much this disturbs him. "Do you want to go?" he asks me as quietly as he can.

My fists clench his shirt, and my pain robs me of my careful words. "Don't," I hiss. "Don't let me go." I want to tell him it's because of Anna and Caleb. I can't leave the two of them behind.

Yet, it is fear that keeps me clinging to Finn.

The stags begin to turn back to the Forest, taking their light that glows like the lilies with them. As deer, both fianna and beast, race to the tree line, I hear one last time, *Join us.*

"Not yet," I decide.

Finn looks at me with concern.

Finally, the gigantic stag is all that remains of the herd. Lifting one hoof and slamming it down into the earth with a mighty force, the stag causes the ground to crack open. More commotion starts as the earth near the stag erupts. Dirt sprays into the air as thick cords rise to the surface.

"Those are vines," Finn states, his tone unconvinced.

We watch as the vines twist and tangle amongst themselves. They move on their own, slithering like snakes until the growth layers together so densely it creates a wall. As far as I can see, the vines are crawling forth and combining, forming a barrier.

My back shudders in hot torture. With a grunt, my spine snaps. I lie limply in Finn's arms, unable to say a thing as he props my head against his chest.

I can't come right now, I try to tell the stag. *Please understand.*

With a turn of his head, the magnificent buck vanishes, and suddenly, the world is a thousand times dimmer.

The fianna that didn't make it beyond the vines are pawing at the structure and crying out, over and over.

"The Forest," Finn says, his voice a mixture of awe and fear. "And Norsewood...they're separated from each other."

As the deer and fianna bellow, I begin to hear the steady cheering from the humans.

Finn

ADELAIDE COLLAPSES SECONDS later. She goes limp in my arms and it reminds me too much of a corpse, like a body after a bullet rips apart the vital organs. Parts of her are no longer human, and I'm not sure why that doesn't bother me as much as her being unresponsive does. People are still consumed with fear as they look to the Forest with renewed suspicion. In the evening hues, we cannot see the wall, but we know it is there.

Hoisting Adelaide up, I try to cover the parts of her that are beastly. Two women glance at me as I enter the town, concern tightly worn on their faces as they inspect Adelaide's body split in two. Blood from her transformation clings to my skin.

I hold her closer and give them a daring sneer.

Norsewood is filling up to the brim with an excitement I can't fully understand. Some are baffled at the display before them, a few voices confess their suspicion that they saw a god, but all of them fuse together in joy.

When I round the street, I see Noah standing at the entrance to the inn, his bow loaded with a steel-tipped arrow.

That means—

A swift kick to the back of my knees causes me to tumble forward. Adelaide's body bounces against the stone streets. Hazel pounces on top of me, pulling my arms painfully behind my back until I swear they are going to tear free. Her lips brush my earlobe, possibly an erotic action if in any other situation with any other person.

"Some wild turn of events, hmm? Looks like even the god of the Forest is against you now. But I'm not here for a struggle. Not one bit," she tells me while a finger tickles my neck. "I was hoping now you would start to understand—"

I slip my arm free and slam my elbow into her cheek. She gives me distance, dropping into a battle-ready stance with a sinister smile. Like an exposed fang, Hazel unsheathes two thin boned daggers.

"I have been looking forward to a good fight, Finny. I'm just surprised you would hit a woman."

"You are far from a woman," I tell her.

I swing high, knowing that she will dodge my fist. As she ducks, she flicks her daggers, slicing shallow cuts into my thighs. I accept the wounds as I bring up my knee, catching the edge of her jaw. I grab a fistful of her hair and fling her against the side of a house. I grab her wrists and squeeze until the daggers loosen in her hold. I manage to catch one, which I press against her windpipe. Yet, Hazel surges to life, wrapping her legs around my ribs and squeezing. I wince from the pain, hesitating for just a moment to take the huntress's life.

When her head collides with mine, I see only black. I stumble back, knowing I am completely vulnerable, but I cannot see a thing—

A solid kick to my gut.

I slam into the opposite wall as another blow to my stomach steals my breath.

Hazel leans in close, her retrieved blade delicately easing into my throat.

"You are truly pathetic. If you weren't such an ass, you might be able to see that I'm trying to help you."

A prominent click causes Hazel to peek behind her.

Marshall stands with a rifle posed at the girl.

"You are a terrible little creature," Marshall tells Hazel. "I've put down critters with less of a bite than you."

Hazel laughs, the threat as feeble as a fly. "I have an anger problem."

"Could've fooled me."

"If you don't mind waiting, I'll get to you as soon as I'm done trying to talk some sense into Finn."

The gun fires off, the bullet catching a wooden crate beside me. I can see, from the look in Marshall's eyes, that he notices the proximity as well.

"And I'm impatient," Marshall retorts. "I would hate for this to get ugly. I have a few chickens that get awfully cranky if I don't give them a bedtime story."

Hazel gave him a hard blink. With the distraction, I attempt to both slip from her hold and deliver a swift blow to her side, but she is already out of reach. Gliding around gracefully, she moves too quickly for Marshall to follow with the tip of his rifle.

"In the end, you're only hurting yourself," Hazel tells me from the lip of the alleyway. "When it all goes to shit, pay me a visit, okay?"

In that moment I want to tell her that her name is on a growing list of those who will fall by my hand. That my vengeance will one day find her. But before I can say anything, she is gone.

I bend down and gather up Adelaide in my arms. Despite all the commotion, she has still not woken up. "I owe you again."

Marshall shrugs, slinging the gun across his back. "You're just lucky I came by this way." His eyes settle on Adelaide. "She doesn't look good."

I shift Adelaide's weight. "Don't worry," I say, unsure what extent of truth Marshall wants. Poking my head around the corner, I see that Noah has crawled away from the inn's entrance, no doubt following his sister into whatever hole they inhabit.

Marshall holds the door open for me, saying, "Until the next time your ass needs saving."

I give him a smile. "How about we don't make this a regular thing?"

"Don't worry, it won't. Besides, you don't seem like the type who asks for help a lot," Marshall comments as the door closes behind me.

The girl behind the counter is the owner's daughter, Lila, and when I ask where the fiannas named Caleb and Anna are staying, she gets flustered. To her, Adelaide's protectors are just another mess she has to clean up after. Instead, I ask for an empty room. Lila nervously grabs a key with a worn-out "5" on the tag and attempts to hand it to me.

I blink at her, arms full of Adelaide.

"Oh, I am so sorry," Lila says as she snaps into embarrassed action. She darts from behind her counter and rushes down the adjacent hall. Several rooms later, she unlocks a door and holds it open so I can lay Adelaide down on the single bed.

I nudge the door shut with my boot, cutting off Lila's gawking and ramblings.

My fingers touch Adelaide's wrist, finding her shallow pulse.

I go into the cramped bathroom and return with a wet cloth. I start to scrub away the blood and petals, but Adelaide's body spasms once more. Her right arm snaps at the elbow, blood squirting from dozens of cuts. I hold down her arm as it flails, but the rest of her body is reacting the same way.

I am helpless while I watch her lose one part of herself to gain another.

"You told me not to let you go," I say as I push her into the mattress by her shoulders. Her eyes race rapidly under her eyelids. "You should know by now that I'm not too good at keeping promises."

With a final jerk, Adelaide goes still, sagging into the mattress in exhaustion. Her body starts to reshape, but this time tenderly and subtly until a human girl rests on top of the covers.

Once her final finger cracks into place, Adelaide's eyes open.

"You're okay," I assure her, finding another blanket to cover her with.

"I'm going to ruin these sheets." Struggling to remain awake, Adelaide's eyelids seem to get heavier and heavier with each blink.

"Fortunately, these were trash long before you," I say, trying for humor but landing at blunt honesty. "I tried to find your guardians. Caleb and Anna."

Adelaide sighs. "That is probably for the best."

"I should let you get some rest," I say like a doctor prescribing his patient medicine. Yet, I clearly don't know what is best for her.

As I rise, Adelaide rolls onto her side in an attempt to hide her face from me. She doesn't pull the covers up quick enough to mask the single tear that escapes her eye. It vanishes down her cheek like a shooting star. "I didn't go to him," she tells me. "I didn't go to the Stag."

I wait in the silence, uncomfortably, knowing that eventually she will expect me to say something.

"Why didn't you?" I ask. Because, if it had been me, I would've run. I would've fled.

Even if it means abandoning others, my heart whispers with malice I've become accustomed to.

"I wanted to," she admits. "I would be safe right now. In the trees. With him." Adelaide closes her eyes. "But I don't think I was made for safety and ease."

I exhale and, without my permission, words go with the exiting breath. "That's stupid."

Adelaide and I stare at each other, shocked. Her, because of the words. Me, because I said those words.

"Why did you say that?" Her voice is oddly steady. She doesn't ask "what do you mean?" but instead, "why?"

"Because," I say, pausing because my throat is not big enough for both words and air. "You could have left this behind. You could be safe." Regardless if that was her god or not, it would be a step up from Norsewood.

"I couldn't leave Caleb and Anna behind," she says with an anger curdling beneath the surface. "I will not abandon my people."

I know what words are coming next. I see them, understand them, fear them.

But I do not stop them.

"Maybe you should." Adelaide blinks, quiet as a snowflake. "I don't see them risking their lives. I don't—"

"Because that is my responsibility," Adelaide cuts me off.

"Why? Why you?" I say. But I'm not sure I'm talking to Adelaide. Or anyone in this town. Or anyone in this world. My anger propels me to someplace new. "Why does it have to be you who suffers? Simply because your god deems it fit? You suffer so that others can smile and dance and laugh?"

Adelaide, back against the wall now, lingers on the divide of fury and sorrow.

"You should've left," I tell her, but I'm also telling myself this. "You should just worry about yourself and leave."

While she readies herself for a reply, I desperately want to tell her, *this isn't about you.*

This isn't about me.

"You don't believe I can do it either." It is strange because, in that moment, our voices sound the same. But, how can they? She hasn't experienced a fraction of what I have.

Or has she—?

"That's not what I'm saying—" I attempt.

"Just go." She lies back onto the mattress and pulls the covers up so all that shows is her hair.

I follow her orders, hesitating at the door before leaving. I look at the room and the weight of a thousand memories threatens to crush me. I imagine all the times I should've said something to Jay, that I should've spoken up. Confessed, pleaded, anything. But I was always silent.

"I'm sorry," I tell her as the door closes behind me.

BY THE TIME I make my way home, a steady drizzle has begun to soak the world. With the moon and stars completely blocked by storm clouds, my trek home is one mostly made from memory. The further I get from Norsewood, the easier I find I can breathe. The tethers, the things that bind me, are left behind in town. While Pa is a complication himself, he is practiced madness. I know all the ins and outs of him.

The house comes into view with the vines creeping dangerously close. Unlike the cords that brush against the fields, these seem hungry as they slither and creep closer to the light that illuminates the house.

The front door is opened and swaying in the stormy breeze. The screen slams around haphazardly. Water is puddled around the entrance, and it seems like every light imaginable is on. Stepping into the living room, I find it trashed. Sofa upended, pictures torn from the wall, and windows shattered. I step through the chaos, my boots crunching over glass as I collect the entire scene.

"Pa?" I call out.

He does not answer.

A warning sounds off inside me when I see Pa's favorite painting torn in two. One tattered half remains attached to the rusty nail in the wall while its counterpart lies on the floor, helpless.

"Pa?" I shout, nothing but ghosts howling back.

I turn, ready to begin my search upstairs, when I see the basement door.

Bashed and hanging off the hinges.

I jump down the steps two-by-two until my boots slap the concrete floor. A lantern is flared up in the corner, and I ignore the warnings that Pa may be hiding in his delusions. I get to Pa's desk, and I run my fingers through the ash that has settled on it. Several of his notes and research are burned and disfigured.

I pick up the lantern and I look for her.

When I come up to the table where she should lay, I find nothing but a cotton sheet.

My mother's body is gone.

Adelaide

NO MATTER HOW deep I burrow beneath the covers, I cannot escape Finn's anger. Regardless if he is physically present, his fury remains with me. I close my eyes as hard as I can, but I can't stop replaying his words over and over.

You should've left.

You should just worry about yourself and leave.

I throw the sheets off, sit up, grab the pillow, and begin to pound it against the bed in vivid frustration. I grit my teeth as I smash the pillow repeatedly, trying my fullest to erase Finn's words.

And the thoughts it awakens in me.

You should've gone, my heart tells me in fear. *Your herd is no more.*

Between my shaky breathing, there is a tap at the window.

Yet, from my vantage point, I find nothing but the ghastly streets of Norsewood outside. I remain still and wait, seated on the bed as I take large gulps of air.

Before I give up my watch, a rust-colored doe appears, pressing her damp nose against the pane, pleading for my attention.

I rise, expecting the animal to get spooked once it sees movement. But no matter how close I get, the doe continues to gently tap onto the window. Once I noisily slide the window up, the doe eagerly presses her head through the gap, her nose twitching as she takes in the musk of the room.

I laugh quietly as she licks at my finger. I reach to brush her jawline, but she dodges my touch, prancing back playfully. I try once more, but the doe dances away, hopping youthfully in the empty streets. Her hooves clack on the stones in a rhythm.

"You are playing a dangerous game," I tell her, unable to remove the smile from my face as I watch her thriving with life, bustling with it. I rest my elbows on the sill. "The humans don't look kindly on our kind."

Her golden eyes stay connected with mine, daringly. She must've been one of the many fianna that shifted into their natural form just to be isolated from the Forest a day ago.

The doe swings her head beckoningly. "What do you want?" I ask. She continues the motion, stomping her hooves in emphasis.

I close the window and leave the room. I tiptoe out into the lobby, but after a quick peek around the corner, I can see that the front desk is unmanned at this hour. I leave the inn and round the building to the main street.

But the doe is gone.

Had she thought that I was leaving her? Did the sound of me approaching startle her into fleeing? A sadness, a rather nameless one, settles on me. I imagined her joyous energy would be contagious with just a brush of her fur.

Click, click, click.

Looking over my shoulder, I am positive that the doe has crept from her hiding place, but it is not her I see gliding down the dimly lit street. Completely at ease within the confines of the human settlement, a magnificent stag moves toward me without a worry. He struts stoically, at peace in this terrain.

I take a step rearward.

As he gets closer, I identify him as one of the bucks who stood beside the colossal stag. His fur hums with a golden energy and delicate white flowers are spotted throughout his coat.

When he settles before me, my entire body trembles. Exhaling, the stag envelops me in a cloud. My head barely reaches the top of the stag's shoulder, and I wonder how hard he'd have to kick me to end my life.

He exposes his flank to me, and I see a single lily on his shoulder blade. The edges of the petals are rimmed with a violent red. Drops of said color drip onto the ground as if the flower is a wound on the stag.

I make eye contact with him, raising my hand slowly. I wait for approval, but he remains still as stone. I move my fingers around the base of the flower and pluck it from the stag with a pop.

Roots begin to twine around my arms, crawling up the expanse of my skin until they slither up my neck. I attempt to throw the flower, but the roots cling to my skin ravenously. The red expands until the entire lily is painted in a rose hue.

I can't even afford a scream as the roots squirm through my lips and into me, and before I—

"You must find me," I hear.

I open my eyes, and a man stands before me. When I blink, he is no longer human, but a stag with antlers that reach up into the sky with the ends becoming stars.

"I do not know where to find you," I tell him, but my words do not come out as a singular noise, but as a chorus of voices. "We are lost," I say, because there are multiples I speak for. I am but just one. I understand that here.

The man extends a hand to us, his skin radiating with the energy of the sun. We have no fright as he lays his palm to our cheek, like a father to his child. Images race before us once his skin touches ours. Blood, too much of it, rains from the sky and drowns squirming bodies. They are running through streets, through the open land, escaping escaping escaping.

"Death," we say. "You show me death."

"I show you the end. Make that what you will."

"What shall we do to prevent this?" we say as we watch several beings die by the hand of a human female.

The stag snorts, and the visions vanish. He stomps his hoof into the earth, and two figures spring forth. One is a tall fianna male with beautiful carved antlers and the other a petite human female. Their eyes are full of love, and the female holds a hand to her stomach, which is larger than usual.

"The Cycle is starting to erode. The events are no longer lining up." The man waves his hands and the two lovers vanish. "This is the future you have sown."

We stand above the world like birds, staring down at the Forest, the Resting Place, like guardians. In a second, the Forest is ablaze. Greedy black flames lick at the green without remorse. It continues until all the land we see is charred and ashen.

Eventually, only stark white bones litter the land.

"This is the future you desire?" the stag questions us.

"We do not wish this. We will serve Fate."

The man nods, and when we blink again, we see a female fianna and a human male. They stand before each other, this time without love in their eyes. They each hold a dagger. Lunging forward, they bury the blades into each other's heart. When they fall to the ground, their blood pools out and a lily the color of snow blossoms.

"Begin again," I hear.

In front of me are endless images of myself. They all stare at me. Some are bloody, others are malformed. They are all me. And they are all their own.

The man reaches down, and he points to a singular location. In my mind, I know where that is. I can see it.

"Begin again."

I open my eyes, and I am alone on the streets.

No lily. No stag. Only the steady dribble of rain against my head.

Find me, the words echo throughout me.

The Cycle is starting to erode.

Finn

I WONDER IF this is how Adelaide feels when she runs through the Forest in her natural form. My legs no longer burn as I cross the terrain, the wind roars past my skin in a violent battle, and my body stretches into limits unknown. My lungs expand further and further until I am ready to slip into the night sky.

Just run, I hear the wind coaxing me. *Run away, away, away.*

Still, I make my way to my destination.

I know the lodge is empty before I cross the threshold. A single hunter sleeps near the fire like a mutt, snoring with several empty mugs around him.

"Garth!" I shout. But only a roaring of snores answers me.

I find a dirty plate on one of the tables and throw it as hard as I can against the opposing wall. As the plate explodes, the snoozing hunter leaps to his feet, fists bundled up for a fight.

"Show yourself!" I scream, pitching two more plates at the wall. I pick up a chair and throw that as well, but it simply bounces across the ground without causing much harm.

"Calm yourself, boy."

I turn to see Garth standing at the other end of the lodge, arms crossed and a look of annoyance instead of smug cockiness. I pick up a mug like it is a weapon.

"Tell me where my—"

And casually, without a care in the damned world, Pa appears from behind Garth's shoulder. While he walks bashfully, he does not show any signs of discomfort.

Pa looks...at ease.

"Finn, you are making a fool of yourself," Pa says, and I am shocked by the normalcy of his tone. He is not shouting madness or raving on myths. He is collected and has clear dialogue. "You do not need to make such a fuss."

"But I was at home, and...I didn't know." Pressure builds behind my eyes as my mind tires out. "What is happening? The house is destroyed."

"A little dramatic, no?" Garth comments as he starts to walk, his boots echoing in the hollow space. "There was a nasty storm, Finn. Did you miss it?"

I do not answer.

Pa remains at the other end of the lodge, far from me. No matter how much I don't want that to mean something, it does.

He does not stand by me.

"Pa, let's go back home," I say through clenched teeth. "We have a lot to clean up."

Garth crosses his arms, watching as Pa doesn't budge. "He came to me, you know?"

Pa does not comment.

"He was telling me how unruly you've been recently. How you've harmed him, locked him away." Garth tsks and shakes his head disapprovingly.

"You went to Garth for help?"

Pa shrugs.

"We don't think you are trying hard enough. Your father and I believe you might be slacking at the tasks given to you," Garth informs me, casually, poking at my anger. "You should have found the god of the Forest already."

"You think, huh?" I ask.

Garth nods, unable to hold back his mocking grin. "Your father told me so."

Giving Pa an encouraging nudge on the shoulder, Garth baits him. Pa, unaware how the man plays him, takes an energetic step forward. "It is true, Finn. I've never told you this—"

Garth clears his throat. "Calm down, you goat. If you go too quick, no one will understand you." Garth looks at me and apologizes like a parent would for an unruly youth. "I am so sorry. When he gets all worked up his mouth just runs and runs." He lays a hand on Pa's shoulder. "Remember, we want to be as polished as we can for when she comes back."

Pa nods, taking the advice wholeheartedly. Beginning his tale again, he is almost a completely different person. "It is time you know the story of your mother's death."

I flinch, because the passing of my mother has normally a subject left for Pa's maddened ramblings and speculation. It was never discussed before others.

Garth most of all.

"I found the Stag's home, Finn. I was crying out for him and looking for the garden of myth—oh and your mother was deathly sick, she was—" Pa's sentences start to collide with one another.

Clapping his hands together, Garth chuckles effervescently. "Say it ain't so! What happened, Niall?"

Pa, unable to decipher the fake enthusiasm, continues to tell his tale with a fire in his eyes. "It was in this little field. I carried your sick mother through the Forest until, between steps, the whole world changed. The trees disappeared, and there were—flowers. It was beautiful," he concludes.

"That couldn't have been all, Niall, my boy. What else happened in that grove? Did the Stag himself greet you?"

Pa begins to deflate slowly. "I didn't see the Stag himself. I saw a girl there. The Maiden. She was not happy. She told me to leave. She would not heal Elinica. She even—" He swallows hard.

Garth refused to let it go. "And?"

"The Maiden killed her. But I got my revenge! I sliced her across the face with a blade, right across—!"

With a wave of his hand and a step forward, Garth dismisses Pa. "See, Finn? If your father can find the Stag's residency, shouldn't you be able? You're youthful, smart. Or do you even know how to navigate the Forest without your friend?"

I bare my teeth. "Go to hell."

Fixing his face with a look of contemplation, Garth pretends to consider my suggestion. "I was just worried you might not have had enough motivation to continue hunting. I went and found your father, asked him how you were doing. He didn't have many answers, but it turns out, he was a little lonely."

With patience depleted, I walk away from the two men. I leave Pa there with Garth because, in the end, he is not in harm. Garth is simply using him to further push me, to further tempt me into losing my control.

"Don't forget, Finn," Garth calls after me. "Time is wasting."

Once I'm out of the lodge, I find the two packs placed by the berry bush and I head into town.

Adelaide

WHEN I WAKE, I expect to be clenching a flower. But my hands are empty. No matter how many times I chanted "this wasn't a dream" before I fell asleep last night, the morning light makes me convinces me otherwise. Logic convinced me that a stag couldn't just walk into Norsewood. No matter if he was a simple deer or a fianna, the hunters are more vigilant than ever.

And the flower.

I touch my throat, but there is no pain.

Peeling back the sheets, I find not everything was conjured from my imagination. Blood, dirt, and fur lay thick throughout the white sheets. As I purge the bedding of the filth, I see a stack of clothing at the foot of the bed. I don't question its origin as I change and toss everything tarnished into a basket.

I tiptoe up to the second floor and enter my shared room to find Anna's figure tucked underneath the covers. Her hair is a spectacular mess, and her face a canvas of healing bruises.

Caleb is seated by the window, looking out of the glass at the gloomy streets. I pull up a stray chair and sit down beside him, finding myself equally as captivated to watch the rain fall from the sky. The glass before us fogs up with our dual breathing. I wonder what Caleb's favorite weather is as a human. I want to ask him, but it isn't important anymore.

"I don't think I have much time left," Caleb tells me, finger tracing figures in the moisture. It has been such a long time since I've heard Caleb utter a human word that I find myself savoring the sound of the husk that accompanies his voice.

"You don't know that," I tell him, but we both see the lie. We both recognize the truth.

But the lie is still comfortable.

"I'm sorry I couldn't be a better guide. I wish I could have shown you all that makes the human town special. Gotten you some flowers."

I grab his hand, trying but failing to envelop it with two of mine. "You still can. I'm looking forward to those adventures with you. You just have to hold on. Things are going to get better."

The twinkle in Caleb's eyes only exists for a moment. "That boy. The one who has been protecting you. Is he good?" he asks while drawing a poorly proportioned person onto the glass.

"What do you mean?"

"Is he different from the other humans?"

Last night slashes through any previous memory of Finn. It clouds me, fuels me, but I must push past it. "He is good," I admit. "He is unsure of himself. He is..." I look at Caleb's hand. "He is hurt. And I don't think he's healing."

Caleb nods. "Everything, human or not, hurts. We are all feeling some kind of despair."

The truth of his statement settles me. "It would be nice not to have pain."

"Without the pain, you wouldn't know the joy."

When I look at Caleb, his words become real. Anguish and despair from the trials placed before me claim dominance of my human heart with each passing day. But, when I look at Caleb, when I find him smiling at me with squinted eyes, a feeling unlike any other ripples through me, shattering all the hopelessness I felt.

With just a single smile, he has undone me.

"Would you promise me something?" he asks.

"Of course."

"I want you to kill me. If the time comes."

At first, I'm sure my ears have deceived me. I know the things Caleb has just spoken aren't real. "What are you saying? Caleb, I would never do that."

"You can say no." He can no longer look at me when he speaks. "It's just...I know it's changing me, Adelaide. I know that eventually I won't be the same. And I don't want to hurt her anymore."

When Caleb begins to cry, his tears summon forth my own. "I know it isn't fair to you. I know what I'm asking is too much. But I can't ask her to do this. I can't."

"I'm going to save you, Caleb. You and all the other ferals. I can do this. That is why I am human. That is why I was born."

This time, Caleb's hands find mine. He squeezes them with just enough pressure that the pain in my chest lessens. "You have become human for a much different reason. You are kind, intelligent, and courageous. You may be the Maiden, but you are also Adelaide, and I think both of those are equally important. I have often thought it cruel that you must take on both roles at once. Human and Maiden. Because I would like to believe that Adelaide, without all the burden, would be a joyful, carefree being." Caleb's index finger sweeps at the tears I didn't know were falling. "You can't do everything. You can't be everyone's savior."

"I will save you," I insist. I cast my arms around his shoulders, clenching him so closely that our heartbeats become one.

Caleb's voice, close to me, hums against my skin when he speaks. "No matter what happens, just remember that I am proud of you."

When he releases me, he tries to hide his tears. Yet, as he wipes the moisture away, a faint smear of red is left behind.

As he turns away, I see a single tear of blood pooling up in his eye.

WHEN FINN FINDS me, I'm seated outside the inn. As they pass, the humans praise the "glorious wall" and the protection it gives the citizens of Norsewood. The humans, in true fashion, completely disregard how the vine wall appeared or who created it but worship the structure for the protection it now offers them.

Yet, a more heinous thing is being whispered.

Finn settles down next to me, placing a pack down against my leg. "Have you been listening to them?" I ask instead of greeting him.

"I try not to," he replies, rubbing at red and agitated eyes.

"Are the crops dying?"

Finn shrugs. "I'm not exactly a farmer, so my answer might not be the one you're looking for. It's been raining enough...that's for sure."

I try to hide my sigh, to consume it somewhere within me, but I fail. "Not like that. I heard a woman saying all her crops withered in her garden. I didn't consider it noteworthy at first...but then another human complained. He said he noticed an entire field drying up." I turn to Finn. "Isn't that odd?"

"It's just gossip," he tells me, tugging at his boots. He pulls at the strings, tightening the laces. "I wouldn't worry about them. Let's get to the wall. We have plenty of troubles to keep ourselves busy with."

That we can agree on.

As Finn and I walk through Norsewood and eventually make our way to the wall, we don't talk about what happened nights ago, days ago, we just focus on the now. On what is before us. Originally, I wanted to yell at him, be cross, but I come to appreciate this silence that doesn't poke at things better left alone.

When the vines tower before us, Finn pulls a hatchet from his pack. He approaches the wall and begins to hack at the structure. The vines fall easily enough, but as soon as a chunk is removed, more slither and reposition themselves to replace what was lost. Finn swings again, and again, and eventually, his arms become a flurry of motion as he set out to tear a hole in the wall.

Finn, lost within the grunts and sweat pouring down his forehead, doesn't hear me offer him aid time and time again. I sit down on the grass, ignoring how damp the ground is after a good rain, and dig through the contents of our packs. I know Finn wants to be in the Forest for more than a few hours, but it looks like the boy packed for an entire week within the trees.

As I sift through the supplies, panic bombards me. The idea of leaving Caleb, even for just a day, causes my hands to shake.

"Why don't you let me give that a try?" I ask when Finn bends over to collect what seems to be a month's worth of air. I don't tell him I want to busy my hands, to lose my thoughts in something physical.

"It won't help," he determines. A response brews on my lips, but Finn continues after one look at my face. "It's not that you can't help. It doesn't matter how many times I swing this damn ax. The wall is...alive?"

I roll my eyes. "Of course, it's alive."

"That isn't what I mean." Finn stands up straight and bends backward, loosening up his muscles. "I'm saying it seems conscious. Sentient. Has a mind of its own."

I rise from the ground and hold out my hand to Finn. "My turn."

Finn doesn't give me the ax. "Adelaide. We need to think of something else. This isn't working."

"Then you figure another option out. I don't want to. Honestly, I would appreciate not thinking right now."

Finn blinks once, his eyes readjusting to see me properly. Without another word, he holds out the ax. When I take the handle, it nearly slips from my grip. I try not to let him see, but I thoroughly wipe the wood against my shirt front.

Flopping to the ground in a huff, Finn stares up at the sky, limbs spread out in exhaustion. "We could try to scale it. Get a ladder?"

"Mhm," I tell him, not really listening. I grip the ax with one hand. Then two.

I try one hand again.

"I wonder if we could burn it down."

"That is not a good idea."

As I step up to the vines, my skin ripples with a shiver. After Finn's comments, it's hard not to imagine this wall sizing me up, laughing at me for attempting to bring it down.

I bring the blade back, close my eyes, and swipe with all my might.

And completely miss.

When I turn, Finn's head is still angled at the clouds, not seeing me at all.

"It might be possible to have a pulley system?" he continues, unaware.

I face the vines. Square my shoulders. And raise the blade one more time.

And with my eyes open, and no matter how close the ax gets...

I miss?

The ax hangs by my side while I stare ahead, confusion numbing all the words Finn continues to mumble. Because my eyes won't believe what I just saw, I raise my hand.

And watch as the vines retreat from my fingers.

They untangle and disappear into the mass. My feet take a step forward, almost of their own volition. I am able to reach through up to my elbow now, and the closer I get, the more the vines untangle, as if they are terrified to touch my body, as if I am a flame they fear.

By now, when I look back, Finn is on his feet, awe etched into the finer details on his face.

When I laugh, he can't help but smile.

Finn gathers up our packs, and when he nears, I take his hand and I pull him along with me.

Eventually, the vines begin to seal back up behind us, trapping us as we move forward. The vines only allow us passage whenever I am within reach of them. Finn is quiet as we are cut off from light and thrown into vast darkness. I do not stop moving forward until spears of light start to poke through the dense vines and I can hear the Forest.

Soon, we are beyond the wall, our feet trudging up dead leaves.

"How did you do that?" he asks with wonder as he watches the wall piece itself back together.

I slide my hand from his. "I'm not sure, honestly. But...what if I could bring the fianna back into the Forest? I could get them back here."

"That would not be wise. Right now, it isn't the humans you need to protect yourself from. Isolating your people would be dangerous." Finn nods in the direction of the Forest. "If a stag of that size was a physical being, I'd expect to find signs of disturbance or even just footprints." Finn starts taking the first steps forward, looking up into the treetops and along the ground for evidence of travel. He studies the world with the eye of a hawk. I, on the other hand, keep watch for the ferals.

We hit a large pool of water where we rest. Finn passes me water and fruit while I soak my feet.

"Nothing," Finn comments as he sits down beside me.

"What?"

"A deer the size of a damned house and nothing to show for it? No tracks, nothing even out of place. Jay once taught me that even a careful bear leaves behind snapped twigs and signs of foraging. A being that large shouldn't be able to go unnoticed." Finn throws a stone into the calm water, a huff escaping his lips in anger.

"Did Jay teach you a lot?"

The question catches Finn off guard. "He was smart," he tells me. "He should have been a scholar. Invented things. Studied the sky."

"It is hard to miss someone each day?" I ask him, knowing that the memories must bring him pain. "Do you think you'll ever forget him?"

He runs a hand through his hair. "It's the worst kind of torture...with each day I hope it will get easier. I keep waiting for the night when I'm lying in bed and realize I hadn't thought of him all day." Finn bites his lip. "No matter how much I fill myself up with other things, drinking, hunting, whatever, there is always a part of Jay that won't loosen itself."

"Like the spike of a porcupine?"

Finn offers me a smile. "Just like that. I keep thinking the next day will be better than the last. One day, I might think about him and smile. But not until..." Finn trails off. "A lot of things need to change before then."

Those last words make Finn look dangerous.

I find a pretty, orange rock with smooth edges. "Did you ever consider asking the Stag to save him? I've heard the human legends. Of what they believe he is capable of."

Finn looks down at his hands, woebegone. "I don't know if he would want that," he admits. "What if Jay would come back to life and hate that I took him from wherever else he was? He might have someone else there. Wherever that may be."

"But you miss him."

"I do. But I also know that wherever he is now, it has to be better than here. Because, in Norsewood, you can't always be the person you want to be. I don't know who Jay would've been in this life if things were different. But I like to believe that wherever he is now, he's that person."

"But I'm sure you made him happy. I'm sure you made a lot of that struggle worth it," I tell him.

Finn meets my eyes. "I hope I did. If only just a little."

IN THE AFTERNOON, we find the fianna village. The bodies that were left behind after the massacre are...strange. At first, the color of the corpses baffles me until Finn clarifies by saying, "The hunters burned the bodies. A handful of people, loud ones, believe you can only kill the ferals by burning them. Making sure the sickness doesn't spread."

"But it isn't an illness," I state.

Finn nods, because he understands. Doesn't mean he can change an entire town's perspective.

"I think we should stay here for the night. But if that makes you uncomfortable, please tell me."

No matter what has transpired here, I can't shake the fact that this is where Jay died. This was the last place he was alive. But Finn stands there, concern angling him toward me.

"I'm okay," I tell him, wanting to fuel him, to try to further build his courage.

"Keep your eyes up. You don't need to see this."

I swallow, and I follow Finn into the closest abandoned house. Finn takes me to the second floor where he finds a small room overlooking the streets below. He takes my pack from me and pulls free a blanket. He hands it to me and moves to the furthest corner of the room, where he places his gun onto his lap. By now, the sun has started to fall behind the trees and the shadows have become larger and far more menacing, making it too dangerous to continue.

"I'm sorry," Finn comments. "I would make a fire, but I don't want the light to attract unwanted attention."

I pull the blanket around my shoulders. "Don't be. I'm warm enough."

A scream rends the night.

Finn is on his feet, looking out of the window before I can even blink. I come up beside him, peering through the gap to the streets. With the fleeting light, I barely make out any of the objects in the village. The bodies that litter the streets look impossibly alive to me. If I focus too hard, I see beings in the darkness that aren't even there.

Pointing, Finn tells me, "Right there." I see a feral limping below us. Behind him, he drags the body of a mountain cat. It hisses and fights back, screaming with the remaining life it still has. The feral does not seem to mind the struggle but keeps a firm grip on the beast's fur.

There is a crash beneath us. A symphony of wood breaking and a body fumbling through the dark. Finn leaps in front of me, hastily squishing me against the wall. I struggle to hear past the pounding of my own heartbeat. We wait, but the noise eventually fades. The house returns to the stillness it once held, and the sound of the mountain cat is no more.

"You should try to get some rest," Finn tells me, and at first, I want to chuckle. How could I calm my blood after that? But when the heaviness of the day comes bearing down, the blanket is right there to lull me under. And I am helpless.

Before I fade, I hear Finn say, "I'm sorry." With one final look, I see the boy looking out over the streets below.

Finn

I WAKE UP Adelaide after patrolling through the village twice. I kept an eye on the building, never too far from it as I scanned the area.

Eventually, I loop back to the spot where Jay died.

At first, it doesn't look different from any other street in Norsewood. The homes are squished against each other, the worn cobble streets are the same warm brown, and—

But I can't ignore the body of the feral that killed Jay.

Even though its body is malformed, the dark pieces of its skin a hideous aftermath, I can still see every detail of the beast's face. I can close my eyes and picture every line of his jaw. Those eyes.

I return to Adelaide as swiftly as possible.

When I poke her gently with the tip of my boot, she jerks awake with a muffled scream. I suppress a smile as she smooths down her hair but gives up and ties it back.

"What's the plan for today?" Adelaide asks me.

I pull out one of the maps from the guild and lay it down on the dusty floorboards. I spread out the paper until I can find our location near the edge of the sketch. "We are here. The fianna village. This is the furthest the guild is allegedly allowed to travel. While I'm sure Hazel and other hunters have gone beyond this, there's no record of it."

She nods.

"Do you think that stag we saw was the Stag himself?" I ask.

Adelaide shrugs. "I've considered it. What do you think?"

"No matter what he was, it was 'other.' Something about him caused you and numerous others to shift."

"If you're asking me to change, I can't guarantee what will happen. Not to mention that I can't decide when it happens. It just...does. When I'm a doe, I have no connection to my humanity. I could just as easily disappear into the Forest and never return."

"I'm just throwing out suggestions. It's possible that, when you're a doe, you naturally go to him." Adelaide processes the words before giving me a nod. "Either way, we have a long day ahead of us. Are you ready?"

When I reach out with my hand to help her up, Adelaide doesn't hesitate to take it, a faint grin on her lips. "Of course."

"YOU DON'T HAVE one?" Adelaide asks, jumping from rock to rock like a child, prancing across the creek with obvious glee.

"I really wish you'd be more careful," I say. Each time her foot lands on a stone, I cringe, expecting the worst. "Those rocks are slick. If you fall in, you'll freeze to death."

Adelaide giggles but continues on her merry way down the creek. I have to increase my speed just to keep up. Her grace, even as a human, is outstanding. She makes her body look like art, while most days I feel like I just wear my skin out of convenience.

"You still didn't answer," she says on the opposite bank of the creek.

I place my hands on my hips and sigh. "No, I do not have a favorite color."

"I think mine is purple. I really like the way it looks. Mostly on flowers. What about food? Do you have a favorite of that?"

I rub at my forehead. "These questions don't seem very important, if I'm being honest."

"They aren't. But that is what makes them fun. You are so serious all of the time." Adelaide makes a mockingly stern face. "Let me guess, your favorite food is beef."

I can't stop the laughter from escaping my lips. "It is not. It would probably be corn on the cob. It is mostly a summer food. But really, you should be careful. You fall into that water—!" I gasp as Adelaide pitches forward but regains her footing quickly. "I really do not like this."

"You're the one who wanted to follow the creek," Adelaide points out.

"Yeah, only because it is easier to map out and easier to follow back when it starts to get darker. I didn't say you should be prancing around like a fawn."

Occasionally, I'll dash a significant landmark onto my makeshift map as we travel, detailing our path. We have been walking for hours now, and I am nervous that the sun will set and we will be in unknown territories. Yet...a dangerous, and stupid, thrill pushes me on. This map, the one I hold in my two hands, is mine. This is my adventure. I am going into uncharted land and discovering it.

This is what Jay and I could have had. This sense of adventure, of potentially finding a place that belonged to only us. I wonder what kind of people we would have been there, if we would be Jay and Finn still, or new beings together.

"Why don't we go up over the ridge?" I ask her. The roar of the water makes it difficult to hear, but it also makes it difficult to be heard, which is ideal. The river has long ago cut through the mountainside, leaving large cliffs to either side of us like walls in the biggest house.

Adelaide jumps to where I stand, and I imagine reaching out and capturing her like one would a skittish bird. She bounds past me, grabs ahold of exposed roots and starts to ascend the sides of the mountain with surprising speed. She moves recklessly from sapling to sapling, kicking down dirt and stones. Once she reaches the top, she holds out her hand for me. She lifts me up with all the strength she possesses, trying to impress me, I'm sure.

My feet touch the Forest floor, and she takes a step back to give me space, but my boot catches on a root and I careen forward. Adelaide, unable to move from my path, follows.

She lands on her back, me on top of her. Her blonde hair blankets the dirt while her pupils swim around in ponds of gold. Her lips, parted in surprised, are still.

It isn't until I say, "This is awkward," that we begin to laugh.

"Normally, I'm the clumsy one." Once I help Adelaide up, she begins to remove twigs and leaves from her mane. "Nice to have it switched occasionally."

I scratch at my head. "I know that—"

I stop.

I lean around Adelaide, my eyes seeking what they saw a second ago.

Adelaide, having turned now, asks, "Are those—?"

"Buildings," I confirm. "Two of them."

Two buildings constructed from river stones, standing together like lovers. The wooden roofs long ago collapsed into the second floors, moss clings to the sides like a coat of paint, and the foliage bursts from the ground and chokes the exterior.

"One of those is a barn," I tell Adelaide, confusion thick in my voice.

She follows me as I approach the stone house. The front door is torn to shreds by creatures seeking shelter. When I step into it, I see a dusty and tattered kitchen and animal droppings. I open cabinets and drawers, but anything left behind has long rotted or eroded into nothingness. Adelaide tiptoes around the furniture and into other regions of the house, finding nothing but spiders and weeds.

"Someone lived here once," Adelaide tells me. "This isn't a part of the fianna village, is it?"

I scratch my head. "I don't think so." I study the structure. "The fianna weren't pleased with the guild when they initially gave them the fianna village. They don't want structures in their domain," I tell her, discrediting the fianna.

Next, I walk over to the barn. Inside are rusted tools that are lost to me, overgrown stalls, and several full body skeletons of different livestock. Adelaide does not make a noise when she sees them but bends over to pick up several bones. A thick tree trunk splits from the floor and bursts from the roof, the bark cracked and aged.

"These were farmers, weren't they?" Adelaide asks.

I nod. "These can't be the only homes. Come on."

We keep the stream to our right as we continue through the Forest. My head aches as it tries to process what those buildings mean. What could a farm in the Forest possibly benefit? There was no mention of anything outside of the village that had been constructed in the Forest. It was often dreamed of, thought of, possibly planned, to dig into the Forest and its resources, but never acted upon. There was no documentation on other buildings this far out. The hunters, out of any other collective groups in Norsewood, would have the information about that.

Was it possible that it was even hidden from them? I cannot be the first fool with a desire for adventure and mischief.

Adelaide is silent beside me when all I really want her to do is talk about all that is happening within my head. She lags, her earlier pep diluted.

Then, amongst the trees and bushes, an abandoned town appears.

At first, I can only see a few buildings built closely to one another, but as we near, I spot the overgrown streets and a low fence made of stacked rocks. Some of the buildings lean too far to the right, others look ready to collapse with a simple push. Here, there are bones upon bones. Not all of them animal.

The first human skull I find has a crack across the forehead.

I look over my shoulder to find Adelaide is walking further down the street, trailing her hand against the walls absentmindedly. She studies the structures vaguely, not as interested as me in the mystery they pose.

"What do you see?" I ask her, walking a distance behind her.

"This was once a human town," she tells me. "The buildings, the bones, all of it is human. But what happened? You know nothing of this place? Looks too large to become forgotten."

I shake my head.

Adelaide disappears within the maze of the town, and I let myself lose her. I take time to pinpoint several locations in the town. Blacksmith, possible bakery, a medical center. All that is left behind in the dust and neglect is outdated.

Most of the equipment and rooms look like they were ripped out of some ancient storybook. The furniture looks primitive as well. I find myself in a tiny graveyard beside the village, where each tombstone is hidden under overgrown grass. The names on the stones are illegible after years of being victim to the elements.

I get to the center of the buildings and find a statue standing erect still. It looks to be the focal point of the town. I jump onto the dais where it rests and start to pull at the vines that choke and hide the features of the statue. I grab my knife to help cut my way through the dense weeds until I can see the face—

Adelaide?

I jump off the platform and pull the remaining vines down with me. Once the statue is exposed, I can clearly see that it does, in fact, resemble Adelaide. Her eyes, her nose, her mouth, all curved, angled, and set just like Adelaide. Her hair is different, but the build, the posture, all of it replicates the fianna Maiden. At the base, by her bare feet, is an engraved passage with a line slashed through it. *"Maiden of the White Lily. Savior of Moss Oak."*

I notice phrases etched along the granite. I wonder if they are further praises, but as I lean in, I see that they are anything but.

Fraud.

Enchantress.

Someone has chipped at her eyes until nothing but hollow spaces remain. Across her brow are the words, *"Begin again."*

"That's not comforting."

The sound of her voice causes me to jump in place, but I try to hide my fright as she comes to stand beside me. "It's possible the Maidens of the past were also not looked upon very highly."

If Adelaide is at all disturbed by the statue, she does not make it known. She merely traces the words with her index finger. With her standing beside the figure, a chill ripples through me.

"This had to have once been a human town. One that was eventually overrun by the Forest," I say. Each year, Norsewood lost more farmland to the vegetation that sprawled closer and closer to their homes.

"How long has Norsewood been around?" she questions as she runs her fingers through the weather worn grooves.

I shrug.

Adelaide swings behind the statue, her head poking around to study me. "What do you think those words mean? Begin again?"

I scratch the back of my neck. "I could have been an old children's song. A lullaby or..."

"Or the words could refer to the Maiden herself? It might've been a phrase passed down. One that belongs to the line of Maidens."

"She looks like you," I tell her. At first, Adelaide just takes in the figure, not entirely convinced.

"She is another Maiden of the white lily. She must have completed her pilgrimage. Found the Stag." When she says the words, she seems downcast by them.

"One day, you'll have a statue," I tell her. I stand in front of her, and I imagine her likeness frozen forever. Would those who carve her capture the gentleness in the eyes, or the light that exudes from each smile? She has such soft features that I doubt stone could convey them. "Just imagine."

Adelaide glances up and down the streets. "Maybe once this is all over...the fianna could live here. Further from the humans."

I nod as a sting of odd sadness pricks me.

"This could have been a home for you and Jay," she says. "I could see you two happy here."

I swallow the lump in my throat and force myself to say, "Yeah? How so?"

She points to the tiniest building in the town. "You'd live there. Because I don't think you need a lot of space. I imagine you'd grow a garden right there." Her finger leads me to a patch without trees or other rough shrubs. "I'm sorry, though. I don't know enough about Jay. Would you help me? Where would he go in here?" Adelaide looks to me, a pleasant smirk on her lips, and the pain in my chest lessens, with just a stare from this girl.

"I think he'd want to build a fence and keep a few sheep. Or pigs." I collect each little detail in the town, letting it unfold in my mind. "He'd definitely clean the streets, fix up the buildings. He wouldn't want it to look like a ghost town."

"Of course not," Adelaide confirms.

In an uninvited wave, memories of Jay bombard me in a fury of blows, but instead of trying to fight back, I let them smash into me. I allow them a place in me. "He used to love painting when he was younger. He was terrible, but that didn't matter to him none. I could see him painting the houses, each a different color or design.

"And you could be whoever you wanted here," I say, the words just rolling off my tongue. "A million possibilities for anyone. All you'd have to do was just reach out and grab them."

"I'd want to live there. With Caleb and Anna. In that place." Adelaide drops her bag and ruffles through it before she pulls out a corded rope and hands it to me. "I want to see that place exist, Finn. No matter what I have to sacrifice."

In this future, Adelaide imagines a sanctuary for her people, a world devoid of ferals, and a Jay who is alive and smiling.

But why does it sound like a future without her in it?

"I'm going to shift," she tells me.

Adelaide

FINN SEEMS LOST for words as he attempts to keep up with me. By now, I have tied a knot around the statue's leg and I instruct Finn to look over it, confirming that it is secure, but he doesn't seem capable of moving. I strip until I stand in only my underwear.

"I hope you know I was just speculating before," he tells me, still holding onto his end of the rope with a lost expression. "If you shift, any ferals in the area might flood us."

"I thought you were an accomplished hunter?" I tease. Finn is far from accepting my attempt to deflate the situation.

"You don't even know how to change forms," he repeats, but now he has laid down his own pack and begins tugging at the rope. "You don't need to do this."

I pull back my hair and tie it so that it doesn't hang in my face. "It makes sense. It is possible that, like the ferals, I could draw the Stag forth. I would focus on him...like a...?"

"Compass," Finn finishes, but adds, "and it might be suicide. You will be vulnerable, and you will be risking your life. And it isn't smart. You could die."

"You've told me. Three times now." I grab the rope from him. "Tie this around my neck. When I shift, I won't be able to escape."

"And I am to protect you in this process? That means harming and or killing ferals. You do understand that, right? That I won't hesitate to kill if it means protecting you?" His eyes bore into mine, his face grim but determined.

"I do understand. Now, tie this around my neck."

Finn moves behind me, leaving the rope slack against my collarbone. After he has tied it as proficiently as he can, he starts to unearth all his weapons. "I'm going to be positioned in that building," he tells me, pointing to the largest structure in the town. It is one of the only places with a roof intact. "I'm going to sit at the peak. From there, I will have view of you and the surrounding streets. We are running out of light, though." He clenches his eyes shut. "You don't—"

I sigh in annoyance as I tear his knife from his side. "I'm deciding this. Now, go."

Once he is gone, the sounds of the Forest are all that keep me company. Irrational fright shortens my breath as I examine the fattening shadows. Unlike in Norsewood, nothing is hung up high to illuminate the darkness that brews monsters.

I stare at the knife in the dwindling light.

I hear a whistle and I look up to see Finn stationed on the roof, roosting like a crow.

I collect a steady breath and hoist the knife before me, then bring the tip down into my opposite arm. The pain is immediate, and my heart screams at the absurdity of wounding myself. I hiss as blood, hot and angry, flows from me onto the streets below. I lower myself to the ground, my head already light. I wait, patiently, but the suffering is human and customary. My limbs remain intact and my skin is loose and whole.

Pain, pain has to be the key, I tell myself. Each time I shifted, or almost did, my body was filled to the brim in such agony. Yet, looking down to my unresponsive hand, I fear the damage I may have done to my body.

I reach for the knife once more, and a dangerous thought crosses my mind. It flashes so quick that I do not have enough time to consider it before my bravery, my foolishness, lasts.

If the Stag watches, if he does truly wish me no harm, he will stop this. He won't let this happen.

He's watching, I try to encourage myself.

I aim the blade over my heart, and I plunge it down, down, down—

Before the knife can pierce my heart, my body rips into pieces.

Finn

I WATCH AS Adelaide's body unravels like a sweater made of wool.

There is nothing beautiful about the transformation. I have seen the act before, but from this vantage point, I can observe the entirety of it. Adelaide's body snaps and restructures itself in a horrendous dance while an inhuman amount of blood pours from her. I see fur that is impossibly white poking from her the areas where her skin is torn in two.

When she stands back up, it is not on two legs, but four. Her fur is unstained by the red. She stares down at the mess that pools at her hooves, slushing in the liquid playfully. She takes a tentative step forward and the rope constricts around her throat. Adelaide jerks her head to the side, fighting the restraint viciously and with a vigor that is hard to watch. She does not stop until her sides are heaving and her neck is rubbed raw.

I look through the scope of my rifle, worried she will end up strangling herself.

By the time Adelaide accepts the collar and begins to munch on the vegetation around her, the Forest is alive with a steady hum.

She eats.

I wait.

I am ready for the ferals, for the onslaught that we have clearly welcomed upon ourselves, yet the Forest is anything but chaos. The bugs are harmonious as the stars snap with light back and forth amongst each other.

Then, the slight vanishes from the sky as the bugs fall silent. Adelaide has her head in the air, body turned attentively toward the trees with a stillness that mimics death.

When I turn, I know that what I see is impossible.

A mighty stag marches through the Forest, each step he takes causing life to blossom at his hooves. As he moves through the trees, shards of life fall from his coat. When each clump touched the ground, it exploded and expanded until a creature emerged from the light. Some were rabbits. Others were foxes. All different but beautiful and vibrant.

Behind him, he leaves a trail of the purest lilies I have ever seen.

As he nears the town, he dwindles in size until he is the height of an average fianna, yet his body is no less magnificent. Birds fly above him in a circle, their cries so joyous it brings tears to my eyes. They dip and dive, evaporating into dust when they collide against his fur. His antlers continue to stretch and grow until they are writhing around the buildings, tangling them so firmly that the structures begin to crack audibly.

Gathered around the perimeter of the town are various animals. Bears rest beside foxes while mice sit on the heads of badgers. All of them gathering to witness a miracle. To worship a god.

The god of the Forest.

I can't stop shaking.

When the Stag approaches Adelaide, she gracefully tucks one leg beneath her and bows.

A pulse of wind ripples from him, and my tunic and hair flail from the warm sensation. The spectating wildlife bows as well, all in unison.

The Stag and Adelaide merely stare at one another. Nothing stirs, nothing changes. I do not know how long they are locked in each other's gaze, but it feels like a lifetime. My own eyes are fixed onto the Stag, my mind battling with what I see before me. The Stag is supposed to be a legend, a myth, but how could I deny the deity any longer?

Does that mean not everything is a myth?

I try to stop myself before I think it because I know it will have a poisonous hold on me, but before I can clamp down my thoughts, I hear—

Does that mean I can save Jay?

Then, against my will, that is all I can think about. I remember all of Pa's feverish studies and all the stories he spun about the blood of the Stag. The power of the god. I could see Jay laughing, I could see him dying, I could see him over and over and over—

I see the life literally falling from this god—

I see Jay smiling—

I see just a drop of blood—

I see an end.

The Stag leans forward and presses his snout onto Adelaide's forehead. Like a pebble disrupting the surface of a pond, the rope shakes from the doe. Raising to his full height, the Stag lets out a bellow, a soft and gentle noise that causes Adelaide to bounce in place, a dull glow beginning to flicker through her fur.

The Stag turns back to the Forest.

And Adelaide follows him.

No. My heart screams as the Stag begins to swell in size, growing with each step. The animals cry out together, and while I know they cheer to their god, it unnerves me.

"You can't leave me," I say, hoping against logic that Adelaide will hear me. That maybe he will hear me.

My finger shakes on the trigger.

The blood. It can cure anything.

Adelaide wants a cure for her people. She wants to protect those who follow her.

If she had the blood, she could do just that.

She wouldn't have to follow the Stag into the Forest anymore. She would be the savior of her people. If she left it would be ruined. She would leave her people behind.

She just needs a drop—

She needs this.

When I pull the trigger, I close my eyes for just a second.

The bullet hits the Stag neatly in the chest. He stops, and the world around him does the same. The animals come to a halt, the plants still, and my heart races. Then, the Stag's front legs buckle. When he opens his lips, I do not know what I expect, but—

A scream loud enough to paralyze me rings through the air. The trees shudder and the birds cry in the sky as winds far more vicious then a tornado sweeps around the town. Pain explodes across my stomach as the wind punches into me. My boots leave the solid foundation and I fall through the air, down, down, down—

Until I crash onto the street.

I collide with the stone, but the impact's pain is nothing compared to the agony deep in my organs.

Once the pain has retreated into a bearable throb, I climb to my feet and pull up my shirt to look for a wound amongst all the smooth skin.

As I race to the center of the town, the Forest comes back to life in a roar. Birds shriek and the bugs shout in anger. The wind that rocks the treetops is frightening as I look for Adelaide. When I find her, she is lying against the street, human. I drop at her side, locate the *thump thump* on her wrist, and drape a blanket over her.

From the corner of my eye, I see a hoof.

I don't want to look at first. I don't want to let my eyes travel anywhere else but Adelaide. I don't want the truth of my actions to come to life.

But I've already fucked this up.

The body of the Stag lies several feet away.

Walking closer, I expect the body to leap up, for the now-average antlers to pierce me. I look at the fur of the Stag, at how it no longer glows but is a plain, boring brown.

This can't be a god.

I listen to my thoughts, as they turn and bite at one another.

Gods do not die.

I stare at the hole in the creature's chest. At the wound I created. I investigate the Forest, but the animals are gone, the path of lilies is gone.

But the wind still howls.

I drop to my knees and empty out my canteen. I try to convince myself this is no god, over and over until it is the vilest song I've ever heard.

Yet, no matter how many times I tell myself a god does not bleed, I continue to collect drop after drop of blood.

Adelaide

MY DREAMS ARE violent.

In them, I am being torn limb from limb, but each time I lose an arm or a leg, another grows back into its place seamlessly. Humans reach and tug at me while fangs sink into my skin as if it was fresh fruit. No matter how much I scream, they do not release me. They kill me over and over. I die a thousand deaths in the span of a blink.

Within the dreams, I see a familiar face, cast in darkness—

Finn.

Holding a gun.

Pointing it at me.

I OPEN MY eyes my eyes to find Finn carrying me through the darkness. I am draped across his arms with a blanket covering my skin. Through the shades of night, I can see the strain on Finn's face as he treks through the Forest.

"Just a little further," he tells me. He doesn't look down, but he still knows I'm conscious. "We are almost at the fianna village."

"How?"

Finn grunts while he steps over a fallen tree. "I took a lot of breaks," he tells me in explanation.

Fatigued, I permit him to carry me all the way to the village. Only when we arrive at the same building we stayed in before do I convince him I can take the steps myself. I tighten the blanket around me, knowing I am naked, but not having enough energy to truly care as I wobble up the stairs. I enter the closest room and collapse into a corner.

Finn, dragging, does the same on the opposite wall.

It matters little that my eyes adjust to the darkness, for I can barely keep them open. "What happened?" I ask him, the words sounding fluffy. Not sharp enough to be distinct.

For a moment, I consider that Finn has fallen asleep. He has been quiet for so long, but eventually his words jolt me awake. "I think he came. To that town."

"The Stag?"

I think Finn nods. That or his head bobs in slumber. "Yeah."

I press my fingers into my eyes, wishing I could remember anything. "You aren't sure if it was him?"

"I wasn't. He was...special. That much I know. Animals followed him. New life...dripped from his fur. Yet..."

Finn doesn't finish his sentence.

"Did he leave?" Panic shocks my heart back to life. Blood flows so forcefully that sleep is cast away from me like rain clouds against a hearty wind.

Finn is silent.

I clap my hands together, only realizing after the fact that it probably wasn't the wisest of things to do this deep in the Forest. At night.

"Damnit, I'm awake. You didn't have to scare me like that," Finn gasps from his corner. He sits up straight and drags his pack onto his lap. "He...he walked up to you. Put his nose on your head and you..." Finn fumbles with the straps. "You shifted and collapsed on the street."

I tilt my head in confusion. "Why would he do that? Touch me?"

"I'm not sure." Clenched in both of his hands, Finn holds his water jug. "He did leave you something. I mean, he left *us* something."

He holds out his canister.

I take it softly.

"What is this?"

Finn does not answer.

I give the jug a shake and the contents whirlpool near the bottom. I open the cap, and the smell of iron fills my nose. "Is this...?"

"Blood," he confirms.

Every inch of me crackles with electricity. "How? Whose?"

"When I found you, there was a lily beside you. Filled with blood."

"What if it was mine?"

He shakes his head. "It wasn't."

I stare down at the container in my hands and watch as it shakes and shivers with me. I place the cap back on and tighten it in fear.

"I already split it into two canteens," he tells me. "That one is yours. I have my own."

"But just this little bit? There can't be enough in here to save everyone. To cure the ferals," I ramble. I don't even voice my doubt that this might not even work.

What did I do with the blood? Have them drink it?

Would there even be enough for Caleb?

"I don't understand."

Finn shifts in the shadows. "I don't either."

If it was the Stag, he wouldn't have left his blood behind if the legend wasn't true. It might be a temporary fix, but the promise of saving Caleb is infectious.

Everything will work itself out. I can save Caleb and then I can figure out the rest.

I turn that joy on Finn. "Do you understand what this means?"

Finn does not respond.

"You could save him."

Finn lies down on his side and uses his pack as a pillow. "I'm not sure he'd like who I am anymore." He pauses. "In the morning, we will make way for Norsewood."

The statement and Finn's lack of excitement confuses me.

He's just nervous. He doesn't want to accept that there might be hope until it's right in front of him.

I don't let it faze me.

Because this is almost over.

Things are going right.

No matter how tired I am, sleep cannot override my excitement tonight.

WHEN WE ARRIVE at the vines, they separate as I approach, just as neatly as they had before. I turn to take hold of Finn's hand and see the fatigue clinging to him. After a late start to the day, Finn continues to lag.

His hand in mine is like holding a fish fresh from the stream.

On the other side, with the trees behind us, and the sun bleeding into the clouds in a collection of warm hues, a lump forms in my throat as I pull my hand from Finn's.

What happens after this?

I stare over the green hills, finding the tips of Norsewood in the distance.

When I turn to look at him, his eyes are downcast. His hands are balled up and his jaw is tight. "I guess we go our separate ways from here, huh?"

He rubs his nose. "Yeah."

Why does this feel like a goodbye?

"If this works, and you bring Jay back, where will you go?" I ask, but what I really want to say is, *where will I be able to find you?*

"I don't know," he confesses to me.

I try to look past what this moment signifies. I attempt to focus on the happiness that will follow in these next few hours. What will happen when I present Caleb to the council as he is now, twisted and dangerous, and splash him with the blood? Will he transform before their eyes and become every bit of truth and evidence they need?

I take a step forward because, eventually, one of us will have to. If no one moves, nothing will change. I turn, getting one last good look at Finn. "Thank you," I tell him, and my heart threatens to make the words choppy in delivery. "I owe you."

"Would you do anything to save those you love?" Finn asks abruptly.

I hold the canteen with the Stag's blood, giving it a shake. "I would."

"But what if someone else did anything. What if, when we are trying to do the right thing for us, we do the wrong thing for someone else?"

"I'm not sure—"

Finn cuts me off with a wave of his hand. "It's nothing. I'm sorry. I'm just rambling."

I know that isn't the case, but I allow him the falsehood.

"Good luck, Maiden," Finn Hail says as he passes me and walks down the hill until he leaves me with the setting sun.

Finn

FIND JAY.

That is all that matters now.

Gods be damned, save Jay.

Once I am prepared, I lie in the high grass for hours, waiting and watching as the guild members, one by one, trickle from the building. Some might go to patrol the town, but others, with their new tolerance, would find themselves at the pub. When two-thirds of the hunters exit the lodge, I take my chances with the remaining members and, with the setting sun, creep into the building.

As soon as I enter, I see not a single body fills the common area. Voices echo in the kitchen, but none of them bother me as I dash to the back of the cabin. Briskly moving down the hall, I keep my hand against the wall, counting in the darkness "one, two, three" as my fingers tab against the doorknobs.

And at the fourth door, I lean my ear against the wood, listening as patiently as my terrorizing heart will allow me to. I smack my knuckles twice, but after no response, I enter the room.

Into Garth's study.

As I swing the door open, I am ready for Hazel, Noah, Garth, or even a feral to be awaiting me, teeth and guns eager to bring this all to a halt.

Yet, this is nothing. Just a desk. A fireplace. Books. Papers.

No Garth.

I go to the only bookshelf in the office and I push at the structure, using my shoulder to get a better angle. Hesitantly, it starts to slide on the hardwood flooring. Novels and bundles of research documents crash nosily to the floor.

A single door steadily emerges from where the shelf once stood.

Once upon a time, I had found this door ajar. I had, without permission, barged into the lead hunter's room to find Garth pulling the bookshelf back into place. Yet, despite what I told the hunter firmly and calmly, I had seen the hinges of the door right as the books settled.

I open the door just a crack and slither into the darkness. I nearly fall down a set of steps but manage to gain my grip on the railing before it's too late. A soft glow peeks out from around a corner, giving me minimal, yet ample, sight of the stairway.

The steps lead to a room twice as small as Garth's office with stone walls, crammed shelves, and another desk. Pushed up against the furthest wall are two tables wrapped in white linen.

The sheets cover lumpy mounds.

I take my canteen in a hand that shakes like hummingbird's wings while the other moves for my pocket.

"You little rat."

I turn on my heel, having already prepared for an attack, but Garth's boot is still unexpected. My fingers are crushed beneath the sole, the canteen cracking against the floor while I collided with the stone wall.

Lurching forward, I dive for the canister in a panic, but Garth kicks the jug further from me. I cry out as he clenches his fingers around my throat and he pulls me to my feet with that one point of contact. I lash out with my boots, but Garth slams me into the wall, knocking me dizzy for a devastating moment.

While I am dazed, Garth retrieves the canteen with his free hand.

"Well, I'll be damned. You risked breaking into my office because of this, eh?" Garth asks as he holds the jug before my nose. "Am I supposed to believe you truly found a god in that damned Forest?"

I struggle against his hold, using my fingers to pathetically reach for the jug while making room to say, "Please."

Garth is silent for a moment, then bursts out laughing. "You really expect me to believe you found some magical beast in those trees?" He pulls the canister back and his fingers work at the lid. "You are a sensible boy. You should know that—" Garth's words are cut short once the top pops off and he gives the contents a whiff.

Even from here, I can smell the rot of flesh so strongly that I gag.

In shock, Garth recoils from the odor.

Slackening his hold.

I unsheathe my knife and bury it into Garth's forearm. With a shriek, he no longer holds my windpipe closed. I duck in time to dodge the swing from Garth's other arm, bringing up both of my hands, wrapped around my dagger's hilt, at the same time.

Into Garth's sternum.

Blade first.

Garth takes the first step backward, calmly and quizzical. Once he inspects the dagger sticking from his gut, his next step gives beneath him, bringing him to his knees.

"How—" Garth takes a ragged breath as the pain steals his concentration. "What—?"

As quickly as I can, I pull my knife from Garth's belly. Standing up, I notice the man who tortured me for years looks much smaller huddled up.

He looks like Jay did.

Holding in his guts like a—

I pull a glass vial from my pocket. I hold up the contents so that the lanterns stationed on the walls illuminate it. "I hid the blood. After I left—" I shake my head. "Once I had it, I transferred it to this little bottle."

"But you—"

"Pretended it was in the canister. Acted panicked. It was a risk. But it worked."

When he laughs, blood slathers his lips. "You think you're clever."

I say nothing.

"I thought you were better than your father. Less maddened," he spits. "Do you really think you have the blood of a god?"

I find that no matter what words I could offer up to Garth, it wouldn't matter much. I could not explain what happened in that town, in those trees.

"What do you think will happen if you do bring him back?" Garth seethes. "You think that boy could ever go walking through Norsewood? They'll burn him—"

My fist collides with Garth's cheek. The man falls backward, his massive frame sprawling out like a bearskin rug. I watch his chest, but it rises and falls unsteadily. I give his boot a kick but gain no response.

Holding the vial preciously in my palm, I turn back to the two tables. I take hold of the first sheet and tear off the cloth before I lose the courage—

And I find the body of my mother.

I nod, because I knew Garth had her somewhere. Her skeletal form does not hinder me.

I reach for the second sheet. I hesitate for a sliver of a moment when I think about what Jay's ghastly image will be after being dead this long, but I push that aside when I yank off the linen—

And find pillows. Just pillows.

I hear a click by my head.

Cold metal presses into my skin.

"Turn around, boy."

I do as he says, pivoting until I see Garth's now bloody grin. He holds a rifle's barrel to my forehead, one eye already squinted.

"Hand me that vial."

My fist gets tighter.

"Make one wrong move, and your brains will be on the wall before you can blink."

"I thought you didn't believe in fairy tales?" I bait Garth. Even with a bullet poised to kill, I am calm. "Now that you're dying, do you plan to use the blood to save yourself? I didn't think you were as weak as my father—"

Garth jabs the barrel at my head with enough force that my own blood trickles down my nose.

"Where is he?" I ask quietly. "Where is Jay?"

"I'm not your father," Garth bites at me before spitting up a wad of blood by my foot. "You think I keep corpses around? Jay Alder's body was burned, just like all the others."

My knees shake and my head sings.

I remember the bodies in the fianna village.

I imagine Jay's amongst them.

"We held a funeral for him. You weren't even there. Of course, little Mrs. Alder cried over an empty casket, but she didn't know that. She didn't know that Hazel burned her son's body the day you drug it back to Norsewood."

Every word that leaves Garth's mouth breaks me. I am no longer able to keep up my façade of courage and strength. Tears, hot and ugly, roll down my cheeks.

"Everything you did was for nothing," Garth tells me. "Even as you die, Hazel is taking care of that subhuman Maiden. She'll collect the blood and return to me. And with the Maiden gone, the council—"

Before Garth can speak another word, a dagger pokes through his throat. He drops the gun to the floor and grasps at his neck uselessly, hands smearing blood down the front of him. He staggers briefly before crashing onto the floor in a final thump.

I find Pa holding a bloody knife.

Sliding down the wall, I collapse onto the floor, the tears refusing to let up.

Pa scopes up Garth's gun from the floor. "Is that really his blood?" he asks as he looks over the gun. "The Stag's?"

Garth's blood spreads across the floor, eventually touching my boot. I nod to Pa, because I don't know if I can do much else.

"How? How did you get it?"

I don't answer him, I just watch the blood get closer and closer until it is soaking my—

"Answer me, Finn!"

"I shot him," I childishly confess. "I killed the god of the Forest. I left him lying in the streets like a—"

"Hand it over."

I look up to find Pa pointing the rifle at me. Unlike Garth, he does not grin or taunt me. He holds the gun with purpose.

I open my palm and study the vial. "You'd shoot your son for this?"

Pa shifts his weight, tucking the butt of the stock deeper into his shoulder. "Give me the blood."

I crawl to my feet, the barrel of the rifle following my clumsy ascent. "Answer me. If I stood between you and this," I say as I hold the glass between two fingers, "would you shoot me?"

Pa is silent.

My throat constricts. "Please. Please answer me."

Pa doesn't. He is quiet when all I need from him right now is just a few words.

"I've protected you for years. I've dealt with Garth so that you wouldn't have to. I protected her." I look at the body of my mother. "Why couldn't I be enough?" And once I've opened up that door, one I never thought would use its hinges, I can't stop. "I was here all along. I was here, with you, but I was never enough. No matter what I did, no matter how much I've protected you from...what I've done for you...I will never be good enough."

Pa clears his throat.

"I just wanted you to be proud of me," I say, despite how the words burn my throat. "And when Jay died, I needed you. I needed someone. But you weren't there. You never were." I stare at my hand. "I'm done helping you."

"Finn—!"

But it is too late.

When Niall Hail dives for the small bottle, it is already too late. The glass shatters against the stones, the drops of blood mingling with the rest of Garth's. Niall, the man who was once Pa, drops the gun and frantically sifts through the red as if the blood of the Stag would be distinguishable from the rest.

"You bastard," Niall snarls as his hands shake. He pounds his fists against the floor and the blood splatters against my pant legs. "You bastard, you bastard, you—"

Niall's fist crashes into my gut.

Doubling over, I open my mouth to get a lungful of air, but Niall grabs my collar and tosses me across the room. I roll across the stones until my head cracks against one of the table's legs.

"You bastard—you are a disgrace, you—" Niall's sentences are broken as he yanks at his hair, staining the black and gray pink. "You will regret this! You are—"

Niall stills like a man turned into a statue. His eyes, still wide and frantic, are unblinking. His lips part, sliding open like the gates of hell, to whisper, "The Maiden."

The pain in my gut transfers to my heart instantly.

"You divided the blood."

I find the gun. Across the room.

"I just have to find her. She must be in town. Hazel is after her now."

I sit up, pulling my legs under me.

"Hope is not lost, yet, my love! Hope is yet—"

I lunge for the gun.

Once I have the rifle in my hands, I turn the barrel to Niall, but he is quicker.

Niall's fist knocks me out before my finger can pull the trigger.

Adelaide

I ARRIVE AT the inn with an impossibly large smile on my face. I even give the innkeeper a "hello" while sprinting up the steps to the second floor. I practically skip down the hallway because everything was going to be okay.

Caleb would be the start of the end.

I'm surprised to find the room of Anna and Caleb unlocked.

I hop into the room, but I do not see either them. Instead, pieces of the furniture are shattered around like puzzle pieces. The walls are marked with red and the paper is shredded. All of it the artwork of destruction.

"The guild came and collected him." I spin to face the innkeeper. He inspects the room with disgust. "He was screaming and attacking his mate. He was acting like a damn feral."

No.

"Who do you think is going to pay for this? Last time I checked, you subhumans didn't have a coin to even spend—"

"Who took him?"

"What do you mean?"

"Which member of the guild collected Caleb?"

The innkeeper crosses his arms and squints. "Why, the only female member. Hazel Golding. Happened to be patrolling our street when the commotion happened."

No. No. No.

I push my palms against my head, trying to calm down the raging thoughts. "Where did they go? Please, tell me where she took him."

"Look here, I don't give a damn if you are royalty. This is my business and—"

My body reacts out of instinct. My knee rises by itself, jamming into the man's groin. He moans and falls forward.

I leave the innkeeper sprawled on the carpet and rush out of the building. In the streets of Norsewood, nothing amiss. The children are laughing and chasing one another, the women are laughing with voices as sweet as chimes, and the men are cursing and making suggestive comments to said women.

It is I who disrupts the calm.

I run down the streets, trying to weave through the people nimbly, but I am not nearly as graceful in my human skin. I end up colliding with a human male three times my size, but he steadies me with a meaty hand. I do not waste my breath apologizing to him despite how kind he looks.

"Have you seen a fianna male come this way?" I barely have enough air to finish my sentence. Most of the words combine in a jumble.

"You may have to be a bit more specific, miss. There are plenty of your kind in our town as of late. What does he look like?"

I want to be angry with him, to tell him I am positive he, like any other human in this damn town, has memorized the face of each fianna he saw so he can keep his distance.

"Well, he is as tall as you, if not a little taller—"

"Hopefully not as fat. That would be horrible, let me tell you," the man comments, laughing with his full belly.

I hold back my annoyance. "And he is—"

A scream splits the air.

I leave the man behind as I continue through the streets. I travel in the direction I believe the shout came from, but the town is alive and bustling in the midday heat. Children squeal amongst themselves, horses whine, and dogs bark back and forth at each other. I spin, searching, searching, searching—

Another scream to my left.

The citizens freeze, making it all the easier to slip through them in the direction of the sound. I pray, silently, as I dash between their bodies, that they will return to their daily routines. *Nothing is wrong*, I will, *nothing is wrong.*

As the town square opens up before me, I see Anna, and I see Caleb.

Horns towering above his head.

Set apart from the withdrawing people, Hazel leans up against a building without a single care in the world. She lingers in the shadows, just out of reach. Her feline eyes catch me, and she gives me a sly grin. "Well, convenient timing. The show is just beginning."

A woman with a babe clenched to her chest retreats as Caleb stalks up to her with his uneven gait. Anna, despite her efforts, cannot slow down her mate. She pleads with him, cries out, but it has no effect. Stepping in front of the woman, a man positions himself before Caleb, sickle in hand. Barking at Caleb, the man demands that he stand down, retreat, anything but progress forward.

Caleb's feet shuffle toward the fountain.

The man, giving up on words, swings the sickle. The blade slices through the air and sinks tenderly into Caleb's shoulder.

I scream as Caleb howls. Roaring in rage, Caleb strikes the man, tossing Anna in the process. As she drops to the ground, I go to her side and pull her head onto my lap. I slap her cheeks softly, but her eyes remain closed. By now, Caleb has thrown both the sickle and the man's hand to the dirt. The human does not wail as I would expect but squeezes his forearm as blood gushes from his wound like a mountain stream.

I look to Hazel, at the girl with all the weapons, and I shout, "Do something!" But the huntress continues to play with the end of her braid. "Please."

She closes her eyes and leans back further.

With a swing of his hand, Caleb's claws slice open the man's throat. As the human collapses, Caleb roars triumphantly.

Anna whimpers, her fingers brushing her forehead as she sits up. It takes but a second for her to clear the fog surrounding her eyes. When she grabs my hands, I notice, strangely, they do not quiver. "Adelaide, please run." Placing her palm against my face, she offers me up a fraction of a smile. "Go to the edge of the Forest. We'll meet you there."

"We have to go," I argue as I watch the humans either fleeing or preparing to bring Caleb to an end. As they circle him, they shout and holler, distracting Caleb with noises and movement. "We can get to—"

Anna shakes her head, acceptance settling on her shoulders like a deadly dress. "I can't leave him, Adelaide." As she speaks, the humans are inching inwards, waving about their weapons as Caleb hisses. "I'm not strong enough to let him go."

"What about me?" I beg, forcing my voice to climb above the clamor. Tears spike my vision as my emotions boil and crackle. "Who is going to look after me?"

The grin Anna gives me, the way her eyes squint at the edges, and the tears that roll down her cheeks, break me into a thousand pieces. "You've never needed anyone to save you, Adelaide. You are a courageous soul, a fire that is uncontainable." Anna, as she stands and begins to walk away, tells me, "And I am so proud of you."

I dive for Anna's hand, but it isn't close enough.

"Please!" I cry as I pivot to Hazel, my body seemingly paralyzed. "I will do anything."

Before Anna can get to her mate, a woman and a man attack Caleb at once.

The woman sticks a thick dagger into Caleb's stomach, twisting the blade before she wrenches it free, causing black blood to pour at her feet. Yet, she does not retreat from Caleb, expecting him to crumble like a fallen leaf.

Caleb has transformed into a monster. One who is invulnerable.

Lowering his head, Caleb brings his antlers into the tender skin where neck meets shoulder, and the woman careens backward.

Her blood splatters onto the flower shop windows.

The man falters in fright at the sight of his fallen comrade. Within moments of the man's hesitation, Caleb seizes control of the situation and jabs his claws into the man's gut. He then leans forward and his fangs tear the man's throat free. Caleb hangs onto the body while it droops to the ground, the blood washing over him like rain.

Anna reaches for him now, her hands seeking to save him. Because that is all she has ever wanted. From the time I have awoken, Anna has cared for her mate endlessly. Anna told me once before that I did not understand love, that I did not know the lengths one would go to protect someone.

But I do. I would do anything to protect the two of them.

When Anna touches her mate, I know that all is well. It is all it takes for Caleb to calm. His shoulders drop, and I know that she is his saving grace.

Caleb turns to Anna.

He raises a single hand.

Then, he draws a single red line across Anna's throat.

My world flickers.

Anna's legs wobble and she sways only once before her body smacks the streets with a thump. Caleb, at first, is frozen in place. Leisurely, he looks down at Anna's body, at the blood soaking his feet.

Opening his mouth, Caleb releases several gurgles before he asks, "Anna?"

While he crouches, his body begins altering itself. The antlers wobble from his brow until they bounce off the stones, fur falls away in clumps, and the black of his eyes recedes. His mighty frame splashes in blood as he collapses to his knees. "Anna," is all I hear him utter.

My heart shatters as he begins to stroke the hair of his dead mate. Tears run down his cheek as his lips move sluggishly.

Would you make me a promise?

By now, three hunters from the guild position themselves around Caleb. All of them raise their guns to him, the barrels glistening in the sunlight.

Would you do that for me?

I rise to my feet, willing my body to take two steps.

I cross the stones, slipping through the puddles of blood. I step over the bodies that are cast around like children's dolls. I have to ignore the eyes that stare lifelessly to the heavens. No matter how much Stag's blood I have, I know I cannot save these people.

I stand before Caleb, who rocks his love back and forth, sobbing.

I reach for the sickle.

I want you to kill me. If the time comes.

The vial, resting against my thigh, is useless to me. I can't save Caleb from this. I can't erase his memories, his actions. I couldn't save Anna. I couldn't bring her back into a world where she died at the hands of her beloved. These are things I can't change.

"Do it," Caleb tells me.

My fist tightens around the handle of the sickle.

"Please, Adelaide. It must be you."

I close my eyes with enough force that I worry they'll pop.

"Please, Adelaide. I can't," he sobs. "I'm sorry. I'm so sorry."

When I stab Caleb the first time, I don't know where to direct the blade.

The tip sinks into Caleb's flesh, and even in this state, he spares me by holding back the moan he wishes to release. My hands shake entirely too much to pull out the blade, but Caleb's hand collects mine.

And he places it against his chest, right above his heart. Where it thumps feebly.

Thud...thud...*thud.*

With his hand guiding mine, the second-strike pierce true.

"Oops, oops, oops!" Hazel suddenly sings as she begins to glide around the town square. Dragging the dead bodies of the fianna closer to Caleb, she stacks them intricately while singing her mad little song. Oops, oops, oops. "My, this was a mess! I don't know about you, but I was scared for my life."

Only Hazel and I exist in the streets. Everything else is dead.

Caleb.

Anna.

I pull out the canteen of blood and unscrew the cap.

As I pour the contents onto the street, I watch it vanish into the sea of red.

Because I don't need it.

It is useless to me now.

Hazel swings closer to me, her boots treading over various limbs without hesitation. "Tragic how some things play out, no?"

I glance at the blade, and the heaviness of this new reality seeps into me. I have lost both Anna and Caleb forever. It doesn't matter what the Stag's blood is capable of, because the Anna and Caleb I knew are gone. They will never return whole. And I can't risk having just pieces of them.

I stare at the sickle.

"Think carefully, princess," Hazel said as she strolls along, hips swaying in an attempt to be seductive.

With legs flooding with power, I lunge at the girl. She quickly dodges the stab aimed for her chest, smacking me across the face with the back of her hand. My vision blurs, but I do not relent. I jab again, but Hazel is too quick. She is an expert in the dancing of blades. Fighting her is as foolish as it would be to outrun a hare.

Hazel slides within my reach, but before I can even register her intentions, she knocks the weapon from my hands. She is sure of each movement, each fiber of her being acting with intent. Between one breath and the next, she drives a dagger through skin.

My skin.

I glance down at the blade protruding from my chest. I reach out for something, even Hazel, to keep me upright. But I grasp only air. I stumble and the ground rushes up to me like a raven diving into the clouds.

Finn

I BLINK IN and out of consciousness. Each snippet conveys the same thing; something is wrong.

It is Niall who carries the body of his gagged and broken son, and my head hangs limply as he weaves through the streets of Norsewood. I hear the screams, I see people running, and I wonder why Niall doesn't do the same. I think that it must be the world ending. All of it going up in flames, but it would make sense why Niall wouldn't run then.

The next image I catch is blood. So thick and encompassing that I imagine it as a pool straight from hell.

"Where is the bottle? Garth sent you to find her and the blood."

"She killed herself!" I hear Hazel snapping. "She smashed the bottle and—"

A crack echoes across the street as Niall's knuckles strike Hazel's cheek. "Get the girl. Get to the woods, we can—" Niall shakes his head, vibrating me in the process. "No. Get the girl. The council will—" Another vigorous shake. "Bring her."

THE CITIZENS PACKED in the council's chambers are trapped and skittish like sheep penned watching as wolves circle the outside. Some of them cry; others shout in fury. I hear only segments of their stories, but the bits that do align are hellish. A feral in the center of town. Death. Blood.

The old men of the council find their seats at the front of the room, their wrinkly faces sour and grumpy. Once they're settled, the lead councilman knocks his gavel against the podium several times, shouting over the madness of the crowd. He tries to control the masses, but it takes a single hunter to shoot into the roof before silence takes hold.

All the councilmembers look at the hunter as if he grew another head.

He shrugs as dust falls from the ceiling.

"Now," the councilman starts. "We are here today to discuss a very serious matter. A fianna staying in the town turned feral and murdered countless citizens. The Maiden of the fianna has been apprehended and is being brought forth to this trial." The councilman broadcasts to the collective, permitting the doors to the hall to open.

All breath in the room is held as the doors are peeled back. A girl is dragged into the room, her hair falling over her face like a blind. I do not need to see her eyes to know that it is Adelaide. Her tunic is stained with blood, and I find myself lurching at her before I can think properly. A hunter stationed behind me pulls at my restraints roughly in response.

Adelaide is placed in a stand beside mine, arms hanging at her sides freely. Her tunic, bloody and torn, shows more life than her.

"Before we begin, I would like to ask Niall Hail to join us."

With that, Niall walks into the room with a cleanly shaven face and freshly cut hair, all traces of blood gone. He looks in control, proper, and human. When the crowd sees the sigil of the lead hunter ironed onto Niall's tunic, they visibly retract. The volume of the conversations is lowered and their anger is subdued for morbid curiosity.

Niall Hail stands between Adelaide and me.

"Garth Roon, lead hunter of the guild, was among the many who lost their lives today. It is a tragedy that leaves me at a loss for words," the councilman states before ironically spewing out more dialogue. "But a new leader must be chosen. Niall Hail, once an esteemed head hunter, will resume the position. Garth was very compliant with the town and the council's wishes. We hope that you will meet the same expectations, Niall."

The people shift, concerned that the man of local legend will be taking a center spot back in the town. Yet, they are far more afraid of what lies outside these walls to matter much about what slithers within.

Niall nods. "Of course. I would just like to mention—"

Coughing, a center councilman cuts Niall off. "Maiden of the fianna, was the feral in the town square not your own guardian? A man you hold in high regard?"

Adelaide remains silent.

"Was this attack intentional?" a councilman asks.

"She controls them!" a voice from the crowd seethes.

"She turns them!" another shouts.

Waving off the voices, the lead councilman addresses the crowd by saying, "The fianna have been visiting Norsewood for generations, possibly since the beginning of our existence. We have sheltered them, protected them, taught them, but what have humans gained in return?" He pauses for effect. "We have allowed their people to kill ours under the justification of a god. We have not been able to enter the Forest for game or supplies due to their faith. We were taught from a young age to respect the beings of the Forest. We were told they were akin to gods, crafted in the image of the Stag. But all of that is at the expense of mankind. We are meant to be dutiful and kind. We are to watch as our young are burned and buried. No more."

Another councilman stands, and for a moment, I think he may tip over and fall, but he catches himself with a hand on the stand before him. "We have suffered too much! Was it not enough that we built them a village and granted them residency within the Forest? For generations, they've abandoned their homes and slaughtered our people. Too many human lives have been lost to the fianna and their faith."

I look to Adelaide, but she has not moved.

A third rises and the crowd is building up pressure like a thunderstorm. Behind me is only dark, dark clouds. "We will no longer let our people become targets of the fianna."

The lead councilman surveys the crowd. "We, as the voice of Norsewood, have come to a decision."

The crowd waits in eager delight. The council is going to protect them, and that is all they hear. They do not realize that an entire species is about to be segregated.

"Effective immediately, the hunters will escort the fianna back to the Forest. Once they are back within the trees, the fianna will no longer be permitted in human territory. Feral or not, the fianna will be persecuted if they tread on human soil."

I look at Niall and I see the glint in his eyes as he declares, "I will be marching them back to their territory immediately. I will guarantee the safety of Norsewood."

My head screams.

"What about the wall?" someone screams.

Niall nods. "That is why I will be taking my son."

The noise in my head doesn't compare to what I hear around me.

"How—?"

"Him—?"

"Silence!" the lead councilman snaps.

Without waiting, Niall hops into his explanation by stating, "My son has traveled with the Maiden deep into the Forest. He knows how to part the vines."

Another woman shouts, "And you trust the son of a Hail?"

Niall smiles. "My son has been very honest with me. He has told me a great many things."

No.

"Does she know?" Niall asks while the crowd continues to rock and sway in their own questions and madness. "Does she know how you gained his blood?"

Slowly, the Maiden raises her head.

"Please, don't—"

"Does she know—?"

"Please!"

"How you killed her god?"

When Adelaide finally looks at me, her golden eyes are wide, and her lips are parted in shock.

"I believe you shot him, right?" Pa continues.

"Silence!" the council commands. They allow the noise to trickle down, but no matter how quiet it gets, Adelaide won't look at me.

She won't turn her head to hear me tell her I'm sorry.

A few voices rise.

"The fianna will be marched to the edge of the human territory. If the wall does not fall, those that reside in our lands...will be persecuted."

There might be some humans who object to such a ruling, but they are drowned out by those who cheer in applause.

I keep praying that Adelaide will look to me.

Please.
Please look at me.
"It is now the age of man. We are no longer the prey. For we are all hunters."
Please forgive me.

Adelaide

HE CAN'T BE dead.

He is not dead.

He can't be.

Before the verdict is even publicized, before the fate of my people is sealed, Hazel weaves through the crowd and plucks me from my stand like a hawk sniping a mouse from the fields. Yet, I don't need to know what these men decide. I already know it in my heart.

I risk a glance at Finn before I'm whipped around the corner—

And he watches me go.

Hazel weaves through the many hallways, not even giving me the privacy of a room before she spins on me and tears off my shredded dress, leaving me partially nude. "We are going to make you pretty, princess of the dirt. All for your homecoming!" Hazel grins as she pulls a new gown over my head, one fashioned from numerous animal furs pieced together. The fabric is rough and agitating.

"You killed them," I say as she fastens the furs to one another.

Hazel doesn't offer a response, just pulls back her teeth in a smile and slams a crown of horns and thorns onto my brow. The hot tickling of blood creeps from my scalp, inching down my nose.

"You can't blame anyone but yourself, princess of leaves. You were weak. You couldn't protect those who mattered most to you. You were even betrayed by a hunter." She pats my cheek with mock sympathy. "I wish someone would have warned you that man is a wicked beast."

I want to desperately to strike her, to cause her harm, but I know that my victory lies within holding my fists at my side, no matter how badly they quiver.

Hazel throws a collar around my neck, pulls my arms back, and binds my wrists together with rough rope. As she works, I tell her, "I want you to know that one day I will avenge them."

She cackles in humor. "Will you throw rocks at me? Poke me with your twigs? Nothing you have will harm me."

"It won't be you who I kill first."

Hazel's hands still, her fingers resting on my skin.

"I won't kill you until after you've watched your brother bleed out at your—"

In her otherworldly way, Hazel wraps her hands around my throat and hoists me off my feet. The girl is a collection of sneers and confidence that make weaker species quiver in fright, but right now, she is only mad. She is serious, all signs of sinister joy drifted away.

"If you touch him, I will cut your limbs off one by one," she threatens.

I wheeze in a breath to tell her, "Your kind declared war. Prepare yourself for the casualties."

"Huntress!"

We both turn.

A hunter with a mask of a bear faces us. Hazel drops me to catch a bundle thrown her way. Unraveling the cloth, she finds an eyeless cougar mask glaring back at her. With the mask against her face, Hazel sways her head around, taunting me.

"I think our little princess is ready for the parade." She places a finger on the feline's chin. "Oh, wait! One more touch." Hazel presses her palm against my forehead and runs her hand down the entirety of my face, smearing blood as she goes.

She steps back and places her hands on her hips. "Perfect."

Outside the council building, the humans cluster together on the streets with fury. They snap at me, every word somehow as clear as the last, growing in intensity.

The first rotten vegetable bounces off my chest.

"Murderer," they say as one.

"Subhuman queen," they shout separately.

I begin to cry when I see the faces of the young, their eyes cast upon me as if I am the foulest of creatures. They hold onto their parents' legs, cowering in fright. I want to reach out to them, to soothe their fears, but Hazel pulls me along by my leash.

"The council has decreed that the deaths of their beloveds are your fault. They even believe you turn the ferals yourself. And no matter how much I tried to reason with them, they wouldn't listen!" Hazel tells me as she leads.

I want to tell the humans, each one, that there will never be a day where I don't feel responsible for Anna and Caleb's deaths. There will never be a time where the weight doesn't crush me.

I also want to taunt them, to laugh at their weak throws and harmless phrases.

Because they can't see the vital parts of me that have already died. They can't smell the rot that has already decayed my heart.

The humans can't hurt me anymore.

Finn

THE GUILD IS dressed in attire pulled directly from a child's nightmare. Their tunics are embellished with animal skins, and they each wear a mask detailed to look similar to the beasts that roam the wild. To the citizens, the hunters of the guild look indistinguishable from one another, and it is brilliant.

Because the masks protect the hunters' identities as soon as the horrors begin.

They begin tearing fianna from the buildings and tossing them out onto the streets. In the beginning, they attempt to be civil and gentle, but eventually, they throw the creatures into the streets like disobedient mutts. Only a few humans stand up to the hunters, refusing access to their homes, but that doesn't stop the purge.

The hunter watching over me gives my back a jab, forcing me to keep moving.

Amongst the chaos, a feral is born.

A fianna male sobs on the streets, his hands clenching his head ravenously. Hunters prod him with their guns, shouting warnings for the fianna to comply. When he throws back his head, horns sprout from his skull, sickly pale and disfigured. His arms begin to unravel as he screams and begs for mercy.

Yet, the hunters do nothing. They wait until the feral is done changing before they end its life.

At the edge of Norsewood, I find Niall Hail presiding over the madness, mask hung across his back, so the people can easily identify him.

Once the hunter deposits me beside Niall, I tell him, "You must be proud."

Niall looks at me with bored concentration. "I could care less about all that is happening here. This is merely the aftermath of whatever Garth had planned."

"You just want to get into the Forest, don't you?"

He nods.

"You claimed you killed the god, no? You'll lead me to his body and I will extract whatever blood is left. I will save Elinica yet."

"You're pretty confident I'm going to assist you."

Niall shrugs. "I assume the Maiden means something to you. Not the same way that the Alder boy did, but still, you care. And she cares for the safety of her people. I would then conclude I have leverage on both parties." Niall waves his hand at all the fianna being brought out of the town like cattle. "None of this entertains me in the slightest."

"I don't remember much about my mother," I state, and I see Niall stiffen at the mention of his lover. Never have I talked to him about her. "I do remember little snippets of her smile, her laugh. Or, at least I think I do. I remember the night that you came home with her in your arms. Her body bloody and lifeless. You asked me to help get her into the basement. You asked me to protect her, to protect you, by keeping that secret."

"Stop your yapping, boy."

But I don't. "The woman I remember, the small bits, would never love the person you are now. If you bring her back, she'll hate you just as much as—"

Niall slaps me across the mouth, and the pain sings in me like a reward.

I smile at him.

"Our esteemed guest of honor has arrived," Niall announces to the gathered fianna and hunters, his calm fitted back into place.

The fianna all turn to watch the Maiden march down the streets. A single hunter pulls her with a rope, the line taut. Adelaide, dressed in a collection of furs and a crown of antlers, is bloodied and filthy. The humans, pressed against the sides of the streets, throw trash and stones at her, cursing her name and her station.

Adelaide, once proud and courageous, hangs her head as she is dragged through Norsewood. I step forward, but my guardian hunter pulls tight at my wrists.

Humans watch her from the doorways and windows, not a single face of joy.

Adelaide halts before the mass of the fianna, and I expect her to call to them, to encourage them to be brave and fierce. Yet, she does not utter a single word. The fianna reach for her, cry for her, but she does not respond.

Niall grabs my arm, pulls me to Adelaide, and places me beside her. "You shall march beside her, Finn. Make sure she stays in line. It was your duty before, so why shouldn't you do it now?"

I shake in fury.

"I do find it rather amusing, though. The maiden and the hunter. Isn't that an old fairy tale?" When Niall doesn't receive a response from the surrounding hunters, he shrugs and leaves me beside Adelaide.

I look at Adelaide's dress, the crown placed on her head, and I open my mouth to say something, anything, but a rough voice behind me warns, "Don't try anything."

And with a shout from Niall, the hunters pull the gathering fianna forward. All of them walk in unison, not even one offers up any kind of resistance. They cry and whisper amongst each other, their utter desperation taking physical form.

The fianna form a single line as they march through the fields, with Adelaide, Niall, and me at the front. Sporadically, gunshots crack like lighting, killing either ferals or those who show even an inkling of disobedience.

"I never wanted this," I tell Adelaide.

The girl continues to walk forward, step following step.

"I just need you to know that. All I ever wanted was to have—"

"You deceived me."

When Adelaide speaks, it sounds like the judgment of a god, or like the Stag himself. She faces me, her eyes the darkest shades of gold while her lips are pulled in a straight line.

I have never wanted so badly to see her smile. "I'm sorry," I say again.

"That doesn't change anything."

Niall halts the march when we stand before the wall of vines and thorns.

Impatiently, hunters roughly gather both Adelaide and me and throw us before Niall. "How do we make a path?" he asks.

But Adelaide does not answer.

A hunter with a cougar mask takes a fistful of her hair and wrenches her head back. Adelaide doesn't even cry out, but the hunter behind me still holds me back from launching myself forward.

"I asked you a question, girl. Answer me," Niall commands.

"One day, you will die," she shrieks. "One day, you will be dirt." She spits at Niall, but the spittle dribbles down her chin pathetically.

Niall pulls a pistol from his belt and snaps off the safety. Aiming at Adelaide's shoulder, Niall looks to me. "I hear this girl has fascinating abilities. She can be fatally stabbed but still live?"

Niall's finger pulls back the trigger.

I dart forward, but I gain no ground. "Don't."

"Tell me. How do we get through the wall?" he asks me this time.

I need to think of something. I can't let the fianna go back into the Forest or—

The gun fires.

Adelaide screams as metal blasts through skin and blood.

Niall loads another bullet into the chamber, ignoring how viciously I fight against my restraints.

He doesn't even ask again, he just aims for another shot, pulls the trigger—

"It's her!" I scream.

Niall holds the gun in the air, staring at Adelaide, at how she bleeds.

"The vines part for her," I tell Niall, but my voice is wheezy and frail. I hear the faint sobs coming from Adelaide and my own heart breaks. "I'm sorry," I tell her again.

Niall hoisters the gun, voicing echoing across the expanse. "Hunters! Guns at the ready!" Crouching, he grabs Adelaide's chin and takes one glance at me. "If this boy is lying, you will watch all of your people die. Do you understand?" Niall waits for but a moment before determining that the Maiden will not answer him.

The cougar mask hunter drags Adelaide to the wall. The vines react as they had before when Adelaide is close, parting until a pathway big enough for a single human is formed. Niall calls the hunters into action, and one by one, he funnels the fianna and humans through the wall.

Gunshots fire off from the other side.

Adelaide, Niall, and I are the last to go through the wall. Niall pulls Adelaide along while the same hunter who has governed me from the council's chambers presses his rifle into the small of my back.

Halfway through, I hear the screams.

When we breach the Forest, I see pure chaos.

Ferals are pouring out against the hunters. As the wall closes behind us, the hunters are trapped as feral after feral rushes at them from the Forest. They must have been lingering behind the wall, waiting. The hunters' self-preservation kicks in, and they ignore the ferals that rip through their defenses and into the heart of the gathered fianna. Endless bodies fall onto the Forest floor, and the screams become a constant ringing.

Niall shouts at the hunter behind me and grabs both Adelaide's and my ropes. He runs down the length of the wall, away from the massacre. Yet, no matter how far we run, I still hear flesh being shredded apart, and commands issued with urgency.

Pausing in a thicket of ferns, Niall collects his breath while surveying the three of us. "From here, we make for the fianna village, and then we—"

"But, sir!" the hunter behind me interjects, stepping away from me and closer to Niall. "What about the others?"

He waves it off. "We don't have time. Now, we have—"

"But, sir!" the hunter insists.

Niall grabs for the hunter and pulls him in close, his face inches from the mask. "I will not tell you—"

The hunter swings the stock of the rifle into Niall's temple. A faint moan escapes his lips as he pitches forward, fanning out amongst the greenery. Once he is downed, the hunter makes quick work of freeing my wrists.

When he is done, he stands before me, removing his bestial mask to reveal—

"Marshall?" I ask bewildered. "What...?"

"Just helping you out. Again," he says as he now works on Adelaide. Even when she is free, the girl remains staring at the ground where Niall rests. "We need to go."

Adelaide, without a word, drops to her knees and fishes through Niall's belt.

We see the dagger at the same time.

I grab her wrist as she unsheathes the blade. Her eyes lock with mine, teeth bared in fury.

"He needs to die." Her eyes spark with rage, shifting from maiden to a warrior. "I will not let the ferals have the satisfaction of killing him."

"Adelaide, you don't want—"

"No!" she shouts, the sound rivaling that of a limb falling from a tree. "You don't get to decide anymore." I shrink as she turns her wrath against me. "Do you have any idea of what you've done? You've betrayed me. Not only me but my people. They are out there." She points ravenously into the trees. "And they are dying. Do you understand that?"

"I know that—"

"You don't get to explain!" Adelaide's voice rises until it is the only thing I hear in the Forest of death. "You did this, Finn Hail. Because of your selfish desires, you have damned my people. You have damned me."

In the space where I was meant to respond, where I would have apologized again, a howl flares to life.

I look up to find ferals crashing through the Forest, galloping to us in a frenzy.

Marshall pulls back his bow and fires two arrows into the distance before shouting, "Leave him! We have to run!"

I yank Adelaide to her feet, taking dagger and anger with me.

"Where should we go?" I ask over the rush in my ears. The trees sway and buck in the agitated wind.

"The Maiden can open up the wall!" he shouts while letting loose another arrow.

"I have to go back," Adelaide says, trying to desperately free herself of my grip, but I keep us running, I keep us moving as the ferals continue to advance. She continues to battle me with the stubbornness of a colt.

"This is no time to be a hero!" Marshall leaps over a fallen log, tripping in the act. "I will take you to my farm. My mother will keep you safe. For the time being!"

"I think that is the best—"

Adelaide comes to a halt, and the strength of her pull is enough to rip me from my feet. I land in the dirt, sprawled out after the whiplash. When I look up, I see that Adelaide is no longer worried about the ferals, or me for that matter. Her eyes are focused on a further point in the Forest. I stand back up and see Adelaide standing in the distance. I spin, but Adelaide is still beside me.

"What in the actual hell?" Marshall yelps as soon as he sees the girl in the distance. "Are there multiple Maidens just lying in wait?"

Adelaide takes a step forward. "She wants us to follow her."

"That girl is you. Does anyone else notice this?" Marshall asks. "Anyone?"

I ignore Marshall. "Adelaide, listen to what you are—"

"No," she tells me. Her hands are clenched into fists, her shoulders are held high. "I'm done relying on you. On anyone."

The girl in the distance beckons us with a single finger. *Come*, she seems to indicate. *Come to me.*

And Adelaide obeys the command.

Adelaide

WHEN THE MAIDEN darts into the wilderness, a trail of lilies breaks free from the earth, illuminating my path. The flowers sway as I race past them, following a trail I had once before.

Always ahead of me, the Maiden with the scarred eye slips in and out of view. Whenever I see her, she is further away, waiting but never agitated that I am not fast enough to keep up.

All she dons is a playful smirk.

You must be quicker, she seems to taunt at each turn. The human boys struggle behind me, trying to keep up. Yet, I have no intention of them following me wherever this Maiden takes me.

You have more legs you can use, she whispers to me.

As I dive through the underbrush, I tell my human skin to shed, to melt away into the whitest of furs. I do not care if I leave Finn or Marshall behind. I want the oblivion, the void of the animalistic mind.

I will save myself.

It is all that I can do now.

My clouded thoughts cause me to stumble over a root. My hands skid across the dirt as I trip, the lilies blanketing my fall. No matter how many feet tread on them, they seem as perfect and soft as ever.

When the lilies come to an end, the scarred Maiden is standing at the end. Beside her is the second Maiden from that night in the clearing. She smiles radiantly at me while her companion only scowls.

I freeze as the two ghostly Maidens move until they stand before me. They lift hands that glow foggily. One rests on my cheek while the other on my bloodied shoulder, and a warmth courses through the entirety of me. I close my eyes as a moan leaves me. A sense of "wholeness" envelops me as all my scrapes, cuts, and aches vanish. When I open my eyes back up, the two are gone, and when I turn to look back, the lilies are as well.

The human boys, limping and exhausted, crawl their way to me, gasping for air. "Where are you running to?"

I study both of their genuine cluelessness. *They didn't see the Maiden. Or the lilies. Only I did.*

"We are here," I state before taking a step forward.

IT HAPPENS AS it did before.

The air grows heavy, becoming as dense as water until I push through the other side. The trees, between one blink and the next, disappear to the sides of us, forming an oval clearing. A field, that stretches as far as the eye can see, is littered with enough lilies to make a snowy-field jealous.

Both boys are in awe of what surrounds them, mouths agape in astonishment. "Look," Marshall says, his finger raised and shaking with disbelief.

Several ghostly figures tend to the lilies with unwavering dedication. After a few steps, each figure fades into nothingness, only to appear miles away. They blink here and there, appearing at random.

"Who are they?" Marshall asks. "They can't be..." He stares at me.

"Ghosts," I tell him. Not sure how, or why, but knowing that they are. "Maidens of the past."

Suddenly, all of them freeze. Some are hunched over, playing with the lilies' leaves, others are in mid-step. As a single-bodied organism, all the ghostly Maidens rise and stand up straight. As one, all their heads turn in my direction.

And as one, their voices coming from all directions, they say, "Welcome home, Maiden."

Next, they all turn and raise a single finger in the same direction. Further into the field.

Without much thought, I step forward and follow their direction. As I move, the lilies before me part, their roots coming to the surface and slithering through the grass like snakes. Each ghost I pass offers me a warm grin before twinkling out of sight. They do not pay much mind to the boys who follow me.

"Lily, lily. Lovely lilies. Bloom, wither, begin again. Lovely lilies," they sing over and over, their voices beautifully intertwined. "Lily, lily. Lovely lilies. Bloom, wither, begin again. Lovely lilies."

Eventually, I see a collection of trees resting on an island. The water surrounding the small island is the purest blue I have ever seen. When my feet brush the bank of the pond, I glance down at the numerous fish that dance and slip around one another beneath the surface. After closer inspection, I can see a single tree on the island, gnarled and twisted with age. Images are carved in the bark, mostly unidentifiable, but some strangely human.

I notice a form huddled between the exposed roots of the tree.

A stag of golden hues rests beneath the glow of the tree while creatures, big and small, somehow weave in and out of his fur. I watch as a fox leaps from the nape of the stag's neck, chasing a hare between the god's legs, before disappearing back into the pelt. Flowers of various styles flourish endlessly about him, crawling over him like birds on a statue.

He is effortlessly majestic. Otherworldly.

He is the Stag. And lilies rest everywhere within sight.

Welcome, Maiden.

The voice echoes through me, as if I'm just a screen the wind curls past. The words enter from every part of me. I hear and feel them all at once.

As the Stag raises his mighty head, he peels back his eyelids to expose two orbs the whitest of fires. His attention centers onto me, and a force of emotion overwhelms me.

I drop to my knees, my face reflecting against the pond's surface. "I am so sorry. I couldn't save them. I couldn't save anyone." My tears, no matter how many fall into the water, do not affect the reflective surface. "I wasn't good enough."

You are more than enough, my daughter. You have always been enough.

Facing him once more, I see a number of the ghostly Maidens surrounding him. Several brush his fur, causing golden sparks to ripple from the hairs while others continue to tend to the thousands of lilies that encompass the clearing. All of them, in varied versions, resemble me. The face is what never changes, despite the hair, the form of the body, the color of the skin. It is always my eyes. My lips.

All of them are me.

"Who are they?" I ask despite already knowing the answer.

My thoughts hum with the voice of the Stag, easing all my fears and anxieties. *She is you. You are her. Past and future, present and always. You are all the same,* I hear the Stag tell me. *One Maiden is all Maidens. It is never who are you, but when are you?*

Roots and vines break from the dirt and gather beneath the Stag's mighty frame. Effortlessly, the foliage raises the Stag into the air. Then, the thick cords begin to twirl together, overlapping one another until four legs appear beneath the Stag's body. Beginning to walk, the wildlife follows its god. Flowers, grass, and animals chase after the Stag's every step.

I watch in awe as his first hoof treads the surface of the water. Without sinking an inch, the beast glides across the blue as effortlessly as he would the fields. The fish swim to the surface, ecstatically jumping before their god.

Once his hooves make contact with the meadow, the flower petals and stigmas radiate effervescently. They glow from within, all of them stretching to get closer to the deer as he makes his way to us.

When he stops before us, my frame trembles, my human body wanting to shed itself and praise my god in my most natural form.

Meeting the fires within his eyes once more, the Stag's presence ignites within me. It wraps around my heart tenderly, the warmth pushing away all the hurt, before flowing into my head. It explores my memories, my thoughts, my everything.

I know you have suffered, the Stag voices, but I am there with him. Watching again how Anna and Caleb perished, how it felt to be mocked by the humans.

He is there to witness my rage, the hatred that burns within my heart.

"Get out of my head!" I hear Finn scream. When I look back, his hands are clenching his skull, his face contorted in agony.

I notice that tears also stream down the boy's face.

I am sorry, my son, for the pain that you have—

"Get out!" Finn roars in a rage so physical it slaps against my chest. "Those aren't for you! You don't—"

Finn suddenly reaches for the knife at his side, pointing it at the god.

"Finn!"

Endless tears flow from the boy's eyes. "I said, get out."

You should not be ashamed, boy. I do not judge your transgressions as harshly as you do yourself.

Marshall reaches forward and lowers the hand that holds the dagger. Finn, swallowing, keeps his eyes locked on the Stag in sorrow, rage, and embarrassment.

I know many things cause you to wonder, the Stag announces, and I know it is not just me who hears his voice. Marshall, Finn, and I are all the same. *Please, ask me anything.*

"The lilies," I say. They are all identical in size and shape. I notice only a few with withering petals.

"They are very special." A Maiden appears beside me, walking out of thin air. Her skin is the gorgeous brown of a doe's fur and her hair is darker than human tar, yet far more beautiful. "Do you not know what lies within? What they hold?"

I can only shake my head, her splendor freezing me.

She holds out her hand and a lily climbs into the air with the elegance of a charmed snake, the stem coiling around her forearm mesmerizingly. She extends her palm—flower and all—to me with a smile. "Please. Do not be afraid."

I take her words as encouragement and reach for the flower, letting the petals brush against my skin. Instantly, a buzz zaps through my fingers, traveling up my arms until my heart is bursting with joy. The emotion overtakes me until I release a smile and strange tears prick my eyes.

A laugh echoes in my ears, but it is not here. The laugh is distant. The joy elsewhere.

I blink, and an image of a child dashes between my lids. A boy chasing his...sister. Wooden sword posed for battle.

"Is this..." The impossibility of my question threatens to hold back my asking. But the Maiden before me, me but not me, gives me courage with just a grin. "Is this a boy in Norsewood?"

The Maiden shakes her head. "No. That boy is not now. He was. Is to be. He rests right now." Before I can say anything else, another lily crawls into her opposite hand. As she holds that to me, her lips turn downwards. "Beware. This is not a life of happiness."

I swallow as I touch the flower. The emotion that slices through my body is not happiness, but terror. In one impossibly long blink, I see a woman cowering in the corner of her home, her face bruised, her tears never ending. In another flash, she is pushing against a man who only seems to fight back all the harder—

The Maiden pulls the lily from me, leaving me with only tears. I see Marshall to my right, bent over, brushing his hand across the lilies, his face flickering through various emotions so quickly it could be viewed as comical.

"She will be rewarded in her next life," the Maiden tells me reassuringly. "She will meet the love of her life. She will be happy."

"I don't understand," I tell her.

"But you do. You just won't say it aloud." The Maiden lowers the flowers back to the ground where they cuddle against the rest. "Be unafraid."

I look to the Stag. "These are...people. They are..."

"Souls," The Maiden concludes as the Stag nods his mighty antlers. "And all of them will be reborn. They live. They die. They are never-ending."

"This is insane," Marshall mumbles, his smile borderline inhuman. "Finn, come here."

But the young hunter's eyes have never left the Stag.

Against my own will, I reach for the Maiden before me. My fingers brush her cheek, and somehow, against logic, they do not pass through her.

"You are—" I start.

"I am you," she adds.

"We are," I start.

"The same," she adds.

You have lived many lives, Maiden.

When the Stag's words finish, the grove explodes with endless Maidens. Some race about naked, others in dresses, more in the form of does. All of them prance and laugh as they play. I notice, as they move, that all of them have a single golden thread coming out of their chests. I follow the strands until they all end up in a single location; the skin above my heart.

All of them sing, "Begin again, begin again."

The Maiden before me takes a step back, and I reach for her, to keep her with me, but my fingers wave through thin air.

"These...are all me?" Marshall asks, his eyes moving rapidly across the fields. What we see must be individual, specific to ourselves.

Finn's gaze is undisturbed.

In a puff of golden dust, the Maidens all vanish, filling the air with shimmering droplets.

Do you want to see the start of it all? the Stag asks, taking a single step forward. The lilies part, creating a circle around where a bright gold flower surfaces. Rising until it brushes my nose, the flower releases a thin cloud of pollen. The particles settle against my skin, giving off a slight burn wherever they land. I blink to clear my eyes, but the searing heat spreads until all I see—

THE GARDEN STRETCHES before me, yet Finn and Marshall are gone. I see the Stag further down, grazing in the grass. He looks younger, the carefree way he prances across the plains giving him a childish wonder. As I watch him, I see the same tree that was centered in the pond, the size of it still awestriking.

Then, time speeds up. The Stag leaps and plays as fast as a hummingbird, the moon and sun go around and around, and the Stag begins to...slow. He doesn't prance with as much life. He becomes...lethargic.

Time crashes back into place clumsily when the tree starts to bloom. Just two flowers. Beautiful, complex, elegant things. As the flowers bloom, they drop to the ground. The Stag sniffs at the lilies, bewildered by this new addition of life.

The Tree knew I was lonely, the Stag's voice finds me. It doesn't matter where I am, it vibrates in my bones. *It knew that it was my turn to nurture life. As it had done to me for endless amounts of time.* Before me, the younger Stag digs a hollow trench with his hooves, nudging the lilies into the dirt, giving them a bed to rest in.

It was my turn to be a creator, he tells me.

This time, when the time speeds up, the Stag is full of life once more. He focuses his devotion onto a single flower, tending to it with meticulous care. He brings his flower water from the pond, he collects the sun in his coat and offers it to his creation. He slices open his leg and...bleeds on the petals, showering them with his life.

I gave everything to it. It was a part of me. It was me, the Stag explains.

Time recoils when a hoof sprouts from beneath the flower.

At first, the Stag is as still as death, his eyes wide as he watches more and more mass spiraling out from the earth. Eventually, the Stag gets over his fear and starts to help, digging free whatever rises.

Then, I see myself.

It is strange, but I know that the deer is me. I see it in her eyes, in the color of her fur, everything that she is. She is wobbly at first, her four legs shaky and new, but the Stag is there to help her, to teach her as a father would. Eventually, the doe prances and trots around the Stag in childlike wonder. Once she is bored of that, she races around the perimeter of the field in a bundle of energy.

It is the first time I notice that their world is rather tiny.

I was, am, will forever be, proud of my daughter. The Stag's voice and words constrict around my heart tenderly. The Maiden of the Stag's heart.

Their lives speed up, the doe a constant energy around the Stag, yet, as the time flies by, the doe stops her leaps and starts to calm herself, as the Stag once had himself. The youth starts to drain from her until I can read the unhappiness from her snorts and the flickers of her tail. A content state that troubles her.

But I could not be everything for my daughter. As the Tree could not be all that I needed. She needed something else. I went to the second flower, the one that I had forgotten, and it was wilting, decaying from neglect. I pleaded to Nature Herself to create a companion for my daughter, to bring life to the second flower.

Nature hears the Stag's plea, restoring the vitality of the lily. Within moments, as it had with the doe, the dirt begins to break and separate.

This time, the Stag does not help the creature free itself.

And sprouting from the earth is a being unlike anything he has ever encountered. This creature does not prance on four legs, but two. It does not have fur as majestic as his own but is nearly bare.

Thus, he was born. The First Hunter.

And that man was Finn.

The boy hid beneath the tree, cowering in the shade at the beings that were different. He watched the Stag and the Maiden, enjoying the sun, playing in the grass, but he was not bold enough to join them.

Days pass by as quick as shooting stars.

I had not created this creature, and because of that, I did not know his mind. The difference that brewed in that space.

After many attempts from the doe, the boy reaches out his hand. She, after waiting for so long, presses her head into his palm eagerly.

And the boy joined her in the fields.

Time courses past me. Occasionally, I come across the Hunter and the Maiden, the two of them full of life, energy, and adventure, even though they do not share a common form. Time and time again they come to me, bounding, and a connection thriving between them.

They are in love, I think.

Finn and I are in love.

The connection that was shared between the creatures transcended form, shape, everything. I had not realized, by calling to Nature, I had somehow bound these two souls together.

My heart stops violently. "This is impossible," I state. I could not love Finn. I didn't...

Another shift, and the boy is at the edge of the fields. I notice now that nothing exists outside of the grass. Everything that falls past the border is...white.

But. I was not enough for the son of the Earth. He wanted more. Like Nature, he wanted to expand. To extend his domain.

I blink.

And I am right beside the boy, the Hunter. He waits until the doe comes to his side before he opens his lips. The language that comes from him is foreign to me. Yet the syllables are shockingly clear as they find an understanding in my mind. "He does not love me the same," the boy states.

The doe shakes her head, clearly trying to dispute him. She stomps her hooves into the ground to exclaim her disagreement.

"He did not create me as he did you," the boy tells the doe as he points back to the Stag who grazes lazily in the grove. "He won't allow my mother's lands to grow. He only allows this small space to flourish. Imagine a world where there were endless fields...imagine a place where there were more people like me?"

The doe cocks her head to the side in confusion, her only response being a quizzical glance.

"He is selfish. He only made one of you. Imagine if there were more of you."

The doe did not completely understand the boy, for her everything was him. She was content with the grove, with her existence.

Yet, the boy's words caused a yearning to grow in my daughter's heart. My neglect inspired jealousy and bitterness to fester within the boy.

"He does not want me here anymore. He would be happy if I left. I am but a pest to him, a mere plaything for his child." The boy turns to the doe, his eyes finding hers, and he smiles. "If I leave this place, would you be sad?"

The doe does not hesitate. She nods vigorously.

"Then...would you come with me?"

The boy, not waiting for the doe's answer, takes a step into the white, away from the grove. As soon as his foot touches the ground, he vanishes.

The doe, fearing the loss of her companion, follows him without hesitation.

Again, the scene changes.

This time, I find the boy, the First Hunter, standing in a sea of green. Endless rows of trees surround him, climbing into the blue sky, swaying in the gentlest of breezes. The boy laughs and spins in circles, trying to take in the world around him.

Finally, his gaze finds a creature similar to himself.

A girl stands behind him. With golden eyes and hair as white as snow.

As soon as my daughter left my domain, her form was tainted. The furs fell from her, and she was given what she truly desired.

Humanity.

The two were in such awe of one another that they didn't notice the grove was nowhere to be seen. Instead, hand in hand, they begin to race through the Forest.

They run, somehow, for days on end. They spend their nights beneath the stars, their days beneath the clouds. The boy teaches the girl his language, and the girl teaches him the way of the land. Together, they discover the world that waited outside of the Stag.

Yet, my daughter was not made to be man. She was made in my image.

The world shifts until I see the boy waist deep in a river, splashing in the water with a childish glee. The girl waits on the bank, studying her love patiently.

Until she doubles over.

The boy does not notice how she suffers at first. While he plays, the girl twists and turns, her body contorting in silent agony.

When she can cry for help, it is too late.

The boy rushes to her side, finding that the girl is no longer human, but a hybrid of both beast and man. Blinded by her pain, she reaches for her lover, for solace, but she is not careful.

The boy's body falls, his blood staining the river crimson.

The Maiden was also the first feral.

Fleeing into the Forest, she cries out to her father, her creator.

Time passes differently in the grove, the Stag explains to me. *The two had been gone for the human equivalent of years, but to me, it was but a breath. When I turned, I noticed that I could not find my daughter.*

The Stag finally leaves the grove himself, dashing into the white after a distant scream. As he runs, a trail of white lilies follows him.

But, when the Stag finds his daughter, it is too late.

I could not save her from the sins of man. She had left, she had chosen for herself, and that was beyond my design. She pleaded for mercy.

I watch as the Stag meets his daughter amongst the rocks and leaves. I witness as he lowers his mighty brow and plunges his horns deep into her chest.

And I saved my daughter.

The next memory that surfaces is of the Stag at the Tree, bowing before it.

I, in turn, pleaded for the Tree to take my life. As I awaited my end, I noticed two flowers before me. I felt the life of my daughter still brimming within. I knew that she would begin again.

The Stag, suddenly, tears the second lily from the ground. He turns and dashes back into the world, leaving his grove behind.

I would not allow man to corrupt my daughter once more. I found the body of the boy, the son of Nature, floating in the river still. In fury, I threw the lily on top of him, casting him from the grove.

Returning to his home, the Stag notices that his daughter's lily has begun to brown. In panic, he tries to water the flower, offer it his blood, but the lily's petals droop, sag, and continue to die. In his last hopes, the Stag takes the lily from the grove and plants it out in the Forest.

Where she flourished.

When I allowed Nature to create Her son, she cursed my daughter. For, without him, she began to wither.

Time speeds up once more. The Maiden is reborn, roaming the Forest as both deer and woman. She exists peacefully until, one day, she finds where the trees end.

I had not known that when I cast out the son of Nature, his soul drifted down the river and floated by on the wind, eventually settling in the Treeless lands.

Where he flourished.
Where the two met, the world began.
—and the scene blends away.

THE CREATION OF all is the first thing I hear when I blink and return to the present time. *That is what you have witnessed.*

I turn, looking for Finn, and find his eyes as wide as mine must be. We mirror each other's fright.

"A cycle," I start, unsure how to finish the sentence. "And that's where it began?"

The Stag nods in approval. *I do not know why, but the souls of the First Hunter and the Maiden are intertwined. Because of that, the Maiden, my daughter, could not exist in this place. Man cursed her with mortality.*

"I'm sorry we're such terrors," Finn finally speaks.

I have, my entire existence, believed the Stag to be god of all. To be a doting father for all creation.

But that is not the truth.

He is the god of the Fianna. Nothing more. The hatred I had begun to brew was nothing compared to the injustice the Stag felt was brought onto him.

You stole my daughter from me. You tricked her into entering the mortal world, Hunter. Because of you, she would live and die, over and over. The Stag shifts his mighty weight, raising his head higher. *Yet, I have tried, each life she is gifted, to bring her home. To cure her.*

"What do you mean?" I ask.

The Stag explains, *the connection that held you in their world was love. It was the companionship to the boy that prevented you from coming home.*

I place a hand against my chest as my heart roars.

I have permitted your lives to continue as one, and for the cycle of time to keep turning. As the ages have passed, you have come to your own conclusion, have you not?

I swallow.

The humanity you wanted is no good. Only darkness resides in man. No matter how many lives you live, you cannot escape that. It hunts you, it chases you. But not here. Here, you would be safe.

"You did this," Finn shouts, his voice cracking with intention. "You pretend to be an innocent bystander."

I have allowed the world to unfold as it wishes.

Finn takes a step forward, and I notice the knife still in his hand. "You did more than that." Finn points to the tree in the center of the pond. Beneath the shade are the two lilies from the vision. The First Hunter's and the Maiden's. They are not pure and white but sagging and begging for life.

Yet, beside the First Hunter's...is another flower.

The Stag is silent.

"You claim that mankind is the true enemy to your daughter, yet you orchestrated the hatred between our species. Doesn't that seem a little backward?" Finn blinks hard, his attention quickly finding a new target. "That flower."

I study the lily as well, but it does not trigger the same response in me that it does Finn.

"I know what I'm about to say might be insane, but hell, have you seen the kind of situation we're in?" Water wells up in Finn's eyes. "That damn flower." Finn closes his eyes and smiles peacefully, despite the tears and trembling lips. "Only one person ever made me feel this way."

Your mind has found the truth. Do not let it scare you.

Finn squares his shoulders, stands up tall, and faces the Stag with the courage of a bear. "That's Jay."

Finn

ADELAIDE IS LOST in her thoughts and Marshall, overwhelmed, crouches over the ground. My throat is my own worst enemy right now, closing so tight that it is a struggle to even breathe.

But I continue.

"You said love was what tethered Adelaide's soul to this world. Yet, you tried to change that. You wanted to remove her anchor."

The Stag waited because he knew that I would not stop.

"You planted another...soul beside the First Hunter's." Regardless of what I say, regardless of the truth that settles in my gut, I can't accept that the First Hunter is me. That we are the same. "You claim to have watched this tale unfold, yet, you were the one controlling it."

Everything I have done, I have—

"You want me to believe that you are merely a spectator in this world. But it's said that each time the Maiden is reborn, the ferals rise in numbers. People die, again and again. Humans blame the fianna. The Maiden. Eventually, that hatred takes shape."

Scenes of previous Maidens being murdered by the humans fills my eyes as I speak. The grove willing offers up its past to fuel my outrage.

"You allow her to be tortured, to be killed. You stand by, and you do nothing. You watch as your daughter moves further and further from humanity and closer to you." I think about how feverishly Adelaide searched for her god, how she believed effortlessly that was her destiny.

And it was. A fate not crafted by herself.

"You baited her into finding you time and time again. The ferals rise. The humans' anger rises. The myths. The legends. All of this so she'll come to find you. And I was just a pawn." I stare at the grass at my feet. "My father found this place, didn't he? He came here, and you killed his love. You caused him to be…"

The human came into my domain, and I simply cast him out.

"It isn't that simple, though. You broke him. You made it so that the only person I could rely on was Jay. You made it that my father would never show me—" I can't finish my thoughts, so I simply growl in the back of my throat.

You became closer to the one you cared for. If you did not suffer, you would not know compassion—

"That isn't for you to decide!" I scream.

"How could you?" Adelaide asks her god with a subdued voice.

From the beginning, man tempted you, Maiden. You wanted to be with him, wanted to live his life. To make you happy, I allowed it. I allowed you to, each life, live beside him. To find him.

"Each time she was reborn, she was a blight to humanity. Each life she lived, it was hell." I cast my accusation at the god, throwing it at his feet.

She would suffer for but a breath before existing in bliss for eternity.

Adelaide shakes her head, tears crashing down her face. "I did not ask for this."

"You toyed with my life." It doesn't matter what came before this moment, all the times that man has suffered because of a god's anger, but in this life, I lost Jay. I watched as he died. "You took him from me."

I did not kill the boy. The world continued to turn—

"Because of your inaction, your games, he died."

The Stag moves forward, the flames in his eyes sparkling brighter.

"You wanted your daughter." I look back at Adelaide. "Well, here she is. Take her."

Adelaide recoils, backing up. The Stag begins to near his daughter, and as he moves, his frame shrinks until he is the size of an average fianna.

Adelaide's eyes switch between her god and me.

This has all been for you, the Stag tells her. *And now, the bond is weak. It is weak enough to break.*

I see Adelaide's mind, her soul, at work. She looks at the flowers beneath the tree, she sees the life they lack.

She does hate the humans.

She must hate me.

If you stay too long in their world, you will begin to change. You will lose yourself. You will suffer. But here, you are safe.

This time, Adelaide looks down at my hands.

"Finn—!"

Before, in a town where nature had reclaimed it, I had aimed my gun at a god. I felt my demons rise and choke me. The guilt was thick and impossible to accept, and at that time, I did not know if the choice I had made was the correct one.

But now, my soul soars as I plunge my dagger through the Stag's chest.

The Hunter

I SINK THE blade deeper into the god, twisting the handle as I dig. "This time, it should count."

Instead of blood leaking from the wound, thick cords of golden light slither from around the knife. They wrap around my hand, my arms, and eventually my entire chest.

You are a fool, the Stag tells me, and I can hear it in his voice, that he is dying. The radiance of his coat is dimming, his antlers are withering. *Without me, you will truly die. The cycle will end.*

I try to remove the knife, to stab the creature again, but I am locked in place as the tendrils of gold continue to encompass my body.

Beneath me, the ground cracks and splinters into pieces. The lilies, one by one, flicker out. Their light dims until they are just regular flowers.

You have damned the world, Hunter.

"I have freed it," I say.

As the Stag dies, the grove begins to collapse. I do not know where Marshall or Adelaide are, but I start to sink into the soil. The cords have begun to darken, turning into ropes of black. Slowly, they work their way into my body, breaking through my flesh to find my organs, my blood.

"You did this," I tell the god as he dies. "You wanted this hatred. This anger. You wanted a fury powerful enough to break destiny."

The ground drops from beneath us, and both the god and I fall into darkness.

Even as my eyes, heavy and tired, begin to droop, I think of Jay, over and over. I see his smile, his death, his laughter, his blood.

All of it.

Perfectly intertwined.

It does not matter how I found him. It does not matter how our lives came to be.

I would do anything for you, he had once told me.

And while I held him, while he died, I was silent. It is now, more than ever, that I wish I could have told him the same.

It is only right here, right now, that I can finally prove I would do *anything* for the boy I miss every day.

The Maiden

WHEN THE STAG falls, the flowers begin to wither.

They start to brown, slowly at first, but eventually they lose their petals and disintegrate into ash. As they disappear, every painful cry buries beneath my skin. A barrage of images courses through me till my very being is stretched over an eternity of lives. I see deaths, births, rebirth, and death again. I see happiness and darkness walking side by side. I scream, I laugh, I sob, I feel the highest of joys.

Then, as the Stag finally crumbles to the ground, the memories fade. When Finn tips over, they completely vanish.

Between the god and boy, I run for Finn.

"Finn!" I scream, the ground beneath him breaking and sinking. "Finn!"

Marshall grips my hand and runs toward the exit to the garden. I fight with him, screaming as the body of the Stag starts to slip beneath the ground. I don't turn until I watch as the body of Finn also vanishes.

Passing through the entrance to the cave, we find ourselves in the Forest with our next step. Dazed and momentarily confused, it is Marshall who regains command of his body first. He continues to run, keeping a tight hold on me.

The ground continues to shudder and shake. Several trees cry out as their roots burst free from the dirt. When they collide with the ground, a loud explosion sounds off.

Before us, I see the wall of vines. They no longer stand erect, though. As the ground tosses and turns, the vines slowly begin to collapse. Marshall keeps running, does not even slow down as we approach the tangled mass quickly. Even when we stand before it, Marshall shoulders into the vines. They snap easily as he plows through them. They are as frail as dried-out twigs.

Breaking free, Marshall collapses onto the field of green. He tumbles and rolls, his arms and legs bloody. I fall with him, hitting the dirt hard. I get to my hands and knees and stare back into the Forest. Tree by tree, it slowly starts to unravel.

No, I think. I try to get to my feet, but I am too weak. "Finn!" I shout, hoping that he might hear me, that he might come running out of those trees.

We could have had a second chance, I want to scream. *We could have done it over. We could have fixed it the next time.*

I scream and scream, but I'm not sure what comes out of my mouth any longer.

"What's going to happen now?" Marshall asks from beside me.

I put my face in my hands, wiping at the tears, trying to push away all the despair.

When I pull them away, my palms are streaked with red.

I notice a single dark vein.

Marshall studies my face, the tears of blood, and the black strings growing beneath my skin.

"War," I tell him as the world begins to crumble. "A war has begun."

And the cycle ends.

Acknowledgements

I'm awkward and uncomfortable around emotions, so this is probably going to be really weird. I want to first thank all the people that have impacted me up until this point in my life. This book is a milestone and culmination of endless amounts of support, love, and encouragement so I apologize if I miss a few people. If I did forget you, tell me and I'll buy you Chinese food or give you a tough truth.

This story wouldn't be anything if it wasn't for my mom, who read me a story every night before bed and nurtured my love for books and adventures. And to my dad who told me "accomplish what you can in one day, don't stress the rest" but never doubted I could conquer the world in a single day.

Thank you, Grandma Shelby, for insisting we go book shopping and out to eat every time I call, and for showering me in love and acceptance always. Over the years, you've bought me numerous books, and now, I hope, I can finally repay you with this one.

Big shout out to Madcap Retreats where I learned from some amazing creators, met some lifelong friends, and completed my first draft of *Foreign to You*.

I don't know if I should thank or fear you, Cristina Santos. You were one of my first beta readers and after your honest and amazing advice, I scrapped 100k words and rewrote my entire story to what it is now. I'm afraid to have you beta for me again...just kidding! I think...

Because of Jenna Shaffer, I never needed to look up inspirational quotes on my bad days. You are such a positive light to this world and your constant enthusiasm and encouragement held me up when I didn't even believe in myself. You started a fire in me and never let it go out.

To Sabina Post, who is a courageous writing goddess. Thank you for letting me rant to you endlessly and for all the incredible advice you've given me. When the world realizes how brilliant and gorgeous your writing is, don't forget me, m'kay?

Thank you, Janna SENSENIG (that is still weird to me), for reminding me, that despite it all, I deserved to be loved and am loved. Thank you for editing the first draft to *Foreign to You* and becoming the best thing that ever happened to Matthew. Also, thank you for still laughing at "dartslip" with me and believing that we truly did see that cat.

To Matthew Sensenig, who has always been a brother to me. You were always there, fighting by my side, regardless if it was countless aliens, over leveled monsters, or my own personal demons. Thank you for hugging me that night in the woods and for always being better than me.

To Justine Goldsborough, who somehow found sympathy in both the Black Knight and Akechi. But most importantly because you used that same heart to stick with me, through thick and thin, always telling me that I wasn't the villain of my own story. And to that same girl who sat on the bench at the top of the hill and said, "If you're with me for the rest of my life, I won't need anything else."

To Greg Stief, who once said, "Okay Gourgle," and I've never stopped laughing to this day. Also, to the boy who held my hand that one summer night as we sang along to "A Whole New World." I cried and smiled and when you asked what was wrong, I told you "I'm just happy." But, I forgot to add "finally."

For everyone that knows me well, this one won't surprise you. But thank you Maggie Stiefvater. Thank you for signing so many of your books to your #1 fan (because I'm cringy like that) and for giving me Ronan and his story when I really needed it most. Side note; I tried to build an altar for you, but my friends stopped me. All I can do now is apologize.

Finally, thank you to Mrs. Hackman-Rupp who impacted my life beyond words. Each time I draft something up to thank you, I'm not satisfied. It's never enough. You believed I could be a writer, believed I had a purpose, and the fact that I can't hand this book to you and say, "This is because of you," guts me. But I know, one day, I will be able to tell you all about it.

About the Author

Jeremy Martin, born and raised in Lancaster County Pennsylvania, considers himself to be a part-time writer and a full-time mess. If he isn't nose-deep in a book, he's obsessively playing video games, re-watching *The Office* for the umpteenth time, or lost in nature. *Foreign to You* is his debut novel.

Email: jeremy.jem21@gmail.com

Facebook: www.facebook.com/jeremy.martin.3557440

Twitter: @germym21

Instagram: www.instagram.com/germym21

Also Available from NineStar Press

Connect with NineStar Press

Website: NineStarPress.com

Facebook: NineStarPress

Facebook Reader Group: NineStarNiche

Twitter: @ninestarpress

Tumblr: NineStarPress

www.ingramcontent.com/pod-product-compliance
Lightning Source LLC
Chambersburg PA
CBHW032057180726
48284CB00002B/319